Praise for
ISABELA'S WAY

"In this richly imagined novel set in the early 17th Century, Barbara Stark-Nemon takes us along as her main characters, teenagers Isabela and her dearest friend David, flee Portugal in a desperate attempt to evade capture by the Inquisitors who suspect they are 'secret' Jews . . . Beautifully written, this unforgettable blend of carefully researched history and fictional intrigue will keep readers spellbound as Isabela and David's destiny unfolds."
—Jenni Ogden, author of *Dancing with Dragons*, *The Moon Is Missing*, and *A Drop in the Ocean*

"In *Isabela's Way*, Barbara Stark-Nemon successfully weds the relentless danger of life for Jews and 'New Christians' in Portugal with meticulous descriptions of the culture and tools that helped these beleaguered populations survive. Fans of historical fiction—don't miss this beautifully written adventure!"
—Esther Erman, author of *Rebecca of Salerno*

"I loved this book. I thought it was poignant, riveting, historically accurate, and a gem!"
—Genie Milgrom, former president of the Jewish Genealogical Society of Greater Miami and author of *Pyre to Fire*

"A riveting physical and emotional journey, this moving, deeply researched tale has the pace of a thriller, all while examining questions of loyalty, love, and truth."
—Rebecca D'Harlingue, author of *The Map Colorist*

"Stark-Nemon, a published writer, handles things expertly, offering strong characters. The book is also well researched. . . . This novel revisits an old story, but like most familiar tales, it bears repeating. Intolerance will always be with humanity, but so will heroes willing to fight that scourge, even to risk their lives. . . . A well-told story with all of the requisite narrow escapes and memorable characters."

—*Kirkus Reviews*

"Just when you think we're in unprecedented times, *Isabela's Way* comes along to remind us—with vivid language, tangling plot lines, and rich details from five hundred years ago—that we've been here before. Stark-Nemon takes us on a journey full of danger, love, and sacrifice, reminding us of the perishable nature of the human spirit and of our shared responsibility to protect each other from empire, age to age. It's a story that will haunt you as you read tomorrow's headlines."

—Kathy Watson, author of *Orphans of the Living*

"A tour de force."

—David Loux, author of *Chateau Laux*

"The several journeys Barbara Stark-Nemon describes in *Isabela's Way* are more than just treks through suspenseful time and exquisitely described spaces—they are journeys of fortitude, of courage while facing danger, of confusion and self-discovery. Mixing adventure and romance, *Isabela's Way* is a novel of discovery for both characters and readers."

—Michelle Cameron, author of *Babylon*, *Beyond the Ghetto Gates*, and *Napoleon's Mirage*

"Beautifully written and deeply researched, this is an inspiring tale of young love, bravery, and family loyalty."

—Elayne Klasson, author of *Love Is a Rebellious Bird* and *The Earthquake Child*

"A riveting tale of courage and survival, *Isabela's Way* vividly brings the terror of the Inquisition to life. Barbara Stark-Nemon's dazzling prose and meticulous research make this story of a young girl's flight from persecution both timely and unforgettable."
—Florence Reiss Kraut, author of *How to Make a Life* and *Street Corner Dreams*

". . . [a] compelling page-turner . . . full of intrigue, danger, close calls, unfolding romantic love, and the joy of seeing a teenager come into her own as an autonomous, creative young adult."
—*The Indypendent*

ISABELA'S WAY

ISABELA'S WAY

A Novel

Barbara Stark-Nemon

Copyright © 2025 Barbara Stark Nemon

All rights reserved. No part of this publication may be reproduced, stored in a retrieval system, or transmitted in any form or by any means, electronic, mechanical, photocopying, recording, or otherwise, except for brief quotations in reviews, educational works, or other uses permitted by copyright law.

Published in 2025 by
She Writes Press, an imprint of The Stable Book Group

32 Court Street, Suite 2109
Brooklyn, NY 11201
https://shewritespress.com

Print ISBN: 978-1-64742-964-5
E-ISBN: 978-1-64742-965-2
Library of Congress Control Number: 2025909432

Interior design by Stacey Aaronson
Map courtesy of Erin Greb Cartography

Printed in the United States of America

This is a work of fiction. Names, characters, places, and incidents are either products of the author's imagination or are used fictitiously. Any resemblance to actual persons, living or dead, is purely coincidental.

No part of this publication may be used to train generative artificial intelligence (AI) models. The publisher and author reserve all rights related to the use of this content in machine learning.

All company and product names mentioned in this book may be trademarks or registered trademarks of their respective owners. They are used for identification purposes only and do not imply endorsement or affiliation.

Isabela's Way

Author's Note

While the characters in *Isabela's Way* are entirely fictional, the Inquisition was a very real presence in early-seventeenth-century Europe. The Roman Catholic Church established commissions of inquisitors starting in the thirteenth century, giving them the authority to question supposed heretics about their religious practices and loyalties.

The Spanish Inquisition, which encompassed the time of this story, lasted between 1478 and 1834 and included permanent, bureaucratically organized tribunals of clergy and laymen in Spain and Portugal. The tribunals were intended initially to detect crypto-Jews (Jews who had been forcibly converted but continued to practice their faith in secret; they were also called Conversos or, pejoratively, Marranos) and their descendants. These Jews were converts to Christianity called New Christians or, in Hebrew, anusim. Muslims and, later, Protestants were also persecuted.

Many historians assess that the Spanish Inquisition's real purpose was to consolidate the power of King Ferdinand II of Aragon and Queen Isabella I of Castile into a newly unified Spanish kingdom. Its brutal methods led to widespread death and suffering of Jews, Muslims, and other suspected non-believers.

The edict of expulsion of all the Jews from Spain on March 31, 1492, resulted in a massive influx of Jews to Portugal, where, for the next one hundred years, pockets of New Christians lived in small towns and villages and were often able to evade the Inquisitors or escape to other lands. Attempts were made to slow the exodus of Jews and

Muslims, who took with them their skills and resources, and during the union of Spain and Portugal in 1610, the so-called "irrevocable permissions to emigrate" some New Christians had purchased from King Philip III were rescinded. Still, many left Portugal, either clandestinely or by securing permission to take business trips abroad from which they never returned.

My speculation that there may have been an underground railroad—like secret escape network to help Iberian Jews and New Christians to reach safer cities like Hamburg, Amsterdam, and Venice at the beginning of the seventeenth century is indeed just that: speculation. However, there is an intriguing story from the previous century of the legendary Doña Gracia Nasi, a wealthy widow who succeeded in smuggling her late husband's fortune out of Portugal and setting up a secret network to help Jews escape Portugal to Italy.

As for the use of embroidered symbols for visual messaging—there is a rich history of using wearable, portable, recyclable textiles to carry personal and political information from place to place and person to person. A famous example is Mary Queen of Scots, who in the sixteenth century was known for her needlework and its power to communicate messages of her sovereignty, strength, and animus to courts all over Europe through her use of symbols and colors.

Finally, for ease of recognition, I have most often used contemporary names of countries rather than the historical names of states and kingdoms that would be unfamiliar to the modern reader. The map that follows, showing the routes traveled by the major characters, reflects those decisions. A list of characters appears at the end of the book.

I hope you enjoy *Isabela's Way*.

—*Barbara Stark-Nemon*

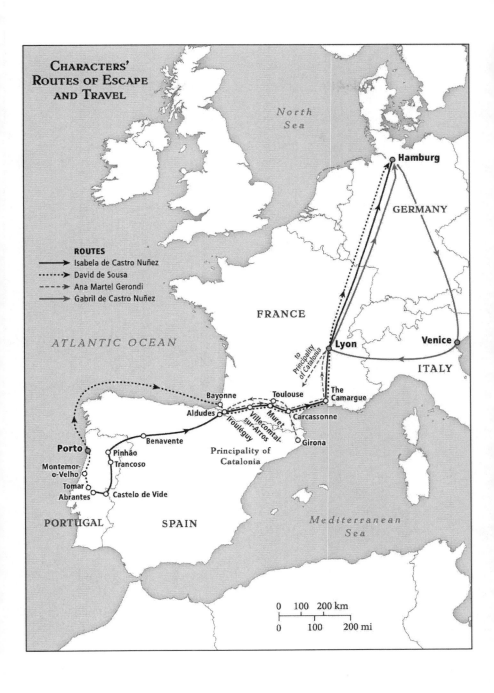

CHAPTER ONE

Abrantes, Portugal

June, 1605

An interrupted life is like a tapestry, begun, then cast aside and picked up again in a year's time. The new stitches must work with the old. They will never match exactly, for the hand that stitches them is no longer the same, but the true artist holds the memory of what the silk seeks to bring to life and makes it whole.
—RUMI

Though she hadn't sewn a single stitch, Isabela cradled a fine linen pouch in her lap, only her mind's eye seeing the profusion of embroidered birds and flowers soon to cover the sacred bag. Her own mother had embroidered the priest's stole that would rest within this burse. It was the first of June, and the piece needed to be finished by mid-July, in time for St. Isabela's feast day. The newly renovated church would require decorated bags for altar cloths, vestments, chalices, ciboria, and cruets, and while Isabela had helped her mother stitch for three years now, this commission was her first solo piece.

Thoughts of her mother brought a familiar, painful seizing at Isabela's center, and she squeezed her eyes shut against the threat of tears and the sorrow of her loneliness. Three long months had passed since the death of Mariem Jessurun de Castro Nuñez in this very room. Isabela cast her eyes to the back of the small but well-appointed space, with its tall cupboards stocked with textiles, silk, and gold and silver thread—the materials from which the de Castro Nuñez family created their famous embroidery.

Her mother had contracted the fever that had swept through Abrantes during the spring. The dreaded red rash had first appeared on her hands and feet, then turned a horrible black, and in three days' time, following the buboes on her neck, armpits, and groin, the headache, belly pain, confusion, and final horror of blood and vomit, Isabela's mother had succumbed, leaving the fourteen-year-old girl alone and devastated. How she had wished to be taken as well, but Isabela remained healthy, even as the plague afflicted surrounding households.

Joao de Sousa, the magistrate of the New Christian community, had assisted Isabela in arranging for the swift burial of her mother, only to fall ill himself and yield his life to the fever within a week. Immediately following his passing, his son, David, though only eighteen years of age, had assumed his father's role, caring as well for his mother and two younger sisters. The epidemic, which had continued to ravage the community in the months that followed, had abated only recently.

The previous winter, Gabril de Castro Nuñez had journeyed to Germany, seeking to conduct his business in that new market as restrictions on his textile trade in Portugal increased. In his absence, Isabela had assisted her mother, but now she worked on her own. She had no brother, no uncle, no relatives at all in Abrantes. Until her father returned, it would be up to her to keep the business alive.

She reached to the floor for her delicately painted sewing basket with its silk drawstring bag, a birthday gift from her mother, then drew her chair into the light of the open door. How different the dry, sun-drenched cobbles looked this morning. Last evening, the Rua Capitão Correia de Lacerda had been deluged with rain, red dirt from the surrounding fields ebbing away. Evening noises were muffled by the soft plinking of raindrops on stone and dust. The scent of wet earth had replaced the stench of waste as rainwater washed the ruin of the day down the hill. This morning was fair, and Isabela set to her task.

She outlined the border on the linen envelope with long satin stitches in the vibrant blue often used in depictions of Santa Isabela, her namesake. Next she carefully drew out gold thread and began to couch the blue, giving it dimension and elegance.

"Isabela de Castro Nuñez!" shouted a voice from the top of road, near the castle gate.

Isabela's hand froze mid-stitch and the songbirds flitting among the blooming tilia trees ceased their calls, as if alert to impending danger. A summons by an official from town or castle never boded well for a New Christian. Only two weeks earlier, the physician Abrao de Medelim had been detained after months of tending to the plague-stricken of Abrantes. When he'd returned to his home many days later, his gaunt visage and silence had terrified Isabela. There were whispered charges that Jews and New Christians were to blame for the deadly fever sweeping the land. Even as the supply of goods from New Christian merchants fed and clothed the townspeople, those same businesses were harassed and taxed unduly. But who would be interested in Isabela?

David de Sousa appeared in the doorway, blocking the stream of morning sunlight and breaking the frozen spell of panic that had struck Isabela. His presence steadied her; she carefully set aside her work, rose, and pulled a shawl from its hook.

"What is it?" she whispered to her friend, her body awash with fear

"I don't know," he said. "I have heard nothing new or worrisome. But you must go. I will come with you."

After glancing around the room, satisfied that all was in order, she stepped across the threshold—as always, kissing her fingertips and touching them to the upper side of the doorframe as she went.

Crossing herself, she stepped into the brilliant morning.

As her eyes adjusted to the light, she turned to her left, straightened her shoulders, and faced the palace guard at the top of the lane, the morning sun directly behind him, blinding her to his features.

He was not alone. A second figure stood to his right and a few steps behind him. Still squinting, Isabela made out the figure of a woman, tall and imposing, the hem of her cape rippling in the breeze.

"Hurry!" the soldier bellowed. "I don't have the day long to stand here waiting."

Isabela scurried up the uneven cobblestones with David de Sousa at her side.

Fear radiated from the warming walls. Not a soul peered from a doorway or grated window, but Isabela could feel collective apprehension in the unusual silence from each house. Even the distant din of hammering and workers' shouts from the Igreja de São João Baptista, the magnificent church being rebuilt by King Filipe at the foot of the hill behind Isabela, seemed muted. Perhaps it was only the rush of blood from her pounding heart that masked the town's noises.

"Say as little as possible," whispered David. "Let us try to understand who this strange woman is."

Steps away from the top of the road, Isabela halted, one stride ahead of David de Sousa, and curtsied quickly. As she rose back to standing, she lifted her eyes for a fleeting look at the woman before her. Taller than Isabela by a head, she appeared to be in middle age, though the skin of her plain face remained only lightly lined. Her simple cloak of light wool did not entirely hide the fine silk brocade and deep orange dye of the dress underneath. Expertly tailored, the ensemble betokened the refinement of its wearer.

"You are Isabela de Castro Nuñez?" the guard asked, no longer shouting but still seemingly irritated. "Who speaks for you?"

"I do," said David at once. "David de Sousa. I am the magistrate's assistant in this quarter. For what purpose do you seek this girl?"

"He asks on my behalf," the woman interjected. She stepped forward and with long fingers lifted Isabela's chin so that she could gaze directly into her eyes. Isabela was held in the older woman's deep brown stare for an uncomfortably long moment. "I am Dama Ana Martel Gerondi. I have come a great distance from my home in Catalonia with instructions to care for the senhorita and see to her future."

Dama Martel Gerondi delivered this pronouncement in fluent Portuguese with an accent that did not sound to Isabela like that of other Spaniards. Instructions? Whose instructions? Questions flew to Isabela's mouth like swallows to a belfry, but she recalled David's advice to say little.

David stepped forward. "I must ask who has sent you and what you intend to do with Senhorita de Castro Nuñez. I am responsible for her and must be assured of her well-being."

As David leaned toward the senhora, the guard moved toward him, but Dama Martel Gerondi raised her hand in his direction and waved him back. She regarded the younger man with the glimmer of a smile.

"Senhor de Sousa," she began, her tone still commanding, though somewhat softer. "If you are interested in the well-being of Isabela de Castro Nuñez, then you and I have no dispute. I suggest we allow the policial to return to his duties, and, Senhorita Isabela, if you will be so kind as to show me to your home, I can perhaps explain further my business here."

Detecting David's nearly imperceptible nod, Isabela performed another small curtsy and waited as Dama Martel Gerondi dismissed the guard with a coin. David offered his arm to the older woman, and Isabela followed them down the narrow way until they reached the doorway to the de Castro Nuñez home.

Isabela slipped in front of her visitors, touched the notch in the doorframe, and then quickly dropped her hand and turned to usher her companions into her home, feeling grateful that she had swept the floor and straightened the room that morning.

Dama Martel Gerondi had to drop her head slightly to clear her headdress through the low doorway; she, too, brushed her hand across the notch in the frame as she passed inside. Isabela wondered if the woman had meant to perform this gesture, something only the New Christians did upon entering their homes, or if the movement had been merely a way to steady herself as she bent through the doorway. To Isabela, the woman's presence filled the previously quiet, pleasant room with the strangeness of the unknown.

"Please, senhora, sit here," Isabela said, gesturing to a finely carved chair with a beautiful embroidered cushion. "May I bring you a cup of wine?"

"Thank you," Dama Martel Gerondi said. "I have journeyed far today already. A cup of wine would be most welcome."

As Isabela moved to the back of the house, she saw the senhora study the blue and white tile surrounding the hearth. Perhaps she noted its quality, along with the intricate carving of the chair she occupied, suggesting a family of means.

David sat opposite her in an upright posture, his face stony. Neither one spoke.

Isabela returned carrying a tray with goblets of wine, eggs, bread, and dried fruit. After serving her guest, she stood uncertainly, still unused to being the primary host to visitors. In truth, visitors had been rare in the plague-ridden town for some time now, and this courtly, exotic woman would have been a rarity in the Castro Nuñez home at any time Isabela could remember.

"Tell me of your parents, Isabela," Dama Martel Gerondi began.

Isabela felt a jolt at her center. From childhood, her mother had warned her to speak carefully to strangers, saying always less rather than more about their family's business and activities. She had expected to be informed, not questioned, and what little presence of mind the woman's gentleness had infused her with fled. Once again, tears sprang to her eyes. No willful squeezing them shut kept the drops from her pale cheeks.

David spoke up quickly. "Senhora de Castro Nuñez was taken by the fever this spring, and Senhor Castro Nuñez has traveled north on business. But I must ask again—under whose auspices do you make these inquiries?"

Isabela shrank from the impertinence of David's demand, but she was eager to hear a response. She watched Dama Martel Gerondi look from one to the other of their young faces and heard her heavy sigh, but she saw no irritation in the older woman's face. Rather, a mask of sadness surrounded her eyes.

"Please, Isabela, sit. I will explain as best I can."

Isabela pulled a stool close to David and waited. Dama Martel Gerondi loosened her cloak, and as it fell to either side, she fingered the magnificent cross that hung from her neck at the center of the orange brocade bodice. The finely wrought gold, filigreed and decorated with vines and tiny flowers worthy of a tapestry, distracted Isabela. At the center, embedded in the filigree, a star of amber picked up the light from the doorway and shone. Isabela had never seen so fine a piece of jewelry.

Dama Martel Gerondi spoke at last, still holding the cross at her bosom. "This has been with the women in my family for one hundred years. My mother and grandmother supposed that it held both secrets and protection. I quite hope they were correct." She stopped, dropping her hand to her lap, looking again to the faces of her young listeners before continuing. "Where I come from, in Girona, there were long ago many families who were . . ." She paused again, glancing first at the door, then around the room, and then finally sipping from her wine cup. "There were families who came to Portugal—to Abrantes. They were New Christians." Again, Dama Martel Gerondi stopped, searching Isabela's face as if for some recognition, some comprehension of this halting story.

Isabela stared back blankly, knowing the woman wished something from her that escaped her utterly.

"Do you seek someone from those families?" she offered. "We know many people here in Abrantes and surely our priest, Padre Alvaro, could help."

"No!" Dama Martel Gerondi said sharply, but immediately lowered her voice. "There is no need for the priest. I have received word from Alemanha." Now her voice became even lower. "You are to travel north. I am to assist you. We are to leave in a month's time. You are to finish what work you are contracted to do before then, and to bring all the tools and silks that you can carry when we depart."

Isabela, stunned into silence, held on to the seat of her stool as if an earthquake threatened to dislodge her.

David abruptly stood, the words exploding from him. "By whose leave do you bring this news? Do you speak with the authority of Gabril de Castro Nuñez? He is the girl's father, and we await word from him as to her future." David stood tall, the muscles in his jaw tensed.

Dama Martel Gerondi sighed but met the young man's gaze. "I do not speak directly on behalf of Senhor de Castro Nuñez, but I believe his wishes are being carried out by another—the one who sent me here." As David prepared to question further, she lifted her hand to stop him and turned to Isabela. "I am not at liberty to name your father's emissary at this time, but perhaps this will assure you of his goodwill in your best interests." She reached into a pouch hidden in the folds of her skirt, pulled out a smaller pouch, and held it in her palm toward Isabela.

Isabela cried out, her hand flying to her throat. "Oh, Papai!"

The pouch, made of fine green silk, had a delicately embroidered wreath of tiny flowers enclosing the initials MJCN. On the last evening before Isabela's father had departed, her mother had presented him with this pouch, containing a dragonfly pin of the finest gold filigree, a gift given to her by his mother. *To keep you safe*, she had told her husband.

Isabela slid the lovely pin from its bag as tears once again slid down her cheeks. David sank heavily into his chair, laying a hand on his friend's shoulder. For all their fierce shows of strength, they were both just grief-stricken children at heart—children who had lost too much too fast. The afternoon light lit the tiny jewels set in the dragonfly's eyes, making them sparkle in Isabela's hand.

Quietly, leaning toward the two young people, Dama Martel Gerondi explained, "The news I bring is frightening, I know, but you must trust that I come only out of concern for your safety and well-being. Both of you." Now she looked directly at David and spoke more urgently, though still softly, glancing again toward the doorway and small window. "It isn't safe for you to stay in Abrantes any longer. The Inquisitors have turned a blind eye to this area for a long while, but circumstances have changed." Looking back at Isabela, she continued, "I believe your father saw this coming and that is why he traveled to Hamburg and hoped to send for you and your mother."

Again David prepared to speak, and again Dama Martel Gerondi stopped him. "I haven't time to explain it all today. I must return to the castle to conduct other business. But I must take a piece of your work, Isabela, as that is what I said I wanted when I asked to be brought to you." Turning again to David, she continued, "Your job will be enormous and dangerous, David de Sousa. Isabela will travel first, but you will be asked to convince other New Christians to leave by ones and twos. I will send a contact to assist with arrangements. And I say this to you both: You must tell no one of what I've spoken today. Do you understand?"

For the first time, Dama Martel Gerondi's forceful bearing wavered as the concern in her eyes deepened, and Isabela felt a new strand of fear tighten around her heart. She stared down at her hands, the pin resting in one and her mother's beautiful work cupped in the other. "I understand," she whispered.

Dama Martel Gerondi turned to David, who only nodded.

Isabela rose, selected a fine linen towel embroidered with bluebirds and a pulled thread nest, and wrapped it with a ribbon. Moments later, with a promise to send a message soon, Dama Martel Gerondi took David's arm and walked out into the noonday sun.

Isabela watched as they continued together up the cobbled road to the castle.

CHAPTER TWO

Abrantes

June, 1605

*Deep in the sun-searched growths,
the dragonfly hangs as a blue thread loosened from the sky.*
—Dante Gabriel Rossetti

*A*na spoke quietly to her young escort as they climbed the hot road toward the castle gates.

"You must convince Isabela to trust me and prepare to travel north. It will not be safe here any longer. It is not safe now. The plague this spring has distracted the Inquisitors, but they will not remain distracted forever. In fact, they will blame the ravages of the plague upon New Christians here, as they have elsewhere."

"Blame?" cried David. "Blame us for the loss of our own families?"

His brown eyes, liquid with pain, also sparked with anger. Ana could see the boy fighting with the man in the rigid set of his shoulders and the twitch of his set jaw.

"And why should Isabela trust you?" he demanded. "Why should either of us trust you? We have no idea how you came into possession of Senhor de Castro Nuñez's pouch. Isabela has lost her mother and longs to see her father again. She will want to believe anyone who pretends to have news of him."

Dama Martel stopped and drew herself up to her considerable full height, nearly as tall as the young man before her. She directed her gaze squarely into his fiery brown eyes. "You do well to protect Isabela and you are wise to question the intentions of a stranger, but you would be equally wise to recognize the danger that lies ahead, even as you cope with your present sorrow. For your own protection, I cannot reveal the extent of my connection to Isabela's father, but you must believe me that he risked much to entrust another to bring his wife's brooch to me and to enlist my help on behalf of his daughter." Lowering her voice, she continued, "I also have risked a great deal just to come here. I ask nothing of you but to aid this young woman and as many others as you can to safety. If you are to hold the welfare of your people in your young hands, then you must learn to judge the sincerity and the honor of others. The weight of a man rests on your fine young shoulders, David de Sousa, perhaps before you are entirely ready, but I beg you, for the sake of Isabela, your own family, and the families of those close to you, heed what I have told you and prepare your people to depart."

Quietly, she added, "I believe this is what your father would have wished you to do—what he himself would have done. I am sorry to place this burden upon you, but the times we live in weigh heavily on us all."

Ana watched as the young man's face froze at the mention of his father, and then contorted with the anguish he tried to control. Resisting the temptation to comfort him, she continued.

"In a week's time, you will hear from a silk trader by the name of Pedro de Martins. He will seek an embroideress, and though he will come to you, you must introduce him to Isabela. He will ask that she travel to the estate of a French nobleman to create the linens and costumes for his daughter's betrothal. He will present you with a pair of gloves, one embroidered, one empty of decoration. Isabela is to copy the designs of the first glove onto the second. When Pedro Martins returns for the gloves, Isabela must prepare to leave Abrantes. He will send a companion, equipped with the necessary papers, to accompany her. She must be sure to take as many of her belongings and the supplies of her craft as will suggest a long journey and much work, but not so much as to suggest she is leaving forever."

David stepped forward. "*Is* she leaving forever, then?"

Ana held the boy's gaze and spoke quietly. "Only the good God above knows that, Senhor de Sousa. Our job is to assist as many of the New Christians of Abrantes to safety as we can, beginning with Isabela. Will you help me?"

The leaves of the tilia tree ceased their fluttering in the stillness of the day's heat. Sweat trickled down the bodice of Ana's gown. Suddenly, she felt an immense weariness. The moment stretched interminably.

"I will." David spoke the words firmly, even as he shut his eyes.

Ana touched his arm softly. "With God's help, may neither one of us regret our promises of today. Thank you."

With a sigh, she turned toward the castle gate, leaving David de Sousa to watch as she summoned the guard.

"But why?" Isabela asked, her fists tight in her lap. "We've managed. I have done well." She cast her eyes down and added, "With your help."

David stood in front of her, captivated by the sight of the afternoon sun pouring through the window onto the flaxen curls that escaped her starched white cap and lace veil.

"I know," he agreed. "But Dama Martel Gerondi brings urgency to news of changes we have already started to see. We are far from the court of King Filipe, but you remember when Michael Perez came from Evora to make his way to Nantes. His father, Almiro, and his brothers—"

"Stop," Isabela cried. "I don't want to remember."

David understood why. The story of the torture of the prominent New Christians Almiro Perez and two of his sons, arrested by the Inquisitors three years previously, had haunted the dreams of many New Christians in Abrantes in the years since. And it was Isabela's parents who had sheltered the third Perez son, Michael, and provisioned him for the long journey north to a small community of Portuguese New Christians in Nantes.

"We are well received at the church here in Abrantes," Isabela said weakly. "We are good Christians."

David looked at his friend's distressed face, her eyes beseeching him not to ask her to leave—to somehow change what was happening that threatened their slow recovery from a cruel spring. For a moment, he could only gaze at the golden curl that escaped Isabela's attempt to tuck her hair behind her ear.

"What happened in Lisbon, and then in Evora, is no longer so far away, Isabela," he said gently, though urgency furrowed his brow. "Somehow your Papai has found this woman to help bring you to him. You must finish the burse for Padre Alvaro as quickly as possible and prepare to work on this glove from a messenger in a week's time."

"And leave? With this stranger?" Isabela's voice broke. "Without you?" Her last words caught in a sob.

"I cannot protect you here, Isabela," David said, bowing his head. "I believe Dama Martel Gerondi is right, and it will only become more dangerous with time. I cannot leave my mother and sisters alone, and I must try to convince the others to leave. But I will follow, Isabela. We will find your father and he will help us settle somewhere far from the Inquisitors."

"How will we find him? How will you find me?" Doubt spread across Isabela's face like an ink stain on a parchment. "I'm scared, David."

In a single stride, he closed the distance between them and wrapped his arms around the slender girl, whose curls barely reached his shoulder. For a long moment, he held her as they'd held each other through deaths and fear in the past months. Then he stood back from her to look directly down into her deep blue eyes.

"I know you are frightened," he said, "but truly, I think this is what your mãe and pai would wish you to do. You must be brave, as you have already been. You must be the smart Isabela now—the only one who could always best me at lessons!"

Isabela's teary face broke into a small smile. She drew a handkerchief from her sleeve and dried her tears.

"Now," said David, returning her smile, "it's time to work. I must go first to my mother and then begin to tell the others."

A week later, Isabela, her summer cloak light upon her shoulders, stepped carefully over the cobbles down the hill toward the Igreja de São João Baptista. Workers had ceased for the day, and only muted noises of the households along the way broke the heated stillness. Late-afternoon light gilded the stone walls and heightened the colors of banners hung over doorways in preparation for Festas de Abrantes.

Isabela felt anything but festive, but she would join her neighbors and celebrate the town in the week to come nevertheless.

She had finished the last stitches of the embroidered bursa only last evening, weeks ahead of schedule, and she carried it now, folded carefully and wrapped in its own cloth, to Padre Alvaro. David's stern warning to say nothing of Dama Ana Martel Gerondi's visit only increased her unease. Padre Alvaro had a way of knowing everything that happened in his parish, and Isabela had to be prepared to parry any inquiries.

She dutifully attended Mass each week, as New Christians were required to do. But her family's relationship to the Church was more rooted in the business transactions of textile and embroidery for the refurbishing of the church than in piety. And while she had accompanied her mother to deliver finished work in the past, she had never thought to attend to the details of compensation or any negotiation that may have occurred. Last evening, she had reviewed her mother's ledger, noting the sums received for previous work. Had her mother set a price for bursas? She had found no such record, and could not recall her mother having worked on such a minor project.

The ledger had shown the sale of a stole for the bishop, dead now for more than a year. Isabela remembered its rich colors and complex design. It had brought one thousand reis to the de Castro Nuñez coffers. Isabela was proud of the work she had done on this bursa, but the linen bag was small and far less significant than the stole, so she had determined to ask only two hundred reis of Padre Alvaro. She had discussed it with David, and he'd agreed that to ask for more could lead to a negotiation for which she was unprepared. In any case, she wished to keep her contact with the padre to a minimum.

She had refused David's offer to accompany her to this meeting. As she reached the foot of Rua Capitão Correia de Lacerda and prepared to step through the side entrance of church, she questioned that bravado. Yet once she entered the church and stood for a moment at the center of the nave, letting her eyes adjust to the cool dark, the vaulted space calmed her.

Pai do Ceu, she prayed, *give me strength and understanding.*

Though Isabela prayed to the Heavenly Father as she knew she should, it was Saint Elizabeth who had always magnetized Isabela to her story of kindness and courage, and this was a church dedicated to her, a former queen of Portugal. So, while Isabela had learned her catechism well and prayed always to Jesus, Mother Mary, and God himself, she drew her connection to the Church from Elizabeth. She silently asked her for her help now as she made her way deeper into the sanctuary.

She found Padre Alvaro in his study. He rose from his writing table, a massive oak piece placed under a leaded window facing west, when she entered. Late-afternoon light flooded the pages of a large Bible and stack of documents strewn across the desk's broad surface. A quill lay on a blotter, its tip still laden with ink.

"Isabela, my child, how good to see you," he said. "We have been graced with little of you these last weeks." The padre was tall and imposing, even without his formal vestments. He wore a simple cassock today, but it was made of fine cloth and fitted his large frame well. A decorated cross lay prominently upon his chest. His piercing brown eyes bore down on Isabela.

She squared her shoulders and resisted the urge to look down. "I'm sorry to disturb you, Padre, but I have come to deliver your order of the bursa."

"Ah, so soon! I didn't expect it for weeks yet."

Rather than reply, Isabela drew forth the stitched linen bag and held it out to the priest. Even under his scrutiny, she could not help but admire her own work: honeysuckle vines, representing the steadfastness of the storied queen; doves and olive branches, depicting her peacemaking; and, best of all, roses, signifying the miracle for which Queen Isabela would soon become Santa Isabela. All, in her estimation, were finely designed and expertly stitched.

Every Christian child in Portugal had heard the story of the virtuous queen who, when forbidden to give food from the royal larder to the poor, disobeyed and hid bread in her basket. When she was on her way to feed the unfortunates, King Dinis confronted her and demanded to see what she had hidden. The punishment for stealing from the king was death. When Queen Isabela reluctantly uncovered her basket, only roses lay within it. The miracle became symbolic of the queen's selfless generosity. Isabela was proud to be her namesake.

"Your work reflects well on the skills your mother taught you," said Padre Alvaro.

"Thank you, Padre," Isabela answered.

"The Holy Queen, the Peacemaker, was known for her virtue and kindness . . .and her loyalty." The padre placed emphasis on this last word. He studied Isabela as he spoke. "She would not brook opposition to her husband or the rule of law. Her efforts at making peace were always to that end." He paused, then continued in a manner that seemed to signify more than a comment about the Holy Queen. "One can only speculate that her disobedience *to* her king and husband was divinely inspired; hence the miracle for which we celebrate her. It is a terrible risk to take, don't you think, Isabela?"

"Yes, Padre," was all she dared reply, and the ensuing silence became uncomfortable. *He knows something*, thought Isabela, *but I mustn't acknowledge that.*

After another long moment, the padre turned to a chest in the corner of the room and withdrew a bag of coins. He counted out a considerable number and placed them in a smaller pouch, which he handed to Isabela.

"There are three hundred reis here," he said. "Fine work deserves fine compensation. I hope you will contribute your skills to the glory of the Church many more times in the future."

Isabela worked hard to maintain an impassive expression.

"Thank you, Padre." She turned to leave the room, but not until she'd returned to the darkening road and begun to climb toward home did she let out the shuddering exhale she'd been holding inside. The padre's scrutiny unnerved her, but she now had a fat pouch of coins hanging from her belt.

David appeared at Isabela's door early the following day. Behind him stood a man of medium height in the dress of a noble house. Isabela drew her mantilla over her curls and rose to greet the two young men.

"Isabela de Castro Nuñez, may I present Senhor Pedro de Martins?" David stepped aside to allow the stranger to approach Isabela.

"Please enter," Isabela said quickly, wishing to shield the visitor from the curiosity of her neighbors.

She showed the two men to the table at the back of the sitting room, where a gentle breeze entered through a small window, bringing with it the scent of rosemary from the garden.

When Senhor de Martins was seated and Isabela had brought cups of wine for all, he withdrew a parcel from his travel coat and placed it on the table.

"I come here at the bidding of Monsieur Raphael de Mercado," he said. "My master's eldest daughter is to be wed, and he has need of a skilled embroideress to assist in the making of her trousseau. He understands that you possess such skills and wishes for you to attend the mademoiselle for the period of the months before her nuptials."

Senhor de Martins spoke Portuguese haltingly, with the peculiar accent of the Basque Country, but his manner was both assured and kind. While he spoke directly to Isabela, he looked also to David to include him in the conversation.

"Your travel expenses will of course be paid," he continued, "and you will live in the household with all proper protections and comforts. Additionally, you will be paid well for your work. By way of introduction, my master wishes for you to reproduce a design from this glove to its mate. If this is agreeable to you, I will return in a week's time to retrieve the glove." Senhor de Martins moved the parcel toward Isabela.

The glove was made from the finest goatskin, softened and stitched to a size suitable for a man with large hands.

"These are gloves for a man," Isabela said, looking to Senhor de Martins.

"Yes, they are to be a gift to the young mistress's betrothed."

Isabela studied the construction of the unworked glove first; the reinforced seams and even thickness of the white leather bespoke fine workmanship. The gauntlet had been cut as part of the original glove, not worked and added later. Though this would make her work more difficult, it was another sign of the quality of the piece.

Isabela had only worked on fine goatskin a few times, and she recalled her mother's instruction to take great care with each stitch, as unpicking would leave unsightly holes in the leather. Additionally, the material required a needle that was strong and yet not so thick as to render Isabela unable to embroider the fine designs that lay before her.

The embroidery on the finished glove was complex and skillfully stitched. Isabela moved her chair closer to the window, where the morning sun pouring into the room ignited the colors of the fine silk threads adorning the glove. Anchoring the outer corner of the gauntlet, a blossom of pomegranate was stitched in rich red, its contours outlined in gold thread studded with pearls; it was so beautifully done that Isabela could nearly smell its sweet scent. A symbol of fertility and plenty, the pomegranate appeared often on church vestments.

The center of the gauntlet had a more unusual design. A lion, stitched with exquisite detail, traveled along what appeared to be a road—not in the proud stance of the king of beasts but stealthily, in a wary crouch. On the inner corner of the gauntlet was a tree with a strong root system, a sturdy trunk, and an elaborate array of branches. Unlike the stout, compact cork oaks of Portugal, this tree was sprawling and lofty.

Isabela flipped the gauntlet up to inspect the back of the stitching, always the test of an embroiderer's skill. She was impressed to see the reverse side protected by a delicate flap of goatskin, though an opening along the innermost seam allowed her to turn the entire piece inside out. She glanced at David and Senhor de Martins, but they were discussing the estate of Monsieur de Mercado. David's gathering of information about this emissary and his master gave Isabela a short time longer to assess the task before her.

The inner side of the glove's embroidery was expertly executed with a minimum of symmetrical stitches. In the center of this backing, hidden when the protective flap was in place, an entirely separate design had been stitched—a symbol unrelated to anything depicted on the outside of the glove. Isabela looked closer, and made out a complex stitched frame encasing a six-pointed star, barely visible underneath the crisscross of lines that backed the stitching on the outer side. Unlike the typical five-pointed design she always sewed, this star superimposed two triangles.

By now, the men had wound down their lively talk and turned to look at Isabela. Something told her to save her questions, though she had many. *Who embroidered this tour de force of a project? What are the meanings of the lion, the road, and the inner design of the star? Why test my stitching skills with this particular piece?*

Instead of asking a thing, she rose and returned to the table, a tentative smile on her face.

"This will be a challenging project," she said, "but I will make the glove's mate."

A look of relief flitted across Senhor de Martins's face. "Thank you, senhorita. Monsieur de Mercado will be greatly pleased." His soft voice became more brisk as he continued, "In a week's time, I will return for the glove, and a fortnight later, we will send a woman of our acquaintance, Dona Simone de Leon. She will assist you in preparing what you need for departure and will travel with you as a companion first to Bayonne and then to Irouléguy, where you will be safe in the house of Mercado."

"Safe?" David and Isabela asked in unison.

Senhor de Martins shifted in his seat. "These are unsettled times everywhere," he said. "Monsieur de Mercado is under the protection of the Good King Henry. And you will be under the protection of his house. I simply mean to assure you that you will be safe and comfortable during your stay."

David leaned back in his chair and turned to Isabela. She met his eyes and found the same guarded look that she was sure he saw in her own. She knew the final decision lay with her. She grasped the small pouch that hung from her belt and felt the delicate metal shape of dragonfly wings through the soft leather. The dragonfly—symbol of change, transformation, adaptability and self-realization. To what changes would Isabela have to adapt? Where would she find the strength? As if the brooch at her waist were flapping its wings, Isabela felt a flutter of warmth travel from her hand into her body and settle in her heart.

Almost as if listening to someone else, she heard herself declare, "I will be ready."

CHAPTER THREE

Castelo de Vide, The Free and Hanseatic City of Hamburg, and Abrantes

June, 1605

Let me fall if I must fall. The one I will become will catch me.
—The Baal Shemtov

Ana Martel Gerondi stood in the garden courtyard of Alfonso Mendes' home in the hilltop town of Castelo de Vide.

"You must guarantee her safety!" Ana stood in front of Senhor Mendes, her hands clenched, voice imperious.

"Dama Martel Gerondi, I believe you know better than to make such a demand. Hashem knows there is no such guarantee." Senhor Mendes spoke firmly but without anger.

Ana closed her eyes but stood tall. She knew Alfonso admired her, perhaps even worshiped her a little. If it would help Isabela, she would use that fact to her advantage. "I understand the risks involved. But she is an innocent. She is valuable to all we are trying to accomplish." Opening her eyes, she leaned toward the shorter man's craggy face. "And I have given my word that I would do all in my power to protect her and bring her safely to her father. Her fate is not only about our endeavor."

Alfonso looked tired. Exhausted.

"Yes," he said soberly, "but her innocence, and the fact that she is under the watchful eye of Duarte Alvaro, complicates our plan. Surely you must understand this, Ana."

Ana's shoulders slumped.

"You know I will do my best," he said quickly. "But you must also know that what we will ask of her is inherently dangerous. It is also her best chance to travel openly and safely to Hamburg. We can only do what we can do. Our sages tell us, 'Do not despair once you have entered the path, for the Creator assures us of success if the direction of our aspirations is correct.' Believe that what we are doing is correct."

Ana looked past Alfonso, beyond the low garden wall and down the steep road to the fields at the edge of Castelo de Vide. The early June day was warm and clear, absent the stifling heat that would come in a few weeks' time. A whiff of the lavender just opening their first violet blooms floated on the morning breeze. Ana tried to summon the calm, serenity, grace, and devotion that she prescribed lavender oil to induce. Her expert eye judged that the lavender plants were not yet ready to harvest for the soft grey dye she made each autumn, but oil would already be available in the plants.

Above the scent of lavender she could smell bay leaves from the tree in the corner of the courtyard. If only she were here collecting herbs and flowers for her dyes and medicinals. Perhaps she should take an extra day and do just that. This fertile spot with its explosion of late spring bloom and growth beckoned from deep within her the instincts of a healer and artisan.

And yet her task in this moment was to secure what Isabela de

Castro Nuñez needed to depart Abrantes and make her way safely through a complex route to Hamburg, Germany, to find and reestablish a life with her father. Isabela's skill as an embroideress would help support her journey. What it would do for others must remain secret from Isabela herself.

With a sigh of resignation, Ana turned back to her friend. "Do you have the sampler?"

Alfonso nodded, then turned and withdrew into his modest home.

Ana chose a seat on an iron bench nestled under a luxuriant wisteria. The gnarled plant had been carefully pruned to crawl up the wall in an arch around the bench. She appreciated the other plantings around the courtyard, arranged in stone boxes bordering the patio tiles. Her eyes wandered to the doorway through which Alfonso Mendes had disappeared; her gaze settled on an ornate stone set above the olivewood door. The carved S at the stone's center signaled the home's inhabitant as a New Christian.

Like Ana, Alfonso had been forcibly converted as a child from the Jewish religion of his parents, and he hid all traces of that faith from the eyes and ears of town officials, merchants, and his old Christian neighbors, who called converts like him *Marranos*—pigs. As required, he went to Mass, muttering as he shuffled into the church, "I enter this house, but I do not adore sticks or stones, only the G-d of Israel," and, like others of his hidden faith, he saw to it that his sausages were made from chicken rather than pork, never ate milk with meat, and he kept as best as he could the other rituals of kosher food and the celebration of the sabbath and Jewish holidays.

Just as he secretly maintained these observances, he now further endangered himself by collaborating with a clandestine network established across all of Iberia and now spreading into France and the Palatinate to conduct crypto-Jews, the Marranos, from Portugal to safety. This border town, high on a hill, had once held a thriving Jewish quarter, but its remnants were now concealed—cloaked in the trappings of crucifixes on walls, church attendance, Sabbath candles lit in pots to hide their glow, name changes, and carefully orchestrated worship disguised as social gatherings.

As the viselike grip of the Inquisition contracted around New Christian communities in Portugal, parents made the painful decision to keep their former Jewish identities hidden from their own children. So, Ana thought, Isabela's innocence extended to the secret of her heritage—a secret that might save her or, if revealed, be her downfall. Now it had become Ana's responsibility to see Isabela through an escape.

Alfonso reappeared with a small leather portfolio, interrupting Ana's thoughts. Wordlessly, he handed it to her and watched as she drew out a folded linen square and spread it across her ample skirt.

Midmorning sun lit the brilliant colors of seven rows of embroidery, each row containing a sequence of symbols, animals, flowers, leaves, and objects. The needlework was exquisite—thread colors in fine gradients creating dimension; stitches of many kinds creating texture and light play; metal threads, pearls, and beads elevating the ornamentation. Ana recognized the dye colors of pomegranate, indigo, and turmeric for the reds, blues, and yellows—these were dyes she regularly made herself, and she also used these plants medicinally in her work as a healer—but there were many other dyes she could not identify.

Similarly, she recognized the images in the embroidered rows that were traditional symbols—the heart for love and for life, the tree for life, the butterfly for liberation, the three triangles for protection, the lion that represented strength and majesty. At this last image, however, Ana looked up at Alfonso. The lion could be the lion of Judah, a fierce symbol of Jewish struggle against tyranny. A dangerous symbol for someone wishing to hide their Jewish identity. In these times, embroidering a simpler cat was safer.

Ana also knew well the symbolism of colors—red depicting positive energy, passion, the blood of life, and the power to guard against harm and promote fertility; blue representing the power of water, the element of survival, and the sky, symbolizing the heavens and spirituality; green signifying youth and new life; black serving as the color of death but also of the ever-present earth.

The sampler was formidable. Isabela was highly skilled, but how would she know to arrange these items into a secret message? As if he'd heard her thought, Alfonso drew a scroll from his pocket and untied the twine that held it.

"She'll be told to embroider cloth strips to become cuffs, belts, headdress ornaments, and other useful items. Here are the codes for each message. She must sew the symbols in the exact order of each code, or the messenger will not understand their meaning. Can she do it?"

Not can *she do it, but* should *she do it?* Ana thought.

Isabela would not know that with her embroidered messages, she would pave the way for an intricate system of safe havens for escaping Jews and New Christians. But Ana knew well that what Isabela did not know could still hurt her.

Alfonso looked at her intently, waiting for a response.

Ana gave him a tight nod. "Yes."

Gabril de Castro Nuñez stood on the banks of the Elbe, hunched into his cape, staring into the vacant eyes of the warehouse windows lining the canal. It was hard to believe it was early June. At home in Abrantes, the mornings would be temperate and clear, and by midafternoon the hot sun would beat down on the cork oaks, though not yet with the fierceness of midsummer. If he closed his eyes, he could almost smell the first pungent scent of lavender wafting in from the fields.

Here in Hamburg, the morning had begun with a cold drizzle and cooler than normal temperatures, but the mounds of grey clouds were beginning to part. Moving down the quay and over the footbridge, Gabril rehearsed his speech to the meeting of burghers, councilmen, and shipping magnates' representatives.

"Gentlemen," he said to himself, "I am here at the behest of Dom Duarte Nunes da Costa, lately of Florence but born and educated in Lisbon, Coimbra, and Bologna. As you may know, he is both merchant and diplomat, and I bring his request . . ."

No, not request but proposal.

". . . And I bring his *proposal* to advance the business interests of you good gentlemen with the textile traders of his acquaintance in Portugal and Italy."

Gabril whispered this introduction again as he approached the heavily barred door. He was early—the nine o'clock bells had yet to sound—so he passed the door and continued his walk, trying to calm his nerves. He knew the business of textiles well and for many years had successfully traded in Abrantes, France, and Spain. But that had been before the Inquisitors had tightened their scrutiny of every aspect of New Christians' daily life.

He and Mariem had chosen to keep from Isabela, their only child, the knowledge of her true religion. In the hope of protecting her from the fear of exposure that haunted all who still clandestinely practiced their Jewish customs and observances, they had raised her as a Catholic. But that protection no longer sufficed to keep his family safe, and so Gabril had come to Hamburg to prepare a new life for them.

"Señor Nuñez!" hailed a voice from behind Gabril.

Startled, he turned to see Eduardo Carel approaching from the footbridge. Scanning the otherwise empty street, Gabril tipped his hat and bowed slightly to the approaching man.

"Good morning, Señor Carel. I am happy to see that you will attend this meeting."

Eduardo Carel stood nearly a head taller than Gabril. His black hair was cut carefully above his doublet and cloak, which were finely tailored and made of good quality wool. A short, well-trimmed beard graced his prominent chin and an aquiline nose centered his fair features. Most startling were the man's eyes: cobalt blue, with heavy black lashes and set under thick brows. Though his unlined face and upright carriage gave the impression of youth, everything about his bearing exuded the competence and confidence of age.

Eduardo clasped Gabril's outstretched hand firmly with one hand and clapped the other on his shoulder.

"Señor de Castro Nuñez, I am pleased to see you as well. I hope your presence here bodes well for your fortunes in business as well as those of your family."

Gabril winced but held the other man's gaze, searching the depths of those blue eyes. "I hope to hear more of my wife and daughter when the next ship arrives from Porto, perhaps as soon as next week, and the conduct of my business here goes well. And you, Señor Carel? How go your affairs?"

Gabril continued trying to read the face of the man before him even during the long pause that followed his question. Eduardo peered into the street in both directions, back toward the door to the warehouse, and then said softly, "I communicated your message, with the package, to my connection in Girona. I believe by now Dama Martel Gerondi has made her way to Abrantes and will have contacted your wife and daughter. But you understand that convincing these men of

Hamburg to pursue the trade agreements we have proposed is crucial to our plan to help our..."

Eduardo's pause caused Gabril to shiver.

"Our clients," Eduardo concluded.

"I understand," Gabril replied. *Only too well.* On the move and gone from home now for four months, he had worked to learn the harsh language of Hamburg and the harsher reality of the narrow space available to a Portuguese New Christian in the commerce of the busy port.

"Perhaps you have heard," Eduardo continued, "that the Wirtschaftsrat has filed a complaint that too many Portuguese Jews and New Christians have entered the business community. Because of our value in trade contacts, we will likely be allowed to continue here, as long as we keep any religious practices secret. The hefty taxes we pay for our trade privileges fall in our favor."

"Yes," said Gabril.

He knew that today's meeting was nominally to further codify this uneasy relationship, which would bring certainty to his own plan to establish himself as a textile agent in Hamburg and finally be able to send for Mariem and Isabela.

In exchange for access to the right officials and the torturous process to apply for an import/export permit, Eduardo Carel had enlisted Gabril in the effort to establish a secret network of sanctuaries for the escape of persecuted Jews and New Christians from Portugal. Gabril had hesitated, having spent years avoiding the scrutiny of officials and clergymen in Abrantes and keeping his identity as a Jew secret under the guise of his parents' conversion to Christianity—but he understood that even New Christians were no longer safe from the Inquisitors in Portugal. Eduardo had promised that Gabril's family would be among the first to be brought out of Abrantes, and so he had agreed, but the danger haunted him.

Mariem knew nothing of his new role, and Isabela knew even less of their hidden identity.

Thoughts of these complex circumstances had filled Gabril's mind for days. Eduardo Carel still stared at him, and despite the cool morning air, as Gabril saw other men approaching from the footbridge, he began to perspire.

Eduardo spoke levelly, keeping his voice low.

"If we can convince this group to accept Dom Duarte Nunes da Costa's application, we will have the last connection we need for the escape network. I wish you the best on your petition."

With these words, Eduardo handed Gabril a small silver medallion and recited what sounded like an incantation, though Gabril caught only a smattering of Hebrew words among others that he could not identify. Before slipping the medallion into his purse, he caught sight of the hamsa imprinted on it—a design of a hand with the shape of the eye at its center that was a protective symbol of kabbalists, a mystical Jewish sect—and had to hide the jolt of shock that struck his center.

Eduardo Carel again clapped Gabril on the shoulder and they turned toward the warehouse door, now thronged with other men waiting to enter.

Isabela sat heavily on a low stool, the garden breeze floating through the small window and bringing welcome cool to the fierce heat of the day. For a week she had risen early and sewn late into the evenings, grateful for the longer daylight hours of early summer. She left shopping and other errands for late morning each day, both to give her eyes and hands a rest, and the only other break she had taken was to attend Mass, making certain when she did that the padre saw her. Every night, she fell into bed at dusk, exhausted.

Finally, the embroidered glove was finished. She expected Senhor de Martins the very next day.

She was preparing to wrap the gloves in a carrying bag when a soft knock sounded on her door.

She froze. Who could be here so late that a first star had already appeared in the darkening evening? Could it be David? But she had just seen him at midday. Perhaps he had news or need of her.

She moved quietly to the door just as another knock came, soft as the first but faster, as though urgent.

"Yes, who is it?" she croaked, her heart beating furiously.

"Isabela de Castro Nuñez?"

"Yes . . . who speaks?"

"Senhorita de Castro Nuñez, I come from Dama Ana Martel Gerondi with an important parcel. I am sorry for the lateness of the hour—I was detained along my way—but I must deliver this to you directly."

Isabela knew the danger of having a stranger in the street before her door, both for him and for herself, but the mention of the formidable Ana overcame her fear. She quickly unlatched the door and ushered the man in, only to find that in fact he was not a man but a boy, not much older than she, and his apprehension seemed to mirror her own.

His sweat-soaked shirt and dirt-streaked face bespoke the hardship of his journey. After securing the door, Isabela pointed to a chair at the table.

"My thanks, senhorita, but I mustn't stay."

"You must be hungry, and surely thirsty, Senhor . . ." Isabela looked expectantly at the boy, but he shook his head.

"It is best if you do not know my name. But here is the parcel." His eyes darted to the ceiling of the small room, as if trying to read from memory. "Dama Martel Gerondi said you must study this well before you send back the gloves and commit the scroll's contents to memory by the time you leave for France." He handed her a well-wrapped bundle the size of a small book.

They both stood for a moment, studying the parcel, as if awaiting instructions. Darkness was now falling in earnest, and Isabela moved to the table and lit a candle. As the flame sprang to life she saw the stamp on the top of the packet, a near-perfect reproduction of the beautiful cross that had adorned Ana Martel Gerondi's bodice on the day of her visit. Spidery ink detailed the filigreed gold and the striking star at the cross's center reminded Isabela of how its amber had picked up the room's light and shone.

Behind her, the messenger shifted from foot to foot. Isabela left the parcel on the table and poured him a cup of wine. As he gulped it down, she pulled half a loaf of bread and some cheese from her larder, wrapped them in a cloth, and handed the bundle to him.

"*Obrigado, senhorita*," he said, already inching toward the door.

She strode past him and unlatched it, and he was gone.

Isabela returned to the table, unwrapped the package, and read until her candle sputtered out in its dish many hours later.

The next morning, Isabela made her way to the de Sousas' home as early as was proper. She had visited David often since their last meeting with Ana Martel Gerondi, sometimes with questions about her imminent departure but often just for the relief of sharing her trepidation. On each occasion the two young people found a way to speak privately despite the fact that David's mother, Adriana, was always watchful. With each visit, their separation drew closer and Isabela's feelings became more fraught.

Just over a week remained before Isabela's expected departure to the house of Mercado in France. When she reached the de Sousa home, David was preparing to leave, as he had to mediate a quarrel between two families in the community, but a single look at Isabela's pale visage caused him to send his sister with a message of delay.

Adriana usually saw to the preparation of dinner, but today it was another sister of David's who moved purposely around the table, setting out the spoons and stirring the *carne de vinha d'alhos*. The rich stew filled the house with scents of garlic, thyme, olives, and wine. The name notwithstanding, the chunks of meat were chicken rather than pork, as was the custom in many New Christian households.

Adriana de Sousa looked aged far beyond her years. Though tidy, her clothes hung on a diminished frame, and her soft grey eyes, once given to sparkle and laughter, were now clouded with sadness and worry. Isabela looked from David to his mother and the older woman nodded, seeming to understand that Isabela wished to speak to David alone.

Wordlessly, David showed Isabela into the garden behind the house—a large, beautifully maintained space filled with the bounty of the season.

David pulled Isabela to a stone bench near the rear wall, and even before he'd found his place next to her she began to pour out the story of the previous evening's visitor. With a quick glance toward the house, she withdrew the packet from her pouch and explained to David the meaning of the sampler and the scroll detailing the code. She handed him the brief note from Ana Martel Gerondi and watched the crease deepen on his forehead as he read.

My dear Isabela,

Enclosed find a sampler of designs which you may find useful in your further pursuits. To augment your income as you extend your travels, I have arranged for small commissions to be directed your way. I must ask that you commit the scroll to memory, and then destroy it; I cannot explain more at this time, but please believe that I seek only to ensure your safety and conduct you to a reuniting with one dear to you. It is my wish that we shall meet again soon, but in the meantime, I pray daily for your safe journey.

Ana Martel Gerondi

"What does she mean, *As you extend your travels*?" Isabela asked, her whisper a quiet wail.

David was quiet for a long moment, then turned to her and took both her hands in his. "I do not know exactly, but I also received a message last evening. Perhaps they are related."

CHAPTER FOUR

Abrantes

June, 1605

A thousand years ago I searched for my star
And the Fados say they have it guarded.
—FRANCESCO RODRIGUES LOBO

"No!" Adriana de Sousa hissed at her son. "You are bewitched by this girl and the *feiticeira* who has influenced her. I will not go, and you will not leave me."

David looked down into the gaunt but fierce face of his diminutive mother, the force of her anger a vibration in the air between them.

"Mamae . . ." He began softly, but his mother's continued wrath kindled his own, and in a harder tone he said, "Dona Martel Gerondi is certainly no sorceress—she risked much to bring word and warning to us from Senhor de Castro Nuñez. And how can you speak of Isabela that way?"

"Perhaps she is not a true Christian and only pretends to believe in order to sell her embroidery to Padre Alvaro. Your helping her will put us all at risk." Adriana's hiss had deepened to a near growl.

David's shock left him momentarily speechless. As he stood looking at her, fear broke through the clouds of anger in his mother's face like shards of lightning in roiling thunderclouds, and he suddenly understood that a madness born of grief and yet another looming peril had supplanted her chronic, quiet sadness.

With an assumed authority he still struggled to feel, he stepped back and spoke quietly but firmly, "Do not ever speak in this way again. It is my job to guide our family and our community in this dangerous time, and you will do as I ask to keep yourself and my sisters safe, even if you cannot yet see the wisdom of this plan. If you care at all for the judgment Papae entrusted to me, you will not afford the spies and gossips around us the chance to endanger us further. You have suffered much, Mamae, . . . we all have." Here David's voice broke, but he stiffened with resolve and continued, "But I will not have you disparage a person who has only ever been our friend and who is now alone in the world and depends on me."

David had never before spoken so harshly to his mother. But now he was the head of the household and of the community. The inner boy faltered, but the man insisted. He watched a single tear brim from Adriana's tightly shut eyes. She did not answer; instead, she turned toward the kitchen and left him standing by the table.

He felt for his pouch, where the note he'd received the evening before still lay, its cryptic instruction as yet unshared with anyone other than Isabela.

> *You must activate an exodus plan for as many community members as possible and then proceed yourself to Toulouse, where further instructions await. Contact Dr. Francesco Sanchez.*

Toulouse? David thought. *That will be a journey of weeks. And who is this Sanchez? What manner of instructions?* The language of the Languedoc was French, not the Spanish that David had minimally learned from the New Christian and Jewish refugees who'd poured into Portugal from Spain after the expulsion of the Jews in 1492. How was he to conduct his family and others to safety without the French language?

Isabela was to go to Irouléguy, but Dama Martel Gerondi's note had said she would travel farther. Would it be to Toulouse? And how would David convince his mother, let alone so many others in the community, to flee—and to do so quietly and quickly?

His belly clenched as thoughts tumbled through his head like boulders down a mountainside of uncertainty. How would he manage?

Adriana entered the church by a side door, near the alcove of the Blessed Mother's statue. She stepped across the narrow rectangle of morning light that fell from the window high above. The huge church was eerily empty, and each step echoed even though she moved softly.

She removed a simple rosary made of jet beads and a wrought silver cross, knelt, and began to pray, the silence thick in the absence of the sound of hammer and chisel hitting stone that had rung out daily for months.

Hail Mary, full of grace, the Lord is with thee. Blessed art Thou among women, and blessed is the fruit of thy womb, Jesus. Holy Mary Mother of God, pray for us sinners now and in the hour of our death . . .

By the third Hail Mary, Adriana had begun to feel the clutch at her center recede, the infusion of warmth that praying to the Virgin Mother always brought. *Full of grace. . . .* Oh, how she needed grace—needed to feel that the Lord was anywhere near her now.

She had come to the church to pray for guidance, for Mary's intercession. When Joao had been alive, he'd known so clearly how to practice Catholic ritual as protection from the Church's and townspeople's scrutiny while privately adhering to the laws of their ancestral Jewish faith within their tight-knit New Christian community. But Adriana had fallen in love with the grandeur of the Church, the orderliness of its rituals, and the embodiment of mysterious beauty and benevolence of the Blessed Mother.

Now she needed all of it to help her find her way. *Blessed is the fruit of thy womb* . . .

A tear tracked down her seamed cheek. The fruit of her womb, David, thrust so young into his father's role in an increasingly dangerous world of Inquisitors, of plague, of strangers delivering menacing instructions from afar. Should she continue to resist? Or was he now no longer a son to be instructed but the head of a family and a community, a man to be obeyed? *Pray for us sinners, now.*

"Good afternoon, Dona de Sousa, how nice to see you here." Padre Alvaro's sudden, silent appearance unnerved Adriana, and she was further discomfited as he knelt next to her in the alcove. "Please, I didn't mean to interrupt your prayers," he said, though his soft, unctuous tone and proximity on the narrow bench suggested otherwise.

Adriana bent her head, though not before she noted his stare at her tear-streaked cheek. She said nothing, fingering her rosary, the burgeoning comfort from moments before vanished.

In a more priestly, sonorous voice, the padre asked, "What troubles you, good woman? Perhaps with God's help we can ease your worries."

With fear seizing her chest, Adriana tried not to gasp as she cast about for something to answer. *What does he suspect? Why has he approached me?* Clutching her beads to her waist to hide her trembling hands, Adriana forced a blank expression onto her face.

"Today I am missing my dear Joao very much, Father. I came to pray for the Virgin's guidance. Oh, and I wished to offer the services of my daughters to help clean tomorrow or on Saturday." Adriana's voice was soft but steady despite the apprehension roiling in her belly.

"Ah, I am sure your life has become more difficult without your beloved husband. And yet your fine son has admirably taken on his father's role, has he not? Why just yesterday he judiciously resolved a quarrel between two families with the madness of the festival swirling about him. That bespeaks a level head, much needed for a boy with so much responsibility. And he advises the poor de Castro Nuñez girl, now that she is alone in the world." Padre Alvaro released an elaborate sigh. "I would be more than pleased to meet with David from time to time—it would be so easy for such a young man to fall prey to dangerous ideas during these unsettling times."

A chill ran up Adriana's spine, sending prickles to the back of her neck. "Yes, Padre, these are dangerous times." In a stronger voice, she said, "And yes, David has worked hard to fill his father's shoes." She was surprised that a small stab of pride pierced her fear as she voiced those words.

"Perhaps I can stop by your house and see David," said the padre.

"Oh, he is out so often," Adriana cut in. "I'll be sure to tell him you wish to see him." Suddenly she wanted to get out of the church and away from this prying priest. Visions of the garden shed, filling with provisions for departing New Christians, crowded into her head.

She rose unsteadily but Padre Alvaro was quickly at her side, holding her elbow firmly.

"If there is anything I can do to ease your troubles, Dona de Sousa, please let me know. I'll be praying for you and for the wise counsel of your son."

Adriana gazed up at the statue of the Virgin, beseeching Her one last time for protection, before stepping out of the alcove and toward the side door.

"Oh, Dona de Sousa, did you not wish to speak to the deacon about your daughters?" Padre Alvaro called after her. "I believe I saw him in the north aisle a short while ago."

Adriana felt his keen eyes on her as she swung around in confusion. Recovering quickly, she nodded her thanks and moved toward the aisle.

The crowded street slowed Isabela's progress but also reduced scrutiny of her movement among the many revelers at the Festas de Abrantes. She made her way down Rua Capitão Correia de Lacerda toward the main square, just beyond the church.

Before she'd gone two minutes, David fell into step beside her, clearing the way for her as the street became even more congested.

"Have you finished the glove?" he asked without looking at her.

Isabela nodded and patted the parcel in the folds of her skirt.

"Why meet in such a public place?" he asked, turning his gaze on her.

Isabela walked resolutely forward. "I don't know." She glanced up at him and then back toward the mass of festival-goers in front of her. "It's what the message from Senhor de Martins said. I'm to meet him in the corner of the square opposite the church."

David's arm looped through hers as he guided her down the road and into the square, the town's central gathering place, currently lined with dozens of booths with food, healers, jugglers, storytellers, barrels of ale and wine, puppet shows, and trinkets. The river Tagus, far below, was crowded with boats pulled up to the wharfs and rafted off each other.

At the corner of the square, Isabela spotted Pedro de Martins, whose searching eyes found hers as she and David approached. He stood before a booth, sheltered from the sun by a beautiful purple tent. In its shade, a lovely woman sat by a table loaded with textiles. On one side were neat stacks of epaulets, neckbands, chest bibs, and cuffs, all embroidered with flowers, animals, fruits, plants, and trees.

Isabela reached out to touch the fine work but hesitated as she looked to the woman sitting on a stool beside the display.

"Isabela de Castro Nuñez," Senhor de Martins said, "may I introduce you to Dona Simone de Leon?"

Startled, Isabela looked from the woman to Senhor de Martins and then to David, who stood a few steps away from the booth, casting his eyes nervously around the crowded square.

Simone de Leon. That was the name of the woman who is supposed to accompany me to France. But it's not time yet. Isabela stepped back, but Dona de Leon spoke quickly to her.

"Senhorita Nuñez, I have looked forward to making your acquaintance. I see you are interested in our embroidery. Your reputation for fine work precedes you." Dona de Leon's voice was low but clear and kind. "Perhaps you have some of your own work I could see?"

Isabela placed a protective hand at her side, where the carefully wrapped embroidered glove lay deep in the folds of her skirt. Should she give the package to this woman? David and Senhor de Martins had now withdrawn into hushed conversation; it seemed she must make her choice without her friend's help.

Before Isabela could decide what to do, Dona de Leon handed a hood band from the stack of embroidered work in the booth to her. "I think perhaps this piece might interest you, though I see from the band of your own hood that you easily accomplish embroidery of this quality."

Isabela absently fingered the flowers and leaves that decorated her hood—the tiny knots of the blue scilla and long stitches of the green ivy were among her favorite motifs. As she studied the band Simone handed her, her eyes widened. On the softest cream velvet, the signs and symbols of the linen square the messenger had brought her—all of which she had already committed to memory— were embroidered in cross stitches, French knots, and couching.

The heart, the tree, the butterfly, the three triangles, and the lion fairly danced across the band, exquisitely worked into a unified design.

Dona de Leon met Isabela's gaze with an intensity that told her this was no casual interaction—no coincidence. The noise and bustle of the festival seemed to recede like a fading dream.

"Hand me the package with the glove as if in payment for the hood band, which you must keep and attach to a hood of your own," she murmured without breaking eye contact with Isabela. "In a week's time, I will return to accompany you to France, but as before, say nothing of our plan. Until then, God speed, senhorita."

Still as if in a trance, Isabela slid the package with the glove out of her skirts and placed it alongside a stack of linens on the table before folding the hood band and placing it in her pocket. Dona de Leon swiftly retrieved the packet from the table and turned toward the trunk behind her wares.

As Isabela turned away from the booth, she found David at her elbow and Pedro de Martins nowhere to be seen. Amid the chaotic bustle of the festival, she tried to tell David of Dona de Leon's message and ask what he had learned from Senhor de Martins, but David silenced her with a squeeze to her elbow as he scanned over the heads of the crowd. When he dropped his head and turned toward her, she caught sight of Padre Alvaro making his rapid way through the crowded square toward them.

"You are here at the market to view the textiles and see the embroidery of others for comparison," David hissed, eyes blazing. "You have sold or purchased nothing."

Isabela blanched. "Why is he watching me?"

David's fierce look silenced her.

The padre was nearly upon them when David turned toward him, a mild, emotionless expression restored to his handsome face.

"Good morning, Padre," he said as the cleric shouldered his way to a spot directly in front of them.

"Senhor de Sousa," said the padre, emphasizing the honorific. "Senhorita de Castro Nuñez." He bowed slightly to Isabela. "It is a lovely day for the festival, no?"

Neither Isabela nor David responded immediately—a discussion of the weather was not first in their thoughts.

"How are you enjoying the festival?" Padre Alvaro pressed on.

"I always like to see the new fabrics and the work of other embroiderers," Isabela responded casually. "It is wonderful to have the festival again after the year of fevers." She kept her voice calm, though the memories of disease and death still weighed heavily upon her.

Turning to David, Padre Alvaro clasped his hands in front of his cassock. "I saw your dear mother in church this week, and she seems so careworn, yet proud of your work with the New Christians. I know how busy you are, but I hope to see you more regularly at mass. And I would be happy to help the community in their efforts to sustain their Christian works, especially as we shortly expect to receive a representative of the Holy Office of the Inquisition. I am sure you will be of great help in our work." He paused before turning to Isabela. "Have you had word from your dear father? His absence must be a continued unhappiness for you."

This unexpected turn of the conversation struck Isabela temporarily mute, and she wished she could appeal to David for a safe answer. Apart from the twitch at the corner of his mouth that Isabela knew to be a sign of distress, he remained expressionless and silent.

"Sadly, no, Padre," she said, "It has been many months since any word has come, though I pray I will hear soon."

"Perhaps one of these textile merchants will have heard of him. Which booth have you visited?"

Isabela glanced toward the purple tent and saw a strange man on the stool behind the display. Dona de Leon and Senhor de Martins had vanished.

"I particularly liked the work of that booth," she replied, "though I have just begun to enjoy the festival."

"I am pleased to see you both working to maintain the legacy of your departed parents, and I look forward to further blessings and good works." With this cryptic pronouncement, the priest nodded in the young couple's direction and turned away into the crowd.

David steered Isabela across the square toward her home. Neither spoke until they had entered the less congested shelter of Rua Capitão Correia de Lacerda.

When she felt the crowd had dwindled sufficiently to assure their privacy, Isabela looked up at David. "Why is he watching us?" she asked again. "Could he suspect our plan? He frightens me." Though she kept walking, she gripped David's arm harder. "And what of your mother? Why did he mention her?"

David breathed out a long sigh. "She is also frightened and doesn't want to face the idea of coming danger. She feels safe here and in her faith, and she does not trust the messages of Dama Martel Gerondi. She resists all thought of leaving."

Isabela stopped and turned to face David. "But you *will* leave, and she will come with you, and your sisters also, yes?"

Searching his face, she saw his warm brown eyes cloud over, and she knew at once that he was contending with a terrible conflict he had kept from her until now. She staggered back.

"I can't do this without you, David," she whispered. "You have to come. I can't leave without knowing we will be together again."

She had never spoken this directly to her friend, to this boy who had so swiftly become a man and who had become so precious to her in a new way since her mother's death. They had never spoken of love, or of their future, but they had also never been apart. Her knees began to tremble and she reached again for his arm.

"I will figure something out," David said quietly. "And I will keep the padre as far away as I can."

Isabela wished to draw him down and seal his declaration with a kiss, something neither one of them had ever before initiated—but they were in the street, so only her pleading eyes sent her message.

CHAPTER FIVE

Abrantes and Hamburg

June, 1605

*Grant, O God, that we lie down in peace, and raise us up,
our Guardian, to life renewed.
Spread over us the shelter of Your peace.*
—HEBREW EVENING PRAYER

The mid-June morning dawned warm and breezy, with the promise of daylight lasting well into evening hours. Isabela had much to do. She cast a critical glance around the cozy room of the only home she had ever known. She had to leave it looking as though she intended to return. The house had to appear tidy but not barren.

Those friends and loved ones familiar with the years of her family's life within these walls would note the absence of the cedar chest, custom made by Gabril de Castro Nuñez for his wife to hold embroidery threads, scissors, needles, and hoops. They would see the empty spaces on the wall where shelves had once held plain vestments, ladies' collars, and gentlemen's cuffs, and which now held a sparse collection of cups and bowls. The wrought silver candlesticks, lit deep within the room and away from windows and prying eyes on Friday evenings, had vanished from their place of pride at the center of the hearth mantle. Isabela's clothing, once stuffed into a corner cupboard, had been removed and packed, making way for those items of her mother's that Isabela could not wear or use and her father's clothing that had not traveled with him to The Free and Hanseatic City of Hamburg.

Is he truly in Hamburg? Why have I not heard from him in months now?

Making her way to the low arch on the far side of the hearth that led to two small bedrooms, Isabela surveyed the nearly full trunk that occupied the large bed in her parents' room. For months she had avoided this room—first to block out the memories of her mother's illness and death, and then because memories of the murmurs and sighs and laughter from a time when happiness reigned in the house made her miss them more.

Over the course of the last week, she had sorted, chosen, and packed for her journey. Her personal items had been easy—her three good dresses, two work dresses, several shifts and bodices, shoes for travel and shoes for living and working in the home of Count Raphael de Mercado, boots and warm stockings for the winter, which would be much colder in the mountains of France. Though she knew nothing of her employer, or of the daughter whose trousseau she would help to create, she hoped that his generous offer of payment and "all protections and comforts" would include the possibility of augmenting her wardrobe as needed.

She packed a tin plate, a cup, a sharp knife, and utensils. She packed her precious book of flowers with illustrations that had inspired so many of her own designs. Her combs, a few ribbons, her hoods, veils, and shawls, and her good, heavy cape were all folded neatly into the trunk.

It had been much harder to choose items belonging to her parents to take. She had spent tearful moments trying to reckon with the likelihood that she would never return to these rooms. What could she remove without signaling that this was more than a short trip to ply her trade? What must she choose to keep the memory of home and family alive and with her in the uncertain days ahead?

Isabela already wore her mother's filigreed golden earrings and delicate sapphire ring. Her breath caught as she recalled the long-ago morning in the garden when her father, holding her mother's hand up to the morning sunshine, told Isabela, "See, *querida*, how the sapphire glows! It always reminds me of your mamae's eyes, and yours as well."

No one had called her "darling" in so long, and she would give all she had to see her mother's blue eyes again.

Isabela quelled these thoughts, as she had so often in recent months, and returned to her packing.

Her father's chests were nearly empty or had gone with him when he departed, but she had chosen a small, well-built cask of his in which to place her valuable items. After emptying it of its items—his large fabric shears, a pair of embroidered cuffs that Mariem had made for him before their wedding, and a sheaf of letters—she withdrew the silk pillow that lined the bottom of the chest. It was beautifully embroidered with pomegranates, a lion, a tree with leafed branches, and a solid trunk. Though not Mariem's typical embroidered patterns, they featured her exquisite stitching.

As Isabela shook the dust from the cushion, she noticed something hard jiggling in the design of the tree branches. Running her fingers over the amber silk and the colored threads, she felt what seemed to be a small piece of metal hidden in a pocket formed in the irregularly shaped space between two branches. Feeling the press of time, she nearly put the pillow back, but curiosity and an unsettling sense of foreboding propelled her to retrieve her embroidery scissors.

She carefully snipped the stitches along the edge of the pocket, and a small key fell into her hand.

Though she had often seen her father use this chest, she had never seen him lock it, nor could she see a mechanism anywhere. Puzzled, she peered at the key, with its tiny, squared end, and then again at the chest, lifting it and studying the bottom and sides. She once again opened the lid.

The floor of the chest was crafted of a different wood than the cedar of its exterior. She tapped the bottom and noted a hollow sound. Moving toward the window for better light, she ran her eyes and her fingers over the wood again, and this time, nearly at the edge of the chest's floor, she found a tiny hole. Working the key gently into the opening, she turned it and heard the softest of clicks. Using the key to lift, she pulled the false floor up and out and stared into the small cavity that lay below.

The space was filled with a bundle of fine parchment, encased in a rougher document.

Isabela glanced around the room, but she was alone, and only the early-summer riot of flowers and herbs looked in from the garden window.

She lifted the bundle and carefully unwrapped the top layer. It was a letter, written in Gabril de Castro Nuñez's strong hand.

My dearest ones,

If you are reading this, I am not there to explain what you find here or protect you from what it means. Mariem, if it is you who has uncovered these documents, you know what they are, and it is my fervent wish that you will take Isabela and flee as we discussed. If I am no longer in this world, you will, G-d willing, have received an instruction and will find your way to safety.

But, my sweet Isabela, if it is you who find your way to these papers, you must know that there is much your mother and I have kept from you for your own safety. We have raised you as a good Catholic, and you must continue to practice in all public ways this religion of your upbringing. Yet, as you know, we are New Christians, and the meaning of that newness we have not fully explained to you. The documents you see here are the marriage papers of your mother and me, and all of our birth records—you must keep them as hidden as I have, for they can only bring danger to you. If I am still in this world, I am trying to establish a new home for us, where we can live in freedom. Follow the signs I have sent your way and know that I love you always.

Yours,
Papae Gabril

Isabela sat down abruptly on the bed, stunned as if a catapult had exploded the walls around her. Shaking, she grasped the fine parchment and carefully unrolled it, revealing a document beautifully illustrated with colorful flowers, animals, and vines. Handwritten script in a language Isabela had never seen filled the center. Within it was a smaller document written in the same foreign script. What was this language? Why were these documents different from those the family had always kept safe in the sitting room chest—her baptismal registry, her parents' marriage record—and what danger did her father refer to?

Another shiver ran through Isabela as she picked out the same symbols in the larger document that decorated the hood band given to her by Dona de Leon, and that had graced the linen square sent by Dama Martel Gerondi. The heart, the tree, the butterfly, the three triangles, and the lion, along with the pomegranate and more of her mother's favored floral designs, embellished the borders of the beautiful parchment.

A sharp knock at the door startled Isabela. With trembling hands, she replaced the strange documents in the chest, stowed it under the bed, and rushed to the door, trying to compose herself.

"Yes, who is it?" she called out.

"It's David," came the urgent reply.

Isabela pulled the door open; David entered quickly and shut the door behind him. He faced Isabela, his face lined with worry. Before she could tell him of her discovery, he clasped her hands and in a near whisper blurted, "The Inquisitors have arrived. The padre has sent a summons directing me to make a list of all the New Christians in our district and to be prepared to detail their affairs and whereabouts. My mother still refuses to leave, though I have urged her to prepare with my sisters. They, at least, believe that we must go."

"What will you do?" Isabela asked.

"I will order her to come," he said. "I head our family now and this is what my father would want. But it will give me pain to tell her so." David moved his hands to Isabela's arms and drew her closer. "There is more. I received a message from Senhor de Martins. You are to ready yourself to leave with Dona de Leon, perhaps as soon as tonight. We cannot write to each other through normal channels for fear of an interception. You must give me something embroidered with a design that you will repeat and send with any message you do communicate to me so that I will know it is safe to receive and respond."

Isabela swayed, dizzied by David's words. Grasping at his sleeves, she stared up at him. She saw both the anguish of the boy she loved and trusted and the weariness and uncertainty of the man burdened with consequential tasks. She would not complicate his challenges.

Reaching up, she pulled his face to her own and kissed him gently. Though tears brimmed in her eyes, she steadied her voice before saying, "I understand. I have prepared for you a set of cuffs. The insides are embroidered with symbols in different colors. I have written out the simple code, which you must memorize quickly. Once you have done so, you must destroy the parchment."

Isabela had worked feverishly to complete the cuffs. Not at all the same symbols and colors that Ana Martel Gerondi had given her, these were flowers, emblems and animals of her own choosing, meant only for David. With her most beautiful stitches, she had sewn an iris as a signal of a message, a heart for her love, a butterfly for the liberation of their escape, blue waves to signify survival, a daisy for loyalty, a candle for light and truth, and, the most special symbol, a hamsa—the stylized image of a hand that her mother had sewn into every one of her items of clothing, though she'd always made clear that it could never be shown publicly.

"It will be like when we were children and made up languages to keep our secrets," Isabela said. "You must always first look for the iris; when you see that, you will know that I intended to send a message." She tried to smile her assurance.

David's eyes widened, but he let Isabela go and she retrieved a carefully wrapped packet from the oak chest next to the hearth. As she slipped it into his doublet, she once more looked up at him.

"I know there is much I have not been told about our lives as New Christians." She held David's eyes. "What do the Inquisitors seek to know about us?"

David took a deep breath before speaking but his voice was unwavering when he said, "They seek to find and root out any evidence of heresy—any departure from the true faith, any remnant of a past religious practice. What they cannot find, they will fabricate." Turning away, David strode to the center of the room.

"But we have been true Catholics!" Isabela cried out. Even as her words rang out, her knowledge of the parchment hidden in the next room sent a shiver through her.

"The truth of our faith seems to be of little consequence to the Inquisition," David said in an anguished whisper. "They will expel, torture, burn at the stake—anything to convict and condemn."

Isabela shuddered. David returned to her side, pulled her close, and found her lips with his own. Holding her face in his hands, he said, "You must go, but I promise, I will follow. Get word to me of your safe arrival in Irouléguy."

Before she could respond, he moved toward the door, and in seconds he was gone.

"Blessed be the Name of the Lord. Into Thy hands, O Lord, I commend my spirit."

Gabril de Castro Nuñez poured out hot wax and applied his seal to the letter he had worked on for the entire morning. The irony of having invoked the Catholic prayer brought a wisp of a smile to his exhausted features. He had come to appreciate the benefits of the prayers of his adopted religion in the many times he had needed to appeal to whatever God above might make his circumstance less intractable. He had no delusions regarding the horrors the Church had unleashed through the Inquisition, but he had also come to understand the power of faith to support and inspire.

He had sometimes felt power in a surge of voices lifted in song or in the meditative hush of the vaulted sanctuary of the Church of St. John the Baptist in Abrantes. At other times, under his prayer shawl, repeating the Hebrew prayer for the dead on the anniversaries of his parents' passing, a sense of his place in the generations that had come before him and that he hoped would stretch forward had filled him with peace.

Ultimately, Gabril was a practical man, and the urgent task before him was to secure a means of earning a living in this new land and bring his family to safety. With a heavy sigh, he rose from his small desk and moved to the sole window in his second-story room. He was as yet unused to living high above the street, though he appreciated the fresher air when a breeze from the canal below brought hints of the river beyond. The houses on Monkedamm were tall and solid, the streets wider in the Neustadt than they were in the older parts of Hamburg. The spires of St. Gertrude's rose protectively to the north, as did those of St. Peter's down the road where it bent toward the Alter Wall.

He picked up the letter, the wax hardened but still warm, and marveled that his appeal to the aldermen of the Wirtschaftsrat had been successful. Ignoring the boldness of the Portuguese New Christians—many of whom, in defiance of the Wirtschaftsrat's edicts, were practicing long-hidden Jewish rituals—the Wirtschaftsrat had granted the Portuguese equal rights for export, import, and wholesale trade. In this, the New Christians were not alone. Other groups of non-Lutherans—English Anglicans, Dutch Calvinists, Catholics, and, recently, some Jews from elsewhere in Europe—were allowed to conduct business according to the value they brought in their contacts from home. None were allowed to openly practice their non-Lutheran religion, but what they did in private, the Wirtschaftsrat chose to ignore. There was even talk, in the close-knit community of his countrymen, of purchasing land on Alter Wall for the construction of a synagogue, should the loosening of restrictions on religious practice continue.

In the meantime, for the first time in more than a decade, Gabril de Castro Nuñez prayed at his own home in his skull cap and prayer shawl, reading from a prayerbook written in Hebrew. Since he'd been freed from the specter of torture and death, the words of his forefathers had slowly arisen amidst his private prayers as often as the Catholic words he'd learned to substitute. As he stood now at the window, he ached to see the faces of his wife and daughter—to hold Mariem and smooth the lines of worry from her forehead, and to tell Isabela all that had been kept from her about her true identity. It had been more than four months since he'd left Abrantes, and his heart was heavy with longing.

He turned back to the letter, the seal now hard and cool. He must now go out into the morning and find the messenger who would deliver it to Eduardo Carel. With this letter, Gabril would begin a commitment to fostering a secret network of sanctuaries for escaping Jews and New Christians traveling from Portugal to France and then Germany.

Never had Gabril engaged in such a dangerous prospect. Secrecy shrouded what he would be tasked to do, and with whom. Terse, coded messages were his only communications. All he knew for certain was that after having studiously avoided overtly political or religious associations all his life, he was now risking his reputation, his livelihood, and perhaps more to reunite his family. In hopes of that outcome alone had he agreed to embark on this perilous path.

With renewed purpose, he descended the steep stairway and set out into the morning.

CHAPTER SIX

Girona and Castelo de Vide

June, 1605

Boldness be my friend.
—William Shakespeare

Ana Martel Gerondi tapped the pocket of her kirtle with her free hand as she hurried through the market square, a basket weighing heavily on her arm. She swung it forward to avoid toppling the fruit on one stand, and again to spare the bursting bouquets of flowers on the next. The profusion of bougainvillea, roses, hydrangea, jacaranda, mandevilla, fuchsia, and lantana filled her senses, overpowering the apprehension that drove her day.

She lowered the basket to her side when the narrow aisles widened enough to allow a faster stride. She wore her simplest grey cloak, though it was warm for the June day, in the hopes of minimizing her statuesque figure. The less she was noticed, the better.

Reviewing her list of purchases and what she had yet to acquire, she kept an eye out for the stall of Diego Ramos, from whom she had purchased herbs, roots, and flowers for medicinals and dyes for many years. Ticking off the needed plants she grew in abundance in her own garden—peppermint, passion flower root, valerian, lavender, rosemary, rose hips, chamomile, and lemon—she mentally listed what still had to be purchased: nutmeg and myrrh for purifying air, cloves and limes for pomanders, calendula and yarrow and elderflower for fever, burns, colic, and blood humors. Packed at home and ready for her upcoming journey were the oak galls, salt, alum, and vinegar that she'd require as mordants to bind her dyes to fabric and thread. Soap root, lupin oil, walnut leaves, and calendula flowers had been made into soaps and shampoos.

Thoughts of the journey ahead once again filled Ana with misgiving. The letter in her pocket from Eduardo Carel had arrived two days earlier, and the plan laid out was daunting. She'd been asked, in previous communications, to assist the conduct of Mariem and Isabela de Castro Nuñez out of Portugal and through France in order to join their husband and father in Hamburg. She'd only learned of Mariem's death after traveling the great distance to Abrantes, formerly a somewhat protected and isolated district but now an unhappy target of the Inquisition's persecution of New Christians.

With the help of Alfonso Mendes and his contacts, she'd managed to arrange Isabela's escape and make her own way back to Girona, where her false identity as an Old Christian and her true work as a healer and dye maker was unquestioned. But now, Eduardo was asking more. He urged her to travel to France and join Isabela on her journey, all the while seeking out and establishing safe havens for refugees along the lengthy and dangerous route. Ana was to use her wealth and her skills as a healer and dye maker as a cover, as she had in her many years in Girona.

Even as she hurried, Ana patted her pocket again. Eduardo—brilliant, beautiful Eduardo. Ana's longing to see her tall, handsome lover made her draw in a breath and slow her pace. Though the very thought of him created a tingle in her chest that spread heat to her neck and arms, she quashed those thoughts. Now wasn't the time. Instead, she must proceed with the instructions in his message: gather her herbs and plant dyes; arrange for transport from Girona into France and toward Toulouse, with a plan to secure safe havens for escaping New Christians along the way; and get herself and Isabela de Castro Nuñez to safety in Hamburg. It was altogether too daunting to consider in its entirety, and so she concentrated only on the next steps.

Back to her list: cilantro and coriander seeds as a stimulant and digestive aid; comfrey for wound healing, joint pain, and skin irritation; woad, indigo, saffron, and madder for dyes.

"Señora Martel Gerondi, what a pleasure," said a low voice in front of Ana.

Her eyes shot up to those of the man across from the herbs she was examining.

It was Andres Henriques, the *notario público* who had handled all of Ana's husband's legal affairs during his lifetime and after his death. When news came that Breno Gerondi had succumbed to plague on a business trip to Italy, Ana had been devastated, and for weeks had been unable to attend to the complex tasks involved in carrying on her husband's business interests or settling his personal affairs. To their everlasting sorrow, they were childless, and so there was no clear heir to take on the business or manage Breno's considerable wealth.

But Andres Henriques was also a close family friend and a compatriot in the close-knit underground resistance group formed to defy the Inquisition and assist those needing to escape it. He shared Ana's history as a born Jew living as an Old Christian, therefore free from the scrutiny and persecution that Jews and newly converted Christians endured. He had come to know Ana well and to recognize her intelligence and self-determination, to appreciate her skill as a healer and dye maker. And so he'd sold Breno's import/export business for a good price on her behalf, and afterward spent many long hours with her acquainting her further with the land holdings and other sources of income that provided her with a handsome living. In finer circles of Girona, speculation had swirled that Andres Henriques, long a bachelor, would seek to make Ana Martel Gerondi his wife. Yet, five years later, they remained close colleagues and friends and nothing more.

"*Buenos días, señor,*" Ana responded, "and always a pleasure to see you as well."

"Allow me to accompany you as you finish your marketing, and perhaps we can have a cup of chocolate," Andres said.

Ana wished to refuse, as there was so much to accomplish before her journey, but something in the tense lines around her friend's deep brown eyes changed her mind and she simply nodded.

She finished her purchases quickly and was soon seated with Andres at a nearby taberna, steaming bowls of hot chocolate before them. She raised her bowl to her lips and sipped gratefully. Though the day was already warm, the sweet, rich drink was a welcome antidote to the queasy sensation that Andres's demeanor had triggered in her.

As soon as the tavern keeper was out of hearing, Andres said in a low voice, "The Inquisitors have closed in on Abrantes, Ana. We believe Isabela has made her departure, but we have not heard for certain as to her safety. Gabril de Castro Nuñez has successfully gained permission to conduct business for merchants in Italy and Portugal, which we hope will allow him to establish transportation routes and"—here, he dropped his voice even further—"therefore safe havens for our . . . friends who must find their way to Hamburg."

Ana sat back in her seat, cupping the cooling bowl of chocolate. Andres's words accentuated the reality of the work that she and other clandestine activists were engaged in. She gazed at his worried face. Did he know about the letter from Eduardo, which was fairly burning a hole in her pocket? Would he attempt to dissuade her from departing?

He looked back at her, a question in his eyes, as if trying to decide whether to speak further. Before she could determine what to say, he whispered, "Those traveling to France from Spain must cross over only near Salamanca, or even farther west. The fighting with France is not going well and Filip's forces cover the roads north and to the west between here and Toulouse. The ocean routes from Porto to Bayonne are plagued by pirates and the British." He leaned even closer across the table. "But my informants also tell me that a priest from Abrantes, a Padre Alvaro, is in collusion with the Duke of Lerma, deploying the Inquisitors to root out networks of New Christians and end the flow of refugees—and their skills and capital—out of Portugal. Do you understand the danger? It comes from all sides."

He sat back, his whole body emanating fear. "What is your plan, Ana?"

Ana could see that he feared for her and dreaded the loss of her.

How much should she reveal to this dear man who had been such a wonderful friend? Without a thought for propriety, she reached out and closed her long fingers around Andre's hand.

"I have been asked to attend to Isabela's escape through France and into Germany. Her own parents are gone and she hasn't anyone to educate her and see to her place in the world. I will make my way with my dyes and my herbs."

This wasn't entirely a falsehood, but the pain in Andres's eyes confirmed that he knew Ana would not, could not, reveal more than she would tell anyone else publicly—this for his own protection. She saw the deepening consternation in his expression as she remained silent, refusing to put him at risk with more detailed information about her secret work.

He sat back with a heavy sigh, seemingly resigned to what she would do and the unknown danger involved. "Is there anything I can do to help you?" he asked.

"Pray for my safe and successful journey." Ana's eyes suddenly filled with tears, the enormity of her task weighing heavy in the air between them.

"That I will do, Ana, but you must know the peril of this journey. The Inquisitors are burning healers at the stake, just like heretics."

Ana's hand pressed the filigreed cross hanging at her chest, the gem star at the center glowing softly in the dim light. "May God protect me, then," she replied with a wisp of a smile, swiftly crossing herself.

Andres shook his head and a reluctant smile softened his eyes as he flagged down the tavern keeper to settle his account.

At mid-morning, the path left the Tagus River and moved through open fields, skirting the occasional hillock and widening enough to allow the wagon, pulled by a single small horse, to ride smoothly.

Isabela had walked nearly the whole of the previous night, first through the slumbering streets of Abrantes and down to the river, where a small barge waited for the two heavily cloaked women and where a young stranger had lifted Isabela's trunk onto his shoulder and carried it to the barge. Silently and in total darkness, the boatman had steered the barge up and across the river, poling and working the long tiller until he pulled up to the opposite shore and discharged the women and their belongings onto a waiting wagon. But the riverside path had been narrow and uneven, causing the horse to pick its way uncertainly and strain at times to pull the loaded wagon. And so Isabela and Dona de Leon had walked behind in the moonless night, sometimes joined by the driver over particularly difficult sections.

At dawn, the path had finally become enough of a road for the women to settle into the wagon bed and sleep. Now, hours later, awaking to the rhythmic revolution of the wheels on the dry hard pack of the road, it took Isabela several moments to remember where she was.

Shifting her sore body into a more comfortable position, she gazed into the deep blue of the cloudless sky. A quiet dread supplanted even the hunger and thirst that had pulled her from sleep.

Dona de Leon had spoken little after appearing at her door the previous night. Isabela had understood that the less noise made that might alert others of her departure, the better. Now, some five leagues into the countryside, her questions and fears arose in full force and she turned to her companion. The older woman lay serenely next to her, hands resting at her chest, eyes lifted to the sky.

"Dona de Leon," Isabela began, "there is much I wish to know of our journey." She had spoken quietly in her halting French, and at first she thought the other woman hadn't heard, as she neither moved nor responded for several long moments.

"We will travel first to Castelo de Vide, and there await further instructions for our journey. No one from Abrantes will expect that we will travel east rather than north or west to the ocean in order to reach France." Dona de Leon spoke in perfect Portuguese. As if she could see the questions swirling in Isabela's head, she sat up and, quietly but harshly, said, "The Inquisitors and your friendly Padre Alvaro will not be pleased to find you gone. It is my hope that your young friend David will be convincing with his story that you are fulfilling a commission and are expected to return. I hope that other investigations will keep them busy long enough for us to reach our destination safely."

"But David is also meant to leave, and to help others leave." Isabela tried to control the panic in her voice.

"Yes," said Dona de Leon, "but the more people that leave, the more scrutiny will be brought to bear on those who remain."

Isabela sat up, then slumped against her bags. Only now did she understand the full extent of the scrutiny and danger she had brought upon David.

In the silence that followed, she choked back threatening tears. She had given herself into the hands of the strange woman beside her, embarked upon a journey, cloaked in secrecy and implicit danger, that would take her away from all she knew and loved. Drawing a deep breath, she sat up once again, swung her feet onto the floor of the wagon, straightened her dress, and reached into her satchel for her combs. She mustn't give in to fear.

"We will stop at the inn in Gaviao for a midday meal and rest during the heat of the afternoon, then continue into the evening." Again, Dona de Leon spoke without looking at Isabela, who wondered what events had shaped this taciturn companion of hers. Instinct told her that the older woman would not welcome questions about her past.

Suppressing her curiosity, she clamped her mouth shut.

The inn was small and simple. Without asking Isabela, Dona de Leon ordered *bacalhau*, the traditional Portuguese salt cod, egg, and potato dish, rather than the local cataplana, a steamed dish of pork and clams.

The food was welcome and tasty. Isabela had eaten only a crust of bread and some cheese since the middle of the previous day.

After their dinner, the innkeeper showed the two women to a small garret room at the top of the stairs, with a window overlooking a kitchen garden and a small olive orchard beyond. No breeze broke the stillness of the afternoon. After securing the door, Dona de Leon matter-of-factly stripped down to her shift and lay on one side of the single bed. Though exhaustion tugged at Isabela, she washed her face and hands of the grime of travel before joining her companion. In moments, she fell into sleep.

After what seemed only a brief rest but turned out to be nearly two hours of slumber, a soft knock at the door woke the travelers, and they were soon accepting packets of cheese and broa and a bottle of beer to bring with them as they continued their journey.

Rested and fed, the horse pulled the wagon with more energy, and in the fading light of evening the travelers came to the foot of a steep hill. Perched at the top and aglow in the evening light sat the Castelo de Vide, surrounded by a walled village.

The women were asked once again to walk to spare the horse on the ascent, and so it was that the long June day had come to an end by the time the small party reached the town gates.

Before they could rouse the gatekeeper, a man slipped from the shadow of the wall and approached the wagon. Tall and dressed in the clothes of a gentleman, he spoke quietly to the driver before leaning over the side of the wagon to address Dona de Leon and Isabela.

Isabela clutched the edge of her seat at his appearance, but when she turned to Dona de Leon, the older woman appeared perfectly composed.

The man did not introduce himself; instead, he studied the embroidered band on Isabela's hood for a long moment, then said, quietly and with authority, "I will ring for the guard and speak to him on your behalf. You will be directed to Rua Nova, to the home of Alfonso Mendes, where you will stay for two nights. You are seamstresses from Covilha, come to acquire woolen threads. Senhor Mendes will direct you to a business on Rua do Arcario, where you will purchase the wool, and he will also give you a volume of the work of Dr. Garcia da

Orta that contains formulas for herbs and medicinals and dyes that you will be asked for later in your journey. Keep it well hidden until you are expressly asked for it."

The oddness of the man's message struck Isabela, but again, Dona de Leon seemed to receive his words with equanimity—so much so that she began to wonder if her companion had actually understood the man's Spanish-accented Portuguese.

Dona de Leon dispelled this doubt when she responded, "Thank you for this information. And who shall we say commends us to Senhor Mendes?"

"You should not say," the man replied. "You are expected." He leaned in over the wagon's sideboard and added, "And go to Mass on Sunday to show your piety. You are strangers here and on your further journey. You will be watched." As he looked to each of the women in turn, the torchlight at the gatehouse caught his face and Isabela noted his black hair and cobalt blue eyes.

"I wish you a safe and successful journey, my ladies," he concluded, and with that he turned toward the bell of the gatehouse.

"Wait . . . senhor!" Isabela surprised herself with her urgency. "Can you get a message to a friend who may still be in Abrantes? He will be worried about my safety."

"It would not be wise to write, senhorita." The gentleman's voice was soft but firm.

"I needn't write; I only wish to see that he receives this." Isabela handed the man a small square of linen, upon which was embroidered an iris and a symbol of a hand, a tiny eye sewn at its center.

The man's eyes widened as he looked first at the cloth and then quickly up at Isabela. In an instant, he seemed to reach a decision. "What is this friend's name?"

When the gatekeeper had been summoned and the wagon had been admitted and finally sent down the Rua Nova, Eduardo Carel leaned his tall, slender frame against the fortress wall and said a quick prayer of thanks, asking the lord to protect the daughter of Gabril de Castro Nuñez on the remainder of a journey that she did not yet know would try to reunite her with her father. He again studied the square of linen in the flickering torchlight. A hamsa, symbol of the hand of God and protection against the evil eye, was as dangerous if seen by an Inquisitor as it was precious as a sign of safety for both Jews and Muslims. Eduardo was certain the girl had been told of the danger of this symbol. Ana would have to remind her.

He sighed, placed the square in his doublet, and, as quietly as he had appeared, stole back into the night.

CHAPTER SEVEN

Abrantes and Hamburg

June, 1605

*For God did not send his Son into the world to condemn the world,
but to save the world through him.*

—JOHN 3:17

David de Sousa stood before Padre Alvaro, willing his eyes to stay on the priest's face, willing his heart not to pound through his tunic, and willing the shiver that ran through him not to buckle his knees. He resolutely kept his gaze on the padre and not the three men who sat behind the massive oak desk in the padre's study, quills in hand, parchments before them.

"Do you understand the gravity of this missing information, David?" the padre asked.

David quelled the moan that rose to his throat before it could emerge and betray the absence of a strong response. For the hundredth time, he wished his father were here facing this crisis, or at least instructing his son from whatever heavenly perch he occupied.

Instead, he responded, "I am at a loss to understand what is missing, your eminence. The tax rolls are up to date and the census is accurate." This David knew, as he had been tasked with accounting and record keeping for several years before his father's death. Since his father's passing, he had taken on the remaining tasks of the titular head of the New Christian community: adjudicating disputes and communicating with civil and church officials. This last was the hardest for David, as he was not yet familiar with all the individuals and ruling systems. What he had learned quite well already was that Padre Alvaro was powerful, presiding as he did over strong ties between church and castle, and that he was not a man to be trusted. Young and inexperienced as David was, he knew the padre was posturing for the Inquisitors.

But what, exactly, is at stake? What does he want?

"We have always had a devout and committed community of believers at Igreja de São João Baptista," Padre Alvaro said. "It is a fine church, and becoming more prominent with the new construction. We don't wish to have . . . dangerous influences bringing heretical ideas. I have reports that strangers have been visiting members of our New Christian community. Surely I should have expected to have received that information from you, shouldn't I, David? And I would hate to have to levy the fines for New Christian businesses leaving Abrantes on the community's remaining residents."

"I'm still not sure I understand what you've found amiss, Padre," said David, though he understood perfectly well that the padre knew a big change was afoot and would squeeze whatever information he could from anyone he could.

"An unusual number of New Christians has left Abrantes in recent weeks, many of whom did not declare their departure or pay the appropriate tax before leaving the city." This last remark came from one of the three men at the desk; reluctantly, David turned to face him.

The Inquisitors were all dressed in heavily decorated clerical garb of fine material and tailoring, as if they were exotic birds who had found themselves in a plain garden. The one who had spoken twirled the quill in his hand as though impatient to record some infraction or damning piece of evidence.

Before David could offer a comment, the man continued, "We are particularly interested in the whereabouts of a young woman of your acquaintance: a Senhorita Isabela de Castro Nuñez. You're acquainted with her, no?"

At this David's pounding heart nearly stopped. He hoped his newly thickening beard hid the loss of color from his face. He held the man's gaze. "Yes, Senhorita de Castro Nuñez is known to me."

"Are you aware that she has departed Abrantes?"

"I am aware that she has traveled to France in the employ of a nobleman."

"Do you find it unusual that a French nobleman would reach so far, all the way into Portugal, for the services of an embroideress? Have they no such skills in France?"

David paused before answering, trying to divine where this line of questioning would lead. "I'm sure I don't know, Excellency." He suddenly wondered if this was the correct honorific for an Inquisitor. He glanced quickly at the padre, whose face remained immobile. Trying to say as little as possible, he still felt he needed to add, "As I'm sure the padre can attest, the house of Castro Nuñez is well known for the quality of its work, and with her mother's death and her father's absence, the work of maintaining the business and her livelihood has fallen to Senhorita Isabela herself. I believe the padre himself has commissioned a number of pieces."

Again, David looked to Padre Alvaro; this time he saw a flicker of a frown cross his face, and David knew he'd made his point.

"Yes, her father has been absent for months, hasn't he?" the Inquisitor asked.

"I believe he must often travel to purchase silks and textiles and to sell his finished work. And then the fevers have made travel a challenge. I'm not certain when Senhorita Isabela last heard from her father." David cringed, knowing he'd answered more than what was asked.

"Do you know when Senhorita de Castro Nuñez expects to return?"

"I do not, Excellency."

A silence fell over the room, the afternoon sun filtering through the leaded glass and the one open window igniting dust motes like tiny fireflies—a small but welcome distraction from David's troubled thoughts.

"And your own mother, Senhor de Sousa. We understand she has also left Abrantes?"

A second Inquisitor, older and more severe-looking, posed this question. David shrank from his cold stare.

"Yes, she has gone to stay with her sister, to help care for my ailing uncle." This was true, but it was not the reason for Adriana Gomez de Sousa's departure. She had gone because she had refused to accompany her son on his planned clandestine exit and was frightened of what she would face if she remained in Abrantes afterward. Her sister lived far to the west, near Coimbra and the port city of Figuera da Foz. But what did these Inquisitors know of his mother and the reasons for her journey?

Silence returned, and uncomfortable though he was, David remained quiet, maintaining a calm exterior despite the fact that every nerve in his body clamored for him to turn and flee. He looked to the padre, who appeared to be waiting for the three Inquisitors to continue the interview. David was surprised to see an expression of uncertainty, even fear, on the padre's face. But then the priest appeared to make a decision, and as he turned back to David, the expression vanished from his face.

"The investigators will be interviewing the members of your

community to make certain there are no lapses in thought or practice as good Christians. We expect your full cooperation."

"Yes, Padre," David said.

"And we expect you will remain available as needed," the priest added.

"Yes, Padre."

As no one said anything further, David stepped back and turned to leave the room.

"Oh, and Senhor de Sousa, do commend us to your mother and tell her we look forward to her return," Padre Alvaro called after him. "Would you like me to send a message to my colleague in Lagos?"

David turned back to look at him. "Oh, I hardly think that is necessary, Padre. I am certain my aunt will have the full support of her church's community and my mother will fit in quite well. But thank you, and please pray for my uncle and those caring for him."

With that, he left the room, stunned at the bravado he had summoned in his responses and hopeful that he hadn't strayed into recklessness. He walked quickly down the long corridor, through the sanctuary, and toward the alcove with the statue of the Holy Mother, where his own mother so often prayed. He paused, genuflected swiftly, crossed himself, and then passed through the side door of the church and into the afternoon light.

Only when he'd made his way through the heat up the Rua Sao Pedro did he begin to assess what had just happened.

In the last week, he had seen to the departure of a dozen families, all those who were willing to leave. Tonight, he and his sisters would escape. A little breathless from the climb toward his home, he felt his chest contract at the thought of the members of the community he would leave behind and what they might suffer after his exit. He had tried with the best of his authority and skill to convince people to depart in anticipation of the scrutiny from the Inquisition that was now beginning, and many had heeded his warnings. But others had not.

If Padre Alvaro knew of David's plan to depart, he wouldn't have allowed him to leave the church—yet clearly he, and the Inquisitors, were aware of movement among the New Christians and were probing for more information. Now he felt his every move would be watched, and so he proceeded with a studied, easy pace toward his home and waiting sisters.

Their packed chests and satchels had been quietly taken from the house that morning in the tinker's wagon during the progress of his normal rounds. For a good price, David had secured the promise that those belongings would be waiting in another wagon, bound for Tomar, that night.

But before he left, he had to finish recording all that would be needed for whomever took over his position as leader of the community, though he feared all the ledgers and parchments would fall immediately into the hands of Padre Alvaro. With that in mind, he had tried to record only what was necessary to comply with the stringent rules governing Abrantes's New Christian community: strict boundaries for residential sections of the town, limited sectors of businesses and punitive taxes on those businesses, fines and other punishments for violations of curfews and commerce restrictions, records of disputes and resolutions within and outside of the sector, and a census that included births, deaths, and entries into and departures from the community.

He would leave it all in good order, though he again fought against the guilty knowledge that others would surely suffer in his stead. His sister Beatriz, who had the kindness of a saint and the wisdom of one far older than her sixteen years, had assured him earlier that week, *You have done all you can possibly do to persuade the others. Now we must save ourselves.*

Why couldn't all the others see that? Why couldn't his own mother?

After casting a final, furtive look down his narrow street, David retreated through the door of the home he would leave within hours, perhaps never to see again.

As soon as he had closed the door behind him, he sighed. "I am certain I am being watched," he told his sisters. "A man followed me home from the church, and I believe he waits at the top of the road."

He paced the small sitting room in silence, then stopped in front of his two younger siblings. "We must think of a way to leave discreetly, and perhaps earlier than tonight."

He looked at his two lovely sisters, their trusting, open faces turned to him, surmounting the fear he knew they must feel.

"I have an idea," Beatriz said.

An hour later, Beatriz emerged from the house and headed up the road, a covered basket swinging from her arm. She stopped at a friend's door just short of the spot where a man in ragged clothes squatted in the shade.

Beatriz knocked and was soon joined by another young woman, and the two began to chat—quietly at first, and then with louder voices punctuated with laughter. As naturally as if she did not know that her life depended upon it, Beatriz held the arm of her friend and moved subtly into the road, blocking the view to her own home and giving her brother and sister a chance to make their hasty exit and flight to the river docks.

After several minutes, the man appeared to rouse himself and stand. Feigning surprise at the sight of a man so close by, Beatriz stepped quickly back, knocking her basket against the house's wall and spilling the oranges she carried, causing a rolling mess. The two young women began collecting the oranges, blocking the man's progress past them even as they profusely apologized and begged his pardon until, clearly frustrated he turned away from the road toward the castle gate and ducked down an adjacent road.

With a swift hug and whispered words of thanks, Beatriz fled in the opposite direction from his and made her own way to the warehouse by the docks where David had told her to meet him.

She ran at first but then remembered herself and slowed her pace. If she were stopped or caught for any reason, they would all be in jeopardy, and so she composed herself and walked with purpose rather than panic.

"The senhoritas are prepared for the arduous walk?" asked the man who arrived at the warehouse deep into the night. "Are you certain you were not followed?"

David de Sousa paused before answering. Of course he was worried for the safety and fortitude of his sisters. The instructions from Pedro de Martins, delivered in whispers by a messenger, had said a trustworthy man would meet them at this warehouse and guide them to Tomar and then to Buarcos, where they would board a boat and sail first to Porto and then to Bayonne. But how did he know this was the trusted man?

The greatest danger was this first part of the escape, now that the alarm over departing New Christians had been raised in Abrantes. With Padre Alvaro's threats echoing in his head, David spoke cautiously.

"We were not followed, and we are as prepared as we can be," he said. "My sisters are strong and used to hard work. If need be, we have brought boys' clothing for them. We have been here for hours already this night. So, unless *you* have followed us here and are planning to arrest us . . ."

A flicker of annoyance appeared in the man's expression, quickly replaced with the calm authority he had previously shown. "If we are to get along on this journey, Senhor de Sousa, I suggest you keep a civil tongue in your head. I am not putting my own life and the lives of your family at risk for enjoyment. As a good Christian, I wish to be of service to those who are being persecuted unjustly, but, as you must know, I do so at my own peril."

Chastened, David bowed his head. "I apologize, Senhor . . ." Realizing he had no name to use, he simply raised his eyes and looked into those of the other man. "It has been hard to know whom to trust these last months."

"I understand, and I know you have borne much responsibility for others in recent months, have had to persuade many people to trust you." Having spoken these words, the man allowed a small smile to soften his face, and he reached into his pocket and pulled out a small square of cloth. "Perhaps this will help you to trust me further," he said as he handed the remnant to David.

A cry left David's lips as he fingered first the beautifully rendered bloom of an iris and then the intricately detailed symbol of a two-thumbed hand that he'd only ever seen on the inside of the cuffs Isabela had embroidered for him. Closing his eyes, he took the first deep breath of air he'd been able to get past the tightness in his chest for days.

Isabela, at least for now, was safe.

Gabril de Castro Nuñez sat on the edge of his bed, elbows on knees, head sunk into his hands. The tattered letter from Joao de Sousa lay on the floor below him, months instead of weeks on its journey bringing the awful tidings of Mariem's death. His body shook as he gasped for breaths, dizzy from the shock.

Between the harassment of pirates and the continuous skirmishes among the British, Dutch, and Spanish navies, the waters of the Atlantic between Portugal and into the North Sea were never entirely safe. God only knew where this letter had gone before reaching him.

And Isabela? A fresh wave of sobs seized Gabril; he rose to his feet and stumbled to the window as though he could find a different world outside than the one he now faced. *Where is she, and how can I reach her? Is she alive? Did my letters to Mariem fail to reach them in Abrantes?* Panic seized him as every element of his plan to bring his family to Hamburg shattered around him like shards of broken glass.

Eduardo. He should now be in Portugal. I must get a message to him.

No longer able to remain in his cramped lodgings with his anguish, Gabril ran down the stairs and out into a June day, its rare, brilliant sunshine and fresh breezes only serving to illuminate his despair. He nearly barreled into a young girl whose golden curls cascaded down the back of her blue pinafore. Her face shone as she pointed up toward a towering chestnut tree, full and fragrant with blossoms.

"*Dort! Ein Bienenfresser!*"

A bee-eater? The child's excitement and her resemblance to Isabela as a child arrested Gabril midstep, and he followed her gaze and her pointed finger. On the tree's lowest branch sat a bird Gabril had never seen before, with an iridescent green chest, a gold throat, and deep orange, blue, and yellow coloring on its wings and back and long tail feathers.

The bird opened its beak to snatch an insect, then chirp its gargling call to an unseen mate.

"*Schon, nicht wahr?*" asked the girl.

"Beautiful . . . yes," Gabril replied in a choked whisper, immune to lovely colors in a world suddenly gone gray.

CHAPTER EIGHT

Girona, Carcassonne, Abrantes, and Tomar

June, 1605

We each decide whether to make ourselves intelligent or ignorant, compassionate or cruel, generous or miserly. No one forces us. No one decides for us, no one drags us along one path or the other. We are responsible for what we are.

—MAIMONIDES

"We follow the Onyar until it joins the river Ter, and we begin our path through the mountains at Medinya. We ride with a merchant and his companions . . . for your safety." His announcement made, the boatman turned away to attend to the departure of the small galiot, its flat bottom and use of both sail and oar an efficient means of navigating through Girona and beyond.

Ana Martel Gerondi settled onto her seat just before the rear mast and surveyed her trunks and parcels. The herbs she had taken for this journey were carefully packed in trunks, folded into cloths or dried and powdered or immersed in oils. Her dyes were similarly stowed, ready for use as she made her way, by turns using her healing skills or her knowledge of dye-making to obscure her more dangerous work.

She closed her eyes briefly and sighed, just as she had when she'd closed and locked the door to her home—furnishings covered, shutters secured, valuables hidden. Her gardens would be tended by the young herbalist to whom she had guaranteed a portion of the harvest in exchange for his assistance.

Eduardo Carel had managed to write her that Isabela de Castro Nuñez had departed Abrantes and was en route to Porto. From there she would sail to Bilbao or even Bayonne and then travel overland to Irouléguy to fulfill her commitment to embroider the trousseau. Ana, meanwhile, would travel to Toulouse where, with any luck, she would arrange to join Isabela and accompany her on the journey north into Germany.

Ana sighed again, knowing that Isabela knew none of this and that so many pieces of the plan Eduardo had fashioned would have to work before the entirety could be executed.

An unusually cloudy June sky hung low over the boat as it cast off onto the Onyar and began to work its way north. Enough of a breeze prevailed so that the sails caught, and Ana pulled her light cloak closer. She was about to reach for her parcel of books when a young man approached.

"Señora Gerondi?" he asked tentatively, pausing a short distance before her.

"Yes," she answered. The man appeared to be no more than twenty, yet he carried himself with an air of assurance mixed with appealing deference. Not as tall as she, he was nonetheless well built, with fair hair that set off his tanned complexion and deep brown eyes. His clothes were simple but finely made and he spoke in a low, melodious voice.

"I am Diego de Leon, at your service, *señora*." He gave a slight bow.

Ana regarded him in silence. In what way was he at her service? She did not recognize his name. As he was certainly not a member of the New Christian community of Girona—not from Catalonia at all, judging by his accent—it perplexed her that he knew her name and purported to be of service to her, so she smiled and nodded in recognition of his introduction, but said nothing further.

Diego moved closer. "My father and I are business associates of Eduardo Carel, and also of your late husband," he said quietly. "I propose to accompany you to France, to protect you on the journey."

So this was the merchant the boatman had spoken of. Ana marveled at the extent of the network Eduardo and Gabril de Castro Nuñez had already established. Without knowing quite why, she trusted this young man immediately, despite his youth and unknown background.

"If I am not mistaken, Señor de Leon, you are not a New Christian yourself, yet you expose yourself to considerable danger." She studied his face closely. "How is it that you come to this unexpected place?"

Diego paused, perhaps taken aback by the directness of the question, then said, "Señor de Castro Nuñez aided my late mother as a young girl. She was a New Christian and a gifted seamstress. She ran afoul of Inquisitors in Salamanca, where her father was a professor, and Señor de Castro Nuñez arranged her employment with a sympathetic abbot at the cathedral, which saved her. She married my father and lived as a Catholic ever since. Helping people, if you have the means to do so, has become a part of my family's creed."

Ana was stunned by this recital, spoken with such sincerity and without artifice. When at last she spoke, it was with a smile. "I shall be most happy of your company and assistance."

Diego returned the smile and, after offering Ana a quick bow, rejoined his companions toward the bow of the galiot, leaving her to marvel at the way of the world. Was it only last evening, when unease at what lay ahead robbed her of sleep, that she'd read from a forbidden volume of Jewish mystical writings about redemption, revisiting the Kabbalist belief that holy sparks of God within each of us are redeemed by acts of goodness that in the end of days will bring all of humankind back from exile to a world of enlightenment? Exile and redemption were now playing out on this boat—she prepared to lead many to escape the Inquisition, and Diego de Leon prepared to risk all to redeem a kindness done to his mother. *What a world, indeed.*

A gentle rain began to fall, and the boatman rigged an oilcloth over Ana to keep her and her possessions dry. The tall houses of Girona, huddled at the river's banks, began to give way to smaller cottages, which then gave way to forests of black pine and cork oaks as they entered the Ter River.

The stench of waste and fish-mongering on the city docks no longer filled the air; instead, piney and floral scents wafted across the water.

By late afternoon, the sails were lowered and the crew rowed the boat to shore at a small inn on the road to Medinya, where the traveling party would begin their trek. As the crewmen began to unload cargo, Diego de Leon approached Ana.

"We have arranged for several wagons, horses, and mules for our transport." He pointed at a low building across the way. "We will stay at this inn tonight and make our way first thing in the morning. Is there anything you need to prepare for the mountains?"

"I believe I have all that I need, but thank you," Ana said. "I am only concerned that my boxes of herbs and dyes are handled carefully."

"I will instruct my men accordingly," Diego said.

The next morning was hot and sultry when Ana joined Diego de Leon's party to begin the ten-day journey over the Pyrenees and on to Toulouse. A comfortable seat had been fashioned for her in the back of one of the wagons, but she often walked along the craggy path, her sturdy shoes and loose-fitting skirt and blouse well suited for the purpose.

At midday, when Diego called for the horses' rest and some shelter from the sweltering sun, the group prepared a light meal in the shade of a pine grove next to a pool at the base of a mountain stream. Ana walked at the edges of the water, stooping occasionally to pick handfuls of watercress and mint.

"Señora," said a tentative voice behind her.

She turned to see one of Diego's workers holding his hat and shifting from foot to foot a short distance from her. His breeches were worn but clean; his linen shirt the same, though stained with sweat from the day's travel.

"Beg pardon, ma'am, but the master says that you are a healer."

Ana stiffened slightly. She was, in fact, well trained in the herbal arts and had even assisted a noted physician in Girona for many years, but in these days of the Inquisition a woman healer could easily be branded a witch and burned at the stake for her pains.

Being careful to neither confirm nor deny this assertion, she asked, "Does something ail you?"

"*Sí, señora.*" Stepping forward, the man rolled up a sleeve to show her a festering wound on his forearm.

"Ah," she said, gently palpating the hot, tight skin around the wound. "Tell me what happened."

"I was loading the wagon a few days ago and caught the rough edge of a crate," he explained. "I pulled out a couple of splinters."

Ana asked him several questions about what he had done to treat the wound and checked him for signs of fever before returning to the wagons, where she retrieved a small chest of herbs.

After cleaning the wound, she applied a poultice of marigold salve and aloe.

The man sat stoically through the process and sighed when she applied the pungent, soothing poultice.

"In two days' time, return to me and I will change the bandage," she instructed him. As she returned her jars and cloths to her chest, she asked, "Where are you from?" He sounded to her as though he was from Catalonia, as she was.

"Besalú," he replied.

She looked up sharply. Besalú had been a protected community for Jews, though those that remained there now did so in secret, under the guise of being New Christians.

"And your name?" she asked.

"To you, señora, my name is Alberto Corvida."

Ana tipped her head in acknowledgment. Corvida was a renowned Jewish family from Besalú. Another New Christian making an escape.

"Very nice to meet you, Señor Corvida," was all she said.

The traveling party wound their way up and around slopes, following valley floors and staying to the east for the shortest routes. Ana felt both vigorous and challenged. The cool mountain air was a relief from the seasonal heat in the lower elevations, though the sun was still strong. In ones and twos, the men came to her for teas of anise, peppermint, and angelica for their stomach ailments, willow bark for toothaches, and salves for their wounds.

In a week's time, they had left the rugged mountains and returned to better roads and the small villages of the Languedoc. In this region, Ana knew, there were feuds and battles related to France's King Philip, and though she'd intended to heed her friend Andres's advice to stay in Spain, traveling west as long as possible, Diego de Leon had countered that the mountain crossing was easier and faster as a means to reach Toulouse. Ana agreed that the need to arrive in Toulouse was pressing, even if she did not understand all that she was supposed to accomplish there. She weighed whether to ask young Diego what he knew of the plan to seek out safe places to hide and lodge New Christians and Jews along the escape routes to Amsterdam and Hamburg, but finally decided to keep her own counsel. She would make possible contacts on the current journey quietly until she learned what awaited her in Toulouse.

Once they found a comfortable inn, Ana arranged for a bath, cleaned her clothing, and returned to the dress of a lady before meeting Diego for the evening meal. Upon arriving in the inn's main room, she noted that he had similarly restored his wardrobe and the bearing of a gentleman.

He informed her that they would detour to the walled city of Carcassonne to conduct business with the wool merchants there, but that within five days' time they should arrive in Toulouse. When Ana asked if he thought there were any dye customers for her, he brightened and said he would make any introductions she wished. She would subtly watch for possible safe places, despite the city's reputation as an impenetrable fortress.

The citadel at Carcassonne was more magnificent than any place Ana had ever seen. With imposing watchtowers and double fortifications, its white stone gleamed in the morning sun. She admired the confident ease with which Diego gained their entrance at the city gates and secured directions to the wool market.

They soon reached the market lane. They left the wagons and the men in the dooryard of a tavern before entering the lane.

When Diego stopped at a merchant's shop, Ana waited outside, marveling at the rows of vendors displaying raw wool, skeins of yarn, large spools of threads, and finished bolts of fabric. She noted the preponderance of dull reds, blues, and olive greens, and she thought of her development of rich purple dyes from elderberry and vibrant yellows from forsythia, marigold, and goldenrod. She had seen all these plants on her journey thus far and wondered why they were not used to create more varied dyes.

She realized she had wandered several doors down the market lane and was about to turn back when an old woman stepped into the lane directly in front of her. Short and slight, barely reaching Ana's shoulder, she was dressed entirely in black, with long wisps of steel gray hair escaping from her hood. Piercing grey eyes peered up at Ana's bodice from her craggy face.

Instinctively, Ana brought her hand to the cross that hung from her neck and which seemed to have caught the woman's fixated attention.

"The Holy Mother saved the song of the boy with pearls at his lips. And death to the Jew who struck him." The woman's sing-song chant rang forth as if from an oracle. She tried to grasp Ana's arm, but before she could reach it, a younger woman flew out from behind one of the market stalls and pulled the older woman back.

"I am so sorry, madam," she said. "My grandmother has lost her wits, and it is hard to keep her silent. She means no harm. Please forgive us." The granddaughter drew the older woman away, throwing Ana an imploring look over her shoulder.

Unnerved, Ana returned to the merchant's shop just as Diego stepped out of the door.

Smiling, he said, "Come in. It seems as if there is much interest in your dyes."

The town of Tomar, with its distinctive seven hills, rose above the surrounding forest and had been visible for more than an hour before the de Sousa party drew near. A night's journey along the Tagus river out of Abrantes had ended with transfer to a wagon and continuation along a road that was barely more than a footpath following a tributary of the Nabao River.

The sight of the Templar Castle, with its monastery and convent, was welcome to the weary travelers. By now David had spoken at length to their guide, who would see them as far as the coastal town of Buarcos. In the dead of night, silence broken only by the rhythmic sound of the barge pole lifting and dropping and the creak of the tiller, Enrique de Leon had quietly explained that he, his sister, and his son, Diego, were part of a network recently created to assist persecuted New Christians by establishing escape routes to safe cities in Europe—namely, Amsterdam, Venice, and Hamburg.

"But how did you know about me and my sisters?" David had asked.

"It's best, for the time being, that you not possess that information," Enrique had said.

Now, as Enrique was speaking to the wagon driver about approaches to the town, the sound of hooves approaching from the road behind brought everyone's attention to a small band of riders. Even from a distance, a banner with Count Miguel de Almeida's coat of arms sent a shiver of panic through David.

"It's the Count of Almeida's men from Abrantes," he said quietly to Enrique.

The other man stiffened and ordered the driver and David's sisters to pull off the road and remain silent in the wagon.

As the count's men halted, surrounding David and Enrique, the apparent leader spoke imperiously.

"We come at the behest of Count Miguel de Almeida and Padre

Alvaro of Abrantes, in service to the High Inquisitor of Portugal. Who goes here, and what is your business?"

David's blood froze and he willed his face to remain expressionless, but before he could even think of anything to say, Enrique replied casually, "Enrique de Leon, at your service, *senhor*. I am here on the business of King Philip. This is my apprentice, Paulo, and those are his sisters, who have been orphaned by the plague and are journeying to a relative in Porto."

"And the business the king has charged you with?" the man asked.

"That is the king's business," Enrique stated flatly.

David was both aghast and awed by the mixture of bold lies and truth that Enrique had just produced as easily as a children's well-known nursery rhyme. The count's official turned to David and asked,

"Your name, *senhor*?"

"Paulo de Silva."

The official stared at David, who did not flinch at the scrutiny.

"Your home?"

Enrique answered firmly, "Salamanca."

At this the official's eyebrows raised. "You are very far from home. What is your line of business?"

"Textiles," Enrique answered, still calm and casual.

The official looked from one to the other; then, drawing himself up in his saddle, he turned without another word and led his party down the road toward Tomar.

As soon as the last of the horsemen had vanished around a bend in the road, Enrique exhaled and leaned against the side of the wagon. Only now did his face show the lines of worry he'd hidden from the count's men.

David, shaken from the encounter, stared at Enrique for a long moment before he spoke.

"Were they looking for me?" he finally asked, his voice shaking.

"It's likely, but we can't know for certain," Enrique replied. "We can only be grateful that none of them recognized you. While we're in this vicinity, at least, you and your sisters must go by the name de Silva. That was quick thinking on your part."

"I was only following your lead, Senhor de Leon." David looked at him with admiration. "I am deeply indebted to you, sir. But why do you put yourself at such risk? I am only a New Christian trying to save myself and my sisters."

Enrique de Leon smiled wanly at the younger man. "I don't undertake this work because of who you are, young man, but because of who I am and who I want my son to be."

This reply struck David to his very center with the weight of a life lesson he knew he would never forget. Stepping forward, he grasped Enrique's arms firmly. "I thank you from the bottom of my heart."

The travelers entered Tomar in late afternoon, the low sun igniting the stone walls of the castle and the abbey with golden light. After they'd threaded their way toward the town center, Enrique stopped to confer with David.

"I think you should relinquish the identity of New Christians and accompany me to the lodgings I have secured as if you are truly my apprentice. And we would do well to stick to this story, if you're certain that your sisters can maintain the deceit."

"They can, and we will," David replied.

"That is good. But if there is a problem, if something happens to put you in danger, here is the entrance to the New Christian section." Enrique nodded toward an arched entrance nearby. "The old synagogue is abandoned, but there is a secret room there in which you could be hidden. If necessary, go to this address and you will be taken care of." He handed David a slip of parchment with an address written on it.

Again, David marveled at the web of connections, the plans that had been put into place on his family's behalf. Had others benefited as he had?

With a pang, he thought of those who remained in Abrantes and would not leave. He thought of his mother and worried about what would become of her. He thought of Isabela and wondered how, if ever, he would be able to join her.

But all these thoughts he pushed away. Right now he had his sisters to protect, and he very much needed to keep his wits about him.

CHAPTER NINE

Castelo de Vide and Tomar

June, 1605

Who can find a virtuous woman? For her price is far above rubies.
—PROVERBS 31:10

Isabela remained kneeling after finishing her prayers, listening as the Igreja de Sao Roque's small choir sang the last notes of the *Sancta Maria*. The morning mass was well attended and the church was intimate, compared to the vast cathedral in Abrantes. The choir's voices filled the sanctuary with ringing harmonies that resonated in the wood at Isabela's knees and traveled up her arms from the pew in front of her to her clasped hands.

While she knew this prayer well, the music was new to her and its beauty filled her spirit. Hidden under her veil, she could forget for the moment that she was in a strange place on a dangerous journey, far from those she knew and loved.

When the last notes faded and the rustling and groans of other worshipers moving back into their seats began, Isabela offered a last appeal to the Virgin Mother: *Keep me safe, keep Father safe, and keep David safe.*

She reseated herself and allowed her mind to wander while the padre delivered his homily. When she and Dona de Leon had arrived at the home of Alfonso Mendes two days earlier, they had been warmly welcomed, made comfortable, offered a room to sleep in, fed well, and left to recover from their long journey. No one had come or gone from the house other than Senhor Mendes and his wife, Dina.

Senhora Mendes was an accomplished weaver, and there were many items of beauty in the house that she had made. Their first dinner on Friday night had been a bounty of roast chicken with potatoes, a vegetable stew, a sweet and airy bread, and a delicious rolled pastry filled with apricots that left Isabela sated and sleepy. Saturday's meal had been a simple fare of leftover stew, bread, cheese, and vegetables, and the day had been spent relaxing, reading, and exploring the Mendes's lovely garden. Alfonso Mendes had been absent most of the morning but had reappeared for the noon meal before retiring to his study.

Early on this Sunday morning, Senhora Mendes had gently woken the two sleeping women and suggested that they accompany her to early mass. As soon as they had dressed, she had led Dona de Leon and Isabela to this quaint church, where Senhora Mendes had greeted and spoken to many others in attendance briefly, introducing Isabela and Simone only when pressed.

Turning to Senhora Mendes now, Isabela studied her lovely profile. Despite her age—Isabela thought she must be nearing fifty—her hair was black and lustrous and escaped her veil in heavy curls; only a few silver strands were visible at her temples. Her skin was alabaster white, with fine lines at the corners of her eyes and mouth. But her most striking feature was her deep blue eyes. They shone with kindness and intelligence, and Isabela thought she could stare into them forever. It had been a long time since someone had taken care of her in such a motherly fashion, and she sank gratefully into the nurture Senhora Mendes offered.

After mass, the women returned to the Mendes home and sat down to a hearty breakfast that Isabela found she was very hungry for. When the meal ended, Alfonso asked Dona de Leon to join him in his library, a room Isabela had not yet been invited to see. Isabela remained with Senhora Mendes, helping to wash the dishes and sweep the floor.

When they'd hung the last of the dishcloths to dry in the sun, Senhora Mendes sat heavily on the iron bench under the profusion of wisteria in the courtyard and patted the spot next to her, beckoning Isabela to join her.

They sat in silence for a while, enjoying the shaded spot and the slight midday breeze that carried the scents of lavender and roses.

"I imagine you were sad to leave your home and travel to a strange place," Senhora Mendes began.

In that very moment, Isabela had been thinking of her mother, and the comment brought tears to her eyes. "Everything about my life has changed, and now I've had to leave Abrantes and the only person I had left. I don't know how my father will find me." Her tears spilled down her cheeks as she blurted out her worries.

Senhora Mendes put a comforting arm around her. "You know, when I was not much older than you, I had to leave my home and travel here to work with a weaver who could teach me more than I could learn at home. Only when I got much older did I understand that I was sent away for my safety as much as to learn more weaving." She held Isabela's gaze and took one of her hands in her own.

"Where did you come from?" Isabela asked. "And what was the danger? Were there Inquisitors?"

"I came from the village of Castelo Rodrigo in the north. We were a small community of New Christians there. We were not wealthy, but we prospered well enough. My father was a physician. My mother was a weaver, but she died giving birth when I was only seven." Senhora Mendes's blue eyes filled with sadness. "My father was away when my mother labored. He was tending to the son of a nobleman. That boy died too. And there was a terrible drought. The vineyards suffered, and suddenly everyone was blaming the New Christians for all their ill fortune. There were threats, and then attacks. My father feared for my safety and despaired of a future for me in Castelo Rodrigo, so he arranged for me to come here."

"Did you ever see him again?" Isabela asked in a near whisper.

"Yes!" Senhora Mendes answered. "When I met Alfonso, we invited my father to come here to live with us. We had many wonderful years together before he passed away."

Isabela smiled through her tears. "If only I could see my father again. And my friend, David."

"Ah, a friend," said Senhora Mendes with a knowing smile. "Is he a special friend? Tell me about him."

And so Isabela did tell her about David—about their childhood, the loss of their parents the previous spring, his assumption of his father's duties, and the challenges leading to their escape.

Senhora Mendes listened quietly, allowing Isabela to pour her heart out. The girl shared all the fears that had filled her, releasing some of the heaviness bottled in her chest. When she finished, Senhora Mendes turned on the bench, took Isabela's other hand, and held both in her own lap.

"I have a story from my village that gave me hope when I was your age. Perhaps it will comfort you as well. It is called the Legend of Marofa."

Long ago in the village of Castelo Rodrigo there was a young girl named Ofa. She was the most beautiful damsel in the region, the daughter of a wealthy Jew. Her father, Zacuto, had earned a large fortune and taken refuge in the mountain town. A young Christian knight, Luis, fell in love with Ofa, but neither his mother, Dona Guiomar, nor Zacuto approved of the courtship because of the difference in their religions. But Luis was hopelessly in love and could not give up his pursuit of Ofa. He devised a plan, convincing some friends to pretend to rob Zacuto so that he could save the older man and win his favor. The plan succeeded, and eventually Luis was allowed to court Ofa. In order for the young people to marry, old Zacuto was required by law to convert to Christianity. He could hide no more. Ofa and Luis married and had many healthy children who filled the village with their families. And the nearby mountain became known as 'Marofa': Love . . . Ofa.

Isabela stared at her hands, which still rested in Senhora Mendes's lap. She understood perfectly well the love that bound Luis and Ofa to each other despite the circumstances that threatened to separate them, for she had come to realize that she had those feelings for David. But why this horror surrounding Jews? She looked up at Senhora Mendes. "What is it about being a Jew that is so awful? Why can't Jews be Jews and Christians be Christians?"

A sad smile settled on the older woman's face. "Wiser people than I must answer that question, dear one. But you must take from this tale the knowledge that the love we give and receive in this life is a source of strength and courage that can sustain us when danger threatens." She gave Isabela's hands a gentle squeeze, and the girl returned the gesture of affection.

The murmur of voices from the library window above the bench rose to what seemed to be a heated exchange. Isabela and Senhora Mendes looked up to the window and then back at each other.

"Before we go in, Isabela, there is one more thing I want to say."

Senhora Mendes looked into her eyes. "The work you will be doing is not only for your livelihood. I cannot explain more to you now, but it is important work that I hope will lead you and others to a safer life. There may also be danger..."

Before she could say any more, the voices inside rose to an obvious argument, prompting her to her feet. "We will finish this conversation later," she said quickly before striding back into the house.

"Isabela!" Senhor Mendes called out moments later. "Please come in."

Isabela hurried into the house and turned toward the library at the far end of the sitting room. It was larger than she'd thought, and she stopped just inside the doorway in wonder. Lining three walls of the room were shelves of books and curiosities made of pottery, metal, and glass. She had never seen so many books in one place. On some of the shelves were open spaces where pictures hung on the back of the bookcase—some paintings, some pages of illuminated manuscripts. A fourth wall of the room was paneled in rich cypress wood bordered with fine carvings.

A massive carved desk occupied the center of the room. Behind it, Senhor Mendes's chair faced the window and the courtyard beyond. Three other chairs were now arranged around the desk, and Senhor Mendes gestured for Isabela to sit in one of them.

Dona de Leon occupied another, sitting rigidly, her face pale and tight. Senhora Mendes entered the room, closed the door, and took the final seat.

Before he began to speak, Senhor Mendes looked at his wife. Isabela saw on her face a small smile but also a look of concern.

"First I want to thank Dona de Leon for her assistance in bringing you here to us, Isabela. I know this has been a most challenging time for you, and that you must have many questions as to what lies ahead." With this Senhor Mendes turned momentarily to Dona de

Leon, but her face remained wooden. "Tomorrow I wish Isabela to accompany Senhora Mendes to a wool merchant's shop, where Isabela will purchase some thread and some fine white linen. The cloth should be cut into strips, as you would use for cuffs or belts or headdress ornaments, and the thread used only to embroider the sequences of symbols sent to you by Dama Ana Martel Gerondi."

At the mention of Dama Martel Gerondi's name, Isabela sat bolt upright in her seat. What had these people to do with the stately woman whose visit more than a month ago had started the unsettling of Isabela's life? But of course, hadn't she used the brooch to convince Isabela that her instructions were from her father? That she was to undertake this journey to join him in some way? She looked around the circle of strangers in whom he had placed his trust. Must she now do the same?

"Do you know her? Do you all know her? Do you know my father? Do you have word of him? What are these cloths for?"

The questions poured out, and Isabela felt suddenly like a child again, with adults speaking over her head as though she couldn't or shouldn't understand. This, after months of being plunged into the adult world to make her own way.

Senhor Mendes leaned across his desk, looking straight at Isabela. "Slow down, *querida*," he said, the endearment slipping from him easily. "Yes, Senhora Mendes and I know Dama Martel Gerondi, and we are helping her to help you. I do not know your father, but Ana has a contact who has been in touch with him, as I believe she told you. And Dona de Leon works on behalf of this same network of people. I can tell you that Dona de Leon's brother and her nephew are working as we speak to assist David de Sousa and his sisters, as well as Dama Martel Gerondi. The hope is that you will all meet somehow in France. I should tell you that Dona de Leon argued strenuously for me not to tell you so much of this . . . for your own protection, in case you are caught, so you would not have information that others could . . . extract from you."

Isabela stole a quick look at Dona de Leon, whose distress was now even clearer on her stern face. But she had more questions for Senhor Mendes.

"What do you mean, 'caught'? And what of these cloth strips?"

Senhor Mendes sighed but answered Isabela directly. "There are many New Christians, and even hidden Jews, who are no longer safe in Portugal and must leave. Some can go to Brazil, some to other parts of the New World, but the Inquisition follows them. We are trying to establish safe passage overland to Amsterdam, Venice, and Hamburg where there is at least a chance of a haven, and where some of our brethren are already established. Your father is one of them, and Dama Martel Gerondi's friend is another. Your embroidered cloths will be a signal . . . symbols of safety that only members of our network will understand. To others they will appear only as decoration. This is why you were given the symbols and the code to their sequences for different messages. I believe you have memorized them all, is that right?"

Isabela nodded.

"If you are seen to be assisting people trying to escape the authorities, it will put you at great risk. The Inquisitors and their deputies are cruel when they seek information. I know you are young to be put in such a position, but our faith tells us, 'Whoever saves one life saves the world entire.' I wanted you to be clear about what you are being asked to do."

Isabela looked at each of the three faces directed toward her. For the first time, she understood the tension and the distance that had marked Dona de Leon's presence ever since they'd met. She and other members of her family were imperiling themselves in service of helping Isabela. The notion of the conflict between doing the right thing and risking one's personal safety hit Isabela like a bolt of lightning. She suddenly felt far older than her years.

"Do you have word of my father?" she asked again.

Now Senhor Mendes smiled broadly. He rose, crossed to the paneled wall, and pressed with both hands along one of the panel's edges. To Isabela's surprise, the panel swung open to reveal a recessed cabinet. Senhor Mendes used a small key to unlock the cabinet, from which he withdrew a large, shabby-looking volume and a letter. He brought both to the desk and placed them in front of Isabela.

"The book is a medical compendium by a native son of Castelo de Vide, Garcia da Orta. I wish for you to deliver it to Dama Martel Gerondi, if you can. It is not forbidden, though he was a Jew; he ended up in India and mostly stayed out of trouble. And this, I hope"—he held up a sheet of paper—"will bring you news of your father. It came only yesterday by messenger."

Isabela snatched the letter, addressed to her mother, and broke the seal to open it. The message was brief but filled her with joy. Papai was alive! Or at least he had been a scant month earlier.

> *My dearest Mariem,*
>
> *I have had no word of you in months now, and I fear that something ill has befallen you or that you haven't received my letters, or perhaps both. I have word that the plague has ravaged Abrantes and also that there is increased pressure on New Christians there. I have sent contacts and funds to help you and Isabela to leave Abrantes and join me here in Hamburg, and I urge you to do so with great haste. I worry for the health and safety of my dear treasured ones. My business interests here are progressing nicely. We shall be comfortable when you get here. I do hope my contact in possession of your brooch has reached you and helped you to embark on your*

journey. I long to hear from you, and more to see you and Isabela again.

All my love,
Gabril

Isabela let the letter drop to her lap. She had shed endless tears for the loss of her mother and now felt a deep sadness that her father's tears had yet to begin when he'd written this letter. But he was alive and wanted her in Hamburg. She would do whatever she could to get there—and with as many others as she could help.

Taking a deep breath, she asked, "When can we go to the wool merchant's?"

David crouched with his sister in the damp confines of the secret room in the old synagogue of Tomar.

"What will happen to Senhor de Leon?" Beatriz whispered. "How will we get to Buarcos?"

David pulled both his sisters close in the pitch dark. "I don't know," he said. "But he is an Old Christian with important connections. I heard him say that he had sent us on ahead of him and was only staying to finish a contract. He sounded confident, but that is when I decided we should leave, in case the Count's men decided to search."

The three siblings had fled through the empty kitchen into the rear garden, each of them with only one small bag in hand, and made their way back to Tomar's New Christian quarter, where they'd hidden in the trees along the wall until the gates opened at the end of curfew that morning. A woman on her way to the market had directed them to the address Senhor de Leon had given to David, and the man who'd answered the door had fed them a meager breakfast and then led them to the abandoned building and this hidden room. After warning them to remain silent, he'd relocked the doors and vanished.

David judged that that had been four or five hours ago. The summer heat didn't penetrate the thick, windowless walls and the sisters both shivered. As he parceled out to the girls the remains of the hard biscuits the man had given them, he worked to keep his fears to himself.

Just when he thought no one would ever come to rescue them, he heard the sound of a key in the door and it swung open, blinding the fugitives with the dim light of late afternoon. A young boy in rough clothes clearly meant for a larger person silently beckoned them to follow him through the side door and onto a footpath that threaded between buildings, through a hidden breach in the town wall, and out to the edge of a field. There, a dilapidated wagon stacked with sacks and barrels sat hitched to a large mule next to a pen full of black pigs. Still silent, the boy motioned the three de Sousas to climb onto the rear of the wagon before following them up.

He opened the first barrel, which lay on its side, and gestured for Roshina to crawl into it. When she hesitated, he demonstrated the handle built into the underside of the top that she could pull closed once she was in, as well as the holes toward the top of the barrel's side that had been fashioned to provide light and air.

The boy gestured to the other barrels, and then to David and Beatriz. They nodded their understanding. Without another word, he released a half-dozen of the pigs, roped them together, tied them to the rear of the wagon, climbed into the driver's seat, and slowly began to drive west from Tomar.

CHAPTER TEN

Castelo de Vide, Hamburg, and Trancoso

June, 1605

A journey of a thousand miles begins with a single step.
—Chinese Proverb

"You will use these bands of linen to embroider one set of messages each, using the symbols from the sampler you were given," said the young woman in the weaver's shop, staring at the embroidered work on Isabela's hood as she spoke.

Isabela and Senhora Mendes stood at the table in the back of the small studio, an array of threads in a myriad of rich colors spooled in neat bundles spread out before them. Surprised by the girl's direct language, Isabela fingered the finely spun threads, both silk and wool, and began to see in her mind's eye the designs she'd committed to memory stitched on the neat pile of fabric in front of her.

Senhora Mendes looked over her shoulder, as if worried that the conversation might be overheard, but although the narrow street outside was crowded with Monday morning shoppers, they were alone with the weaver.

The young woman's eyes darted from the table, around the room, and finally to Isabela, who met her gaze steadily.

"Your thread is beautiful, senhorita," Isabela said softly. "I will be well supplied. I thank you."

The young woman's eyes seemed sad to Isabela—or perhaps that was a look of pity she wore?

After gathering the materials and transacting payment, Isabela and Senhora Mendes left the shop and entered the busy lane. Picking their way over the cobblestones, the women set out to find Dona de Leon, whose errands would finish the provisioning of their journey north to Covilha, Belmonte, and Trancoso. She and Isabela were set to depart the next morning, so this day was to be spent preparing and packing.

Senhora Mendes walked purposefully through the throng, leaving Isabela to follow closely and think. The weight of the embroidery materials pulled at the shoulder bag she hugged close to her body. She understood the designs and their assigned meanings—protection, warning, message to deliver, message to receive, trusted person, untrustworthy person, escape, hide—and how to use them to create the nearly twenty messages she'd been assigned. But how many bands of each should she create? How would she know when to use them? And whom could she trust?

Isabela's reverie came to an abrupt halt as she nearly collided with Senhora Mendes, whose way was being blocked by a man dressed in smart black breeches and an embroidered silk doublet that looked too warm for the late June morning. Isabela stepped to Senhora Mendes's side, noting that the older woman was clutching her market basket so firmly that her elegant fingers were white with the effort.

"Senhora Mendes, how nice to see you," the man said mildly. His fine clothes and calm bearing contrasted sharply with a terrible blemishment of the skin on his face and the backs of the hands he held clasped over his ample belly. Isabela dropped her eyes from the sores and scars, not daring to stare at the disfigurement. "And this must be one of your visitors that we've heard has graced our town. Women with talents in textiles, I believe?"

For an embarrassingly long moment, Senhora Mendes did not reply, and Isabela felt heat rising to her face.

At last, Senhora Mendes spoke. "Yes, senhor, these good friends journey onward shortly, and we are finishing our errands before dinner." Her tone was clipped, and her breach of etiquette in failing to introduce Isabela properly hung in the air of the sunny morning like a poison vapor.

Isabela stood frozen until Senhora Mendes muttered a swift "good day," moved gracefully around the man, and resumed threading through the crowd, Isabela fairly tripping behind her.

Not two minutes later, they came upon Dona de Leon, her baskets laden with purchases. With a bare nod, Senhora Mendes signaled for her to join them as they progressed away from the town center.

They walked in silence. Eventually, Senhora Mendes turned into a narrow lane. She led them quickly down to another corner, and then onto an even narrower footpath. Only after turning onto that path did she finally come to a stop. She was breathing heavily, and there was a sheen of sweat on her brow.

"Who *was* that?" Isabela asked, unable to wait even for Senhora Mendes to catch her breath.

"He is a member of the town council. We don't yet have Inquisitors, but I believe he is in communication with them and is dangerous to us. I don't know what he may know about you, and I didn't want to give him your name. This encounter made me think that perhaps you should travel with a different name, Isabela."

Stunned, Isabela looked from Senhora Mendes's frightened face to Dona de Leon's. *Know about me? Know what? Change my name?* Suddenly, Isabela remembered standing in her own sitting room enveloped in David's fierce hug, willing herself to trust that all would work out. All that bravery now vanished. The fourteen-year-old girl began to cry—deep, racking sobs that deprived her of speech.

Senhora Mendes's long arm drew her into a hug, and Isabela tucked her head under the taller woman's chin.

"How will I do this?" she moaned. "There's too much I don't understand. I'm afraid." With her face pressed into Senhora Mendes's ample bosom, she still heard Dona de Leon's sharp exhale.

Senhora Mendes, her arm still around Isabela's shoulder, turned her up the lane toward home. "You will not be alone, Isabela. Tonight, I will give you the codes that will let you know whom to trust. You are a strong and capable girl, a tribute to your parents. There will be many along the way to help you." Here, she stopped and faced Isabela. "It is true that there will also be some that wish you and others harm. May God keep you safe from them." With these words, she bent and kissed the top of Isabela's head.

Isabela hoped her prayers would be enough.

After midday dinner, Isabela climbed up to the loft that had been her bedroom for the last few days and packed her belongings in her trunk and carry bags, reorganizing her threads and fabrics to include the new purchases and finding a safe spot for the book she was to take to Dama Martel Gerondi. *How will I ever find her?*

Senhora Mendes appeared at the ladder below the loft and called gently to her. Isabela climbed down and the older woman handed her a small book, finely bound in red leather.

"You cannot write to your friend David, or to your father . . . or to me. But perhaps it will help you to write to yourself as if writing to one of us. I want you to have this diary."

Again, Senhora Mendes drew the girl into a hug.

Isabela wished for all the world that she could stay in the safety of those arms forever.

"You are a madman!" The elder man, red-faced, leaned over his massive desk and shook a finger at Gabril de Castro Nuñez. "You can't leave now. And you can't disrupt what we've worked so hard to put in place!"

"This is not some abstract plan, this is my daughter we're talking about. A fourteen-year-old with no mother and a father who is spending his time wining and dining officials on behalf of the comfortable burghers of Hamburg!" Gabril was equally enraged.

The official, head of the newly formed Kehillah, the communal organization of Jews and New Christians in Hamburg, sat back in his chair, his glare replaced by a look of exhaustion.

"We all have sons and daughters, Gabril. And you are hardly safe and sound here. Our permission from the aldermen to live and work and practice our faith only in private homes is tentative at best. You did so much to help us achieve that! Now we must work to bring our brethren safely out of Portugal. Your daughter has a talent. I know the risk she takes, but think, Gabril, of the potential to save lives. And think of the alternative. We have sent more people than we can afford to see her here safely. Ana Martel Gerondi is on her way from Girona to join your daughter. The de Leon family is helping the de Sousa children, Ana, and your daughter. And you know Eduardo will do everything in his power for Isabela."

Now looking more haggard than angry, the official softened his voice.

"What you do here is so important to ensure a secure and stable community for those who come. But be careful, Gabril—even here. There are those who will denounce members of our community to the Inquisition, and while it may not pose a danger for you here, any assets that you have in Portugal or any shipments you send there or to Spain may be seized, and the denouncer will share in the proceeds. So keep your head down. Help us make a safe haven here. As soon as I hear from Eduardo, or any other news of your daughter, I will let you know."

Gabril stared for a long moment at the other man, and then turned without a word and left.

Dear David,

I am writing this in a book you will probably never see, given to me by a very kind woman whom you will probably never meet. I may never see her or you or anyone else I have ever cared about again, but the senhora who gave me this book said it might make me feel better to write to the people I miss.

I sent my first message to you with a man who met us a week ago in the first town on our journey. He was a stranger, but when he saw that I'd embroidered an iris and a hamsa for you, I almost thought he knew I'd sent you my wish for your safety, wisdom, bravery, and good fortune. I so dearly hope you received it.

The senhora asked me not to use real names or places in my writing, in case I am arrested on my travels. As you know, I am going to France to embroider a trousseau for the daughter of a noble house, and we are on our way there after a few days' stop in a lovely little town in the hills where it was nice and cool. I got to shop for some beautiful thread . . . for some other work I have to do. Now we are three days' travel north and will come soon to a town with an important community of New Christians.

Everywhere we go, everyone we meet seems to have secrets, and I expect this next town will have more secrets and be just as mysterious as the last place we stayed. It scares me, but so much has scared me in these last weeks that I just try to move forward each day and hope that the people Papae trusted to send me with know what they are doing.

I wish I knew where you are and that you are well and safe. Are your sisters with you? See, I am asking questions as if you will answer, so instead I will tell you about my journey.

I travel with a woman, I will call her SL, whose whole family is helping people escape, just as you have done. Oh, perhaps I should not be writing this either, but I think you know her brother. She is very severe, and the man I just stayed with says it is because she worries about keeping me safe. Senhora M (that's the kind woman) told me that SL is not a Jew or a New Christian, but is from an Old Christian family. But they believe the persecution is wrong, so they help us.

We have traveled through one or two towns on our way north, and nice people have given us places to sleep along the way. If I am given the right request, I leave a gift of a banner or hood band or cuffs embroidered in a certain design. We travel long hours in the wagon, which is a good thing, as I must make many of these gifts. I hope my fingers are not too tired by the time I reach France.

My candle has nearly burned out, so I must stop.

How I wish we were together again. I so miss you,

Can I sign with love?

I

Trancoso was bathed in golden evening light when the weary travelers arrived after having walked and ridden in the wagon for most of the previous twelve hours. The driver was a new one—a mere boy, it seemed—who was from Covilha but knew the region north to Belmont and now Trancoso well enough. His sturdy little horse was clearly exhausted. When Dona de Leon asked for directions to the address she'd been given for lodging, Isabela was grateful that it took only a few minutes to arrive there.

It was a solid stone house, with an unusual carving of what looked like a cat above the arched doorway. Dona de Leon knocked, and quickly a young woman answered—but rather than ushering her into the house, she said in an overloud voice, "The senhor has left this message for you. Your inn is not far up this road. He wishes for you to send the finished order tomorrow morning."

Isabela could not see around Dona de Leon to the woman in the doorway, but she saw her travel companion's back stiffen.

"*Obrigada, senhora.*" With nothing more than this thank-you, Dona de Leon returned to the wagon and quietly instructed the boy to hurry the wagon away. When he argued that the horse could not go any farther, she grasped him by the arm and hissed, "Go!"

Before Isabela could begin to ask anything, Dona de Leon handed her the message. Hastily written in an awkward hand, it said simply, "Belladonna. For a banner."

Isabela looked up at Dona de Leon, whose face had gone white. Belladonna was one of the symbols Isabela had memorized; it denoted great danger. Reflexively, Isabela turned to look behind the wagon, but no one followed them down the road.

In a short time, the wagon stopped again at a small inn. This time, the young driver did not wait for instructions; he dismounted, removed his horse from her traces, and led her to a water trough at the side of the inn without delay. A sturdy stone shelter with hay stacked next to its open side promised food and rest for the horse.

Dona de Leon motioned for Isabela to join her. Together, they passed inside.

The innkeeper in the tidy common room took no notice of the embroidery on Isabela's hood, nor did he respond to the code that Dona de Leon offered by way of greeting, signaling to the women that they should give only their traveling aliases and be discreet in their conversation.

When they were alone in their room, Dona de Leon slumped onto the ample bed, cast her cloak off, and held her head in her hands. She was clearly frightened, which only increased Isabela's dread.

When she could wait no longer, she asked in a quivering voice, "What does all this mean?"

"You are to make a banner with the belladonna embroidered on it," Dona de Leon murmured. "The house is now under some sort of danger and we cannot stay there; nor can any other travelers escaping Portugal. If we were not all so exhausted, we should have journeyed farther away."

"What kind of danger?" Isabela asked. "Is it because of us?"

"I don't know," Dona de Leon answered. "The woman seemed desperate for us to leave. I felt I shouldn't ask any questions." She sighed, her haggard face empty. "I will go down and order some food for us and see to the boy. You should begin work on the banner."

These last words she said without her normal brusque authority, which scared Isabela most of all.

When Dona de Leon left the room, Isabela took her work bag to the window, which still held the fading light of the summer evening. As they traveled, she had sketched designs on a number of linen strips and begun to outline the symbols and flowers and animals with the appropriate threads. She had not begun even one of the deadly belladonna flowers, avoiding the idea that the danger it represented would confront them, but she began now, and worked steadily until Dona de Leon returned with a maid carrying a welcome repast.

When they'd finished their supper, Dona de Leon undressed and got into the far side of the bed toward the wall, leaving the nearer side for Isabela. But Isabela lit the large candle the innkeeper had given them and continued her work, creating the distinctive purple of the belladonna flower, its central cone of yellow, and its green leaves, so like the tomato and aubergine plants from the same family whose fruits many people still would not eat.

When she was satisfied, Isabela repacked her threads and needles, washed quickly at the pitcher and bowl, and sank gratefully into a deep sleep, filled with dreams of her mother's warm smile, David's fierce hugs, and all the comforts that were now absent from her life.

When dawn had just broken the darkness, a sharp knock at their door woke both Isabela and Dona de Leon.

"Yes," called Dona de Leon.

"There is a gentleman to see you, senhora." The maid sounded tired and annoyed.

Dona de Leon rose. "I'll be right down." She threw her cloak and hood on over her nightdress. "Lock the door after me and don't let anyone but me in," she instructed Isabela. "Where is the banner?"

Isabela pointed out the finished linen, bound in a black ribbon, and lay back in the bed, drawing the bedclothes around her.

Dona de Leon grabbed it and swept out the door.

Isabela tried to remain in the room as she'd been instructed, but she could not. Minutes after Dona de Leon left, she pulled on her own cloak, opened the door quietly, and crept to the top of the stairs.

Below, she saw a short man being led into the common room by the innkeeper, the latter also still in his nightshirt. The visitor was well dressed, though not, apparently, a nobleman. He thanked the innkeeper and turned to Dona de Leon. He greeted her with the correct code to signal that he was a trusted person. Dona de Leon responded in kind.

"I understand you and your companion must leave us soon, no?" the man said.

Dona de Leon did not hesitate. "Yes, senhor, but I have fulfilled the order I was given, and very much appreciate the business."

She handed the man the linen packet; he quickly pulled several coins from his pocket and handed them to her.

"*Obrigado, senhor*," she said.

"*De nada*," he replied, and with a quick bow, he left as suddenly as he'd come.

"I would say it's early to be transacting business, senhora," the innkeeper said wearily.

"I'm so sorry, senhor, but as the gentleman said, we have a very long journey ahead of us and must leave shortly," Dona Leon said. "Can we have our breakfast soon?"

The innkeeper raised his eyebrows and sighed but answered, "Surely, *senhora*."

CHAPTER ELEVEN

Montemor-o-Velho and Toulouse

June, 1605

*And what our fortunes doe enforce us to,
She of Devotion and meere Zeale doth do.*
—EMELIA LANYER

David had long ago left the wagon to his sisters to walk—sometimes alongside the cart, sometimes in back of it—as the solid mule picked its way forward along narrow paths cut into the hillsides. A day's walk from Tomar, the boy driving the cart sold the pigs to a farmer and in the next town bought supplies for the continuing journey.

David thought the boy must be mute. He didn't speak at all, even after the road began to narrow and empty of other travelers and he released his passengers from their cramped barrel imprisonment. David's insistent questions as to where they were going, whether the boy had contact with Enrique de Leon, and who had directed him to help the de Sousas make their escape produced only head nods or shakes or no response at all.

Toward the end of the day they reached the tiny settlement of Caxarias and the boy turned the mule off the road toward a small house set far down a wide path bordered with fields of maize. David had never seen the plant before, except in drawings in books, and he stopped to look at the neat rows stretching in both directions. Everything here was green, though they had left the Nabao River far behind in Tomar, but David noted a sophisticated series of troughs and canals threaded through the fields, so he thought there must be a stream close by.

His reverie came to an end when two herding dogs started calamitous barking, bringing the mule to an abrupt halt. A man appeared behind the dogs to quiet them and then turned to the wagon party.

"*Boa noite*," the boy greeted him in a perfectly normal voice.

So he could talk after all. As David was processing this, the boy produced a parchment from his ragged pouch. The man read it, looked over David and the bedraggled girls in the wagon, sighed, and, before David could step forward to introduce himself, motioned for the small party to follow him toward the house.

He led them along the side to the back, where a large pergola covered with a riot of bougainvillea sheltered a long table draped in purple shade. The man extended his arm to indicate that they should sit and disappeared into the house.

David helped his exhausted sisters down from the wagon and they stood silently together in a small knot.

A small woman appeared, a pitcher and bowl in hand. "Please, come and wash and then sit," she urged them. "You must be tired and hungry." She placed the pitcher and bowl on a stand to the side of the table.

Within moments the man returned, laden with bowls and a loaf of bread. When he'd placed them on the table, he turned to David.

"Welcome, Senhor . . . de Silva," the man said slowly, pausing before speaking the alias that David had made up days ago, which now seemed like eons in the past.

"Thank you for your hospitality, Senhor . . ."

David paused, but the man did not supply his name. Instead, after glancing around, he led David inside the pergola. "The message I received from Senhor de Leon recommends you and your sisters to our care as you continue your journey to Buarcos," he said in a low voice. "Any friend of Enrique de Leon is a friend of ours. Please have some dinner and rest for the night."

"Again my thanks," David said. "Can I assume that Senhor de Leon is safe and well?"

"You can. He awaits you tomorrow in Pombal, a full day's journey from here."

David closed his eyes and his shoulders slumped in relief. After collecting himself, he joined his sisters in washing the grime from his hands and face, then sat gratefully at the table and ate hungrily.

The next morning the three de Sousa siblings continued their journey, this time with a sturdy wagon and fresh mule supplied by the farmer, whose name remained unknown to them. He instructed David to stay on the road until they reached Pombal, and gave them a satchel with enough provisions so that they would not be forced to stop anywhere along the way.

Once again, David marveled at this secret but well-organized network of people known to Enrique de Leon and committed to helping New Christians escape Portugal. Looking back at his sisters—rested and fed, their hair brushed and their dresses neat—he felt he could breathe again, and his thoughts dared to wander toward Isabela. *Where is she?* He reached into the pocket of his shirt and felt the stitching of the iris and hamsa she'd sent him. *Is she still safe?* He silently prayed that someone was protecting her in his absence.

ISABELA'S WAY

It was a long but uneventful day of travel. As the wagon approached Pombal, its ancient castle rose from the plain before them. With no instructions as to where they might meet Enrique de Leon, David slowed the mule and tried to ascertain the lay of the town ahead, which was much larger than he had expected. Forested hills rose on either side of the road, which itself twisted and turned, making a full view of the town impossible.

Just as David decided they should stop and eat the remaining food in their satchel before proceeding any farther, Enrique de Leon stepped out from the trees at the side of the road. After checking to make sure there were no other travelers in sight, David stepped down and greeted the other man with enthusiasm and relief.

"Thanks be to God that you are well, Senhor de Leon."

"And you, David. Senhoritas." Enrique turned and bowed slightly to the girls in the wagon. "We have much to catch up on, but let us get to our inn for some supper and rest. Tomorrow will be another long day. You must all stick to your aliases, and we will continue with the story that you are my assistant and these are your orphaned sisters. We will be passing closer now to Coimbra, where the Inquisitors are said to be establishing a court. Once we arrive in Buarco, with the bustle of the port at Figueira da Foz, we will be safer, but tomorrow we rest in Montemor-o-Velho, where many soldiers inhabit the fortress and the Church of Saint Mary has a very powerful padre sympathetic to the Inquisitors. We must be careful."

David glanced at his sisters. "Our mother is living now with her sister in a village somewhere between Coimbra and the coast," he said quietly.

"You cannot risk trying to see her," Enrique said firmly. "No one must know of your presence or your plan."

David sighed but nodded his understanding. They could not put their escape, or the people helping them, at risk.

The road from Pombal to Montemor-o-Velho broadened and became more heavily traveled as the day wore on. Enrique de Leon set a brisk pace on his horse, stopping only when necessary to greet the occasional fellow traveler or procure food.

The day was fine and the party made good progress. By midafternoon, they'd made it to the ford at Alfaleros, where they arranged for a barge to cross the Mondego River. Soon the castle of Montemor-o-Velho rose into sight on its hill. Around the travel party, a growing throng of soldiers, farmers, horsemen, and pedestrians surrounded them, also headed toward the town.

Soon, fields of maize, wheat, and flax gave way to cottages surrounded by kitchen gardens and then to the gates to the town itself. Enrique handed the false papers to the guard, and when he let them through he led the wagon to a small inn on a side lane below the Church of St. Mary.

The de Sousa sisters wearily climbed down from the wagon and were about to enter the inn with David when Enrique stopped them.

"Remember to say little and be as inconspicuous as possible," he reminded them. "Tonight we will take supper privately and go to our rooms after. Tomorrow is a feast day, and we will attend church as we must. Immediately after church, we will leave for Buarcos." Searching out each of the faces in front of him, Enrique seemed to be waiting for any questions. Hearing none, he stepped back to attend to the horse and mule.

ISABELA'S WAY

The next morning dawned yet another beautiful day, cool but promising early-summer heat by afternoon. Beatriz and Rosinha had done their best between their room's washbasin and the single dress each had kept for occasions other than travel to look presentable for church.

Already, even the quiet lane outside the inn bustled with revelers and men visiting the taverns as the Feast Day of Corpus Christi got underway.

On the short walk to the church, Enrique and David strode ahead of the two girls, forging a path through men already weaving with drink and children crisscrossing the lane with the remnants of sweets covering their lips and hands. Near the corner, an impromptu trio of two guitars and a mandolin played a lively folk tune. Garlands of flowers decorated posts and doorframes. A portly woman dressed in country costume sang lustily with the musicians, perspiring with the effort. Spying David and Enrique, she waved with a flourish of her arm and crossed the lane toward them.

"Senhors," she bellowed, leaning in an unsteady curtsy toward David. She lifted her face, revealing a nearly toothless grin. "Such a fine day to celebrate the body of our Lord." With this, she poked David in the chest. "It's a fine body you have as well." She broke into raucous laughter.

David stepped back, bumping into his sisters and putting his arm out to sweep them toward the wall behind him. Enrique stepped forward, but before he could say a word, a soldier grabbed the tipsy songstress from behind and jerked her back.

"You take too much liberty with the feast day, senhora. Sober up or you'll spend the day in a cell." With that he shoved her back toward the musicians, now who sat silently on the other side of the lane.

Enrique tipped his hat to the soldier, whose gaze swept over the four churchgoers before turning back to a scraggly group of three men and a woman dressed in rags and bound together with ropes around their ankles and wrists.

"Move!" the soldier shouted.

Briefly, silence descended over the whole of the street as the pitiful line made its way into the square before the church.

"Judaizer!" someone in the throng there shouted, and soon other epithets were thrown at the bound prisoners.

"Make way," the soldier shouted. "The Jews will face their fate soon enough."

Enrique stood stock still a step ahead of David and his sisters, the stiffness of his back and shoulders a signal for the other three to remain motionless as well. After the crowd closed around the soldier and his miserable charges, Enrique turned and nodded his head toward the church.

David in turn nodded to his sisters, who had reflexively clutched each other's arms when the people around them began to yell. They relaxed their grips on one another, pulled their veils closer around their faces, and moved with him up the street.

Slowly, the foursome made their way into the crowded square and finally through the massive church doors, thrown wide open for this special Mass.

In the somber quiet of the great sanctuary, Enrique led the way to a side aisle and a pew near the center where they could all sit together. The girls entered first, genuflecting deeply and crossing themselves as they whispered their prayers, and the two men followed. David could see his sisters' pale faces and knew they were still frightened by the episode with the soldier.

Enrique poked David's knee and nodded toward the altar and

David returned his attention to the Mass and went through the motions—responding, kneeling, sitting, and moving his lips where required.

Near the end of the service, just before communion, a commotion at the front of the church engendered a murmur among the congregants and a woman's cry echoed briefly off the stone arches.

"No," she cried again. "She is my sister. A good Christian."

Drowning out the cries, the congregation began to chant: *I believe, O Lord, and I confess that Thou art truly the Christ, the Son of the Living God, Who camest into the world to save sinners, of whom I am first.*

Moving quickly up the aisle toward them, the very same soldier from the scene in the lane dragged a small older woman behind him, gripping one arm, while behind them another woman held her other arm, whimpering as she trotted to keep up.

As the soldier approached their pew, Beatriz gasped and let out an anguished cry. David grabbed her wrist and squeezed it so hard that she yelped again. This time the soldier and the two women stopped abruptly in front of them. The soldier stared hard into David's face, then turned to the women.

"Are these friends of yours? Will they speak to your 'Christianity'?" The sneer made his rough face even harder.

Therefore I pray Thee: have mercy upon me and forgive my transgressions both voluntary and involuntary, of word and of deed, of knowledge and of ignorance, the congregation continued to pray. *And make me worthy to partake without condemnation of Thy most pure Mysteries, for the remission of my sins, and unto life everlasting. Amen.*

Teetering on unsteady feet and shaking with fear, Adriana de Sousa turned away from the shocked and anguished faces of her three children and whimpered, "I told you, I am a stranger here. I know no one but my sister."

The soldier tugged the two women to the rear of the church and out into the throng in the square.

"Monsieur de Bernuy, what a pleasure to meet you, and thank you for taking the time to see me."

Ana arranged her silken skirts on the seat offered by the distinguished gentleman whose salon she had just entered. The liveried servant who had led her through the interior stairs and loggias surrounding the courtyard of Hotel de Bernuy exited as another servant entered with a silver platter bearing a slender bottle and two wine goblets.

Ana had heard of the new glass containers for fine wines, but this was the first time she'd been served from one. She watched with interest as the ruby red wine was poured into her goblet.

Raising her eyes, she saw her host's smile and returned it.

Jacques de Bernuy was the current steward of his family's business in the cultivation of woad and production of indigo dyes. Ana had already proposed to purchase some of the woad indigo to sell to the textile merchants in Lyon, but there was more she wished to understand about the man in front of her before she proposed other possible connections to him.

Ana judged that he was younger than she, perhaps near thirty. He was tall, with a full head of fair hair that waved tidily to his shoulders. His beard and mustache were well trimmed in the style of the day, and he wore a beautifully embroidered doublet with slashed sleeves that revealed the fine linen shirt beneath. His breeches and tall, narrow boots were equally stylish and custom made.

He handed her a goblet and she took a small sip.

"Your wine is as interesting and pleasant as the bottle it came from," she said mildly.

"Thank you, madame, but I am guessing you did not come to see me to talk about my wine. I understand you are interested in woad indigo." Jacques de Bernuy's directness and his dispensation of social niceties surprised but did not offend Ana.

"I am indeed interested in purchasing some indigo dye, but I wonder if you might make some of the plant's roots available to me as well."

"The roots of the woad plant?" De Bernuy's eyebrows rose and he tilted his head slightly.

"In addition to my work as a dye maker, I am an herbalist. I've learned from a Jesuit friend of some useful teas made from the root of the woad plant."

"A Spanish woman working openly as a healer?" He grimaced. "Perhaps your friend the Jesuit will assist you when the Inquisitors find that you are a witch instead. Doesn't that worry you, Madame Martel Gerondi?"

It was Ana's turn to look quizzically at the man sitting across from her. She knew that two or three generations back, the de Bernuy family were Jews who had escaped Portugal and come to Toulouse, where they'd become wealthy merchants and practicing Christians. She gambled that this man's sympathies lay not with the Church or the Inquisition but with the people of his ancestry and the plight of escape that lay in his own family's past.

And yet his part in their conversation had so far been brusque and full of challenge, and she had no wish to be entrapped. She willed herself to adopt an even calmer, more relaxed demeanor and offered another pleasant smile.

"My friend the Jesuit has spent most of his working life in China, attempting to bring the Word of the Lord to its people, yet I believe he would be the first to admit that he has been changed more than he has changed others. He quite believes that his duty is to ease suffering and bring happiness to mankind in whatever form. I don't believe he has found any room at all for the Inquisition in his vocation." Ana paused and, staring directly at Jacques de Bernuy, added, "Nor have I, Monsieur de Bernuy."

There it was. Ana's own challenge hung in the air between them.

After a long, tense silence, Jacques settled further into his chair, crossed his long legs, and in a softer voice replied, "Then, Ana Martel Gerondi, you and I do indeed have business to conduct. But first, can you join me to dine? I would like to show you Chez de Bernuy."

Deep night fell before Ana left Jacques de Bernuy's home, but when she finally did she was greatly pleased with the evening's work. As she'd hoped, she'd been able to buy both the indigo dye and a bundle of woad root, soil still clinging to the dug plants. What she had not dared to hope but had ultimately also received was Monsieur de Bernuy's promise of safe haven for New Christians fleeing the Inquisitors. Chez Bernuy's warren of corridors, rooms, vaults, and passages would make a secure hiding spot for travelers.

Now, Ana had only to wait for word that the particular traveler she had promised to conduct to Hamburg was getting closer to France.

CHAPTER TWELVE

Trancoso and Pinhão

June, 1605

And high above, depicted in a tower,
Sat Conquest, robed in majesty and power,
Under a sword that swung above his head,
Sharp-edged and hanging by a subtle thread
— GEOFFREY CHAUCER

Isabela stared at the cat-like figure carved into the stone wall of a solid house across from the well from which she had filled her water jug. She and Dona de Leon had just arrived in Trancoso, a small, bustling village near the border with Spain. The stone cat bore a clear resemblance to the figure of a lion given to her to embroider as a symbol of strength and safety. And yet she also knew the black cat was a Christian symbol of evil.

She was pondering these thoughts when Dona de Leon tapped her shoulder.

"This used to be a house of worship for the Jews," the older woman said quietly.

"What?" Isabela asked, glancing around to make sure they were alone. "How do you know?"

"The well there was the ritual bath, and you can see the rounded shape of the door—the arch is different than that of other doors." Dona de Leon pointed down the road. "And do you see the niche cut into the stone? That is where the Jews touched their special box when they entered."

Isabela froze where she stood. Everyone in her household always touched the doorpost when entering. *Is that a custom of Jews?*

"And the cat?" Isabela nodded up at the stone figure.

"It may represent the Lion of Judah. Before Our Lord was named the Lion, it was a Jewish symbol of the patriarch Jacob's warrior son, Judah, in their scriptures—a triumph over enemies, over pain and suffering, perhaps even over sin." Dona de Leon sighed as she spoke these last words, then turned to leave. "Come. No more questions now. We have a long journey to the river at Pinhão, and the hills on either side of the river are tall."

The journey was indeed long, the late June heat relieved only occasionally by shaded lanes of maritime pine and cork oak. Simone had hired a wagon with a driver, and the women sometimes walked, sometimes sat in the back, their bundles and Isabela's trunk piled around them, their tired feet dangling. Always, there were curious, sometimes disapproving stares at the absence of a male escort, but Dona de Leon returned such stares with fierce stares of her own.

Stopping only to rest the horse, eat, drink, and cool off at midday, they arrived at the Douro River crossing to Pinhão and the destination from which they were to secure a boat to Porto on the coast after only two days' travel.

When at last they stood on the ferry dock in Pinhão, Dona de Leon looked around anxiously.

"Which way do we go?" Isabela asked.

Dona de Leon shook her head. "I have the name of an inn, but no directions for how to find it," she said. "Let us walk toward the village center and hope we find it."

"I shall be so glad when we arrive in Irouléguy," Isabela said as they began walking. "I am weary of travel." Stone houses crawled up the hills from the riverbank in orderly terraces, white stone and brightly colored stucco gleaming in the sunlight.

Striding purposefully forward, Dona de Leon said without turning her head, "You must realize that your journey has only just begun, child. You are young and strong. Do not complain while you are still safe."

Isabela felt neither safe nor strong. But she pressed her lips together and moved quickly to keep up with the older woman.

Eventually, after asking two different townspeople, Dona de Leon led Isabela to a large inn at the center of the town, where they settled at a table in the corner of the tavern and ordered a meal. Dona de Leon kept a watchful eye on the tavern door, but there were few customers, and none who seemed to interest her.

Isabela ate ravenously and downed first one and then another of the cups of the local sweet wine. Well after their meal was done, they remained seated at the table.

Finally, Isabela asked, "Are you waiting for someone?"

"I did hope to receive a message," Dona de Leon answered.

As if summoned by her words, a young man entered the tavern and cast his eyes around the room until they landed on Dona de Leon. Upon sighting her, he made his way to their corner and sat heavily on a stool at their table.

Without waiting for introductions, Dona de Leon spoke the short, coded words to ensure their security. When the young man responded appropriately, she asked, "Have you instructions for our boat passage?"

"I am sorry, *senhora*, but your instructions are to travel to Irouléguy overland, not by boat," he replied.

Dona de Leon went pale and managed to ask in a strained voice, "But why?"

"I do not know," he said. "Perhaps because Porto is inundated with refugees and the Inquisitors are interrogating and arresting with impunity. But I have been sent to accompany you as far as the French border, where we will meet a chaperone of the house of Mercado who will bear responsibility for Senhorita de Costa Nuñez. If we are fortunate, and the wagons and carriages that have been arranged all work out, we should arrive in Irouléguy in ten days' time."

Silence fell around the table as the women absorbed this news. Looking from one solemn, drawn face to the other, the young man smiled tentatively, reached into his satchel, and pulled out a small bundle.

"I have messages for each of you," he offered.

Dearest Isabela,

If you receive this letter, then you must have safely made it to the north of Portugal or perhaps even into Spain. It feels as though a dozen years have passed since I left you in Abrantes, and I think of you each day. I know you are not supposed to write to me directly, but when I received your cloth it made me so happy to have something that you had touched and that had come from some point in your journey that I had to reply. It will help me to feel less lonely and uncertain to imagine that my words will find you safe and secure . . .

Isabela stopped reading, tears blurring her vision as she bent over the candle in her room above the tavern. She wondered if she'd ever feel safe and secure again, and reading David's words, scrawled in his loopy mess of a scrawl, filled her with a longing that left her barely able to breathe.

> ... *My sisters and I traveled to Figueira da Foz from Abrantes with the help of a man I cannot name but whose sister I believe you are acquainted with. By the time you receive this, I hope we will have sailed to Porto or even continued to Bayonne. Once we are in France I hope to learn of your safe arrival at your destination, and will fervently try to connect with you there. We have eluded danger at every step of our journey, but I fear my mother has not fared as well. We saw her apprehended in Montemor-o-Velho and were helpless to assist her. She, who has been such a devout Christian. I cannot understand what the Inquisitors want. Needless to say, my sisters are bereft.*
>
> *I only hope you are safe and on your way to your new employment. I miss you more than I can say, and wish for all of us a safe journey until we can be together once again. Our world has changed, Isabela, and I have been frightened by what I have seen, as perhaps you have. I promised to take care of you, and I only wish to be with you again so that I can fulfill that promise. Please send me a message.*
>
> *Stay well, and stay safe,*
> *David*

The writing had become rushed and irregular by the end of David's letter, and Isabela could feel in it a haste, the uncertainty, that matched her own. She pulled the worn paper to her chest, her tears now turned to a hopeful joy that David would indeed try to find her and was so far still safe.

She unpacked her box of threads and a fresh linen square and began to once again embroider the iris, symbol of faith, courage, hope, and wisdom, and a hamsa, symbolizing protection from evil.

This time, she would also add a heart.

Simone de Leon sat at the table in the corner of the tavern after sending Isabela upstairs to their room and stared at the letter in her hand. She knew the writing well.

She ordered another cup of wine and prepared to read the words of her longtime lover.

Dearest Simone,

I hope all is well in your journey to bring your young charge to Irouléguy. There is a full moon tonight here in the Camargue and I have just come in from watching the white horses fly across the marsh before their evening sleep. I await your return with as much patience as I can command, but the beauty of this night makes me want you by my side again. Even so, your work is more important than ever—the Inquisitors have begun to arrest the Roma here on charges of heresy. This is preposterous, of course, as none have ever belonged to a church of any kind, but under this threat the bands have melted into the marsh and now avoid Saintes-Maries-de-la-Mer. May the three Marys protect them.

As you requested, I have made arrangements for possible places to stay across Provence and as far as Lyon. Beyond there, I have no influence or contacts.

I love and admire what you do, sweet Simone, but please take care, as danger abounds. Come back to me safely and let us live in this wild land of white horses and red flamingos and the salt smell of the sea. Thank you for your message from a month ago, but please send one again, so I know that you are well.

All my love,
Claudio

Simone sat back in her chair and closed her eyes, blessing Claudio with prayerful thanks for his help even as the very thought of him filled her with longing. She could feel the mistral wind of a Mediterranean summer night on the Camargue, picturing in her mind the many acres of salt grasses, the small hillocks dotting the vast open spaces, and the horses and many birds outlined by moonlight on or above the flats.

As soon as she was able she would return to Claudio, whose politics of resistance and independent mind had forced him to flee Portugal and find refuge among the Roma of the Camargue. These fierce, independent people were persecuted equally by Islamic Turks and the Holy Church and had brought their herds of sturdy white horses to the uninhabited wilds of the salt marshes along the Mediterranean between Marseilles and Montpelier.

Claudio had been born to an Old Christian family, but like Simone he had left its protection in the face of the injustice wrought by the Church through the Inquisition. They'd met at the first clandestine meeting Simone had attended with her brother to create an escape network for the persecuted. Since then, she had learned so much more about him.

Claudio was a whisperer of horses, and he managed the wild

herds in the Camargue as needed for the occasional traveler or merchant. He had become well known all over Provence as a trainer and breeder—a useful cover for the dangerous escape work that engaged them both. How she longed to return to him, as she now understood that she too must forsake Spain and Portugal or be revealed as a collaborator and Judaizer.

With a sigh, Simone picked up the other letter she had received. This one was an urgent instruction: She and Isabela were not to embark as planned on a boat to Porto and then a ship to Bayonne. Instead, they were to make their passage to Irouléguy overland, through the Basque Country of Spain and over the Pyrenees into France. This would, according to the note's writer, take another ten days to two weeks. A pouch of funds to provision them and to hire a guide, as well as several recommendations for whom to contact along the way, had come with the message.

If only she could join Enrique with his young charge, David, and proceed as planned! But apparently it was no longer safe to make the journey down the Douro River to Porto with a young New Christian girl.

She scanned the message again; it was unsigned and in a hand she did not recognize. How much more secure she would feel if the message had come from Enrique himself.

After fingering the two letters for several more moments, Simone cast them into the fire.

A final swallow of the sweet wine brought on a fatigue that was never far from the surface. Simone left her spot by the fire to climb wearily to the bedchamber—and toward the journey that lay ahead.

Eduardo Carel shivered on the cell floor, iron cuffs scraping his wrists and ankles each time he tried to move. Had it been only a day since soldiers had seized him, blindfolded him, and brought him to this dungeon?

The throbbing in his head confused his thoughts. He struggled to remember anything that had occurred in the last twenty-four hours but all his thoughts drifted by, chased away by pain and a dire thirst.

He'd been meant to meet the two groups of escapees from Abrantes: David de Sousa and his sisters, led here by Enrique de Leon, and Isabela de Castro Nuñez, guided by Simone de Leon. David, his sisters, and Isabela were to board a ship to Bayonne, in France, and then move on to the safer protection of Raphael de Mercado in Irouléguy. *How did it all go so terribly wrong?*

A message from Enrique had confirmed that his party had reached Porto. Simone and Isabela were supposed to be coming down the Douro from Pinhão. Eduardo thought he had slipped unnoticed into Porto—until early yesterday, when armed men had broken into his room and arrested him with no explanation of charges. Beatings and wild questioning had followed his hasty transport to this cold, dark cell.

How will I help those young people now?

Another wave of pain and nausea stabbed him from stomach to chest and he retched. The mere turning of his head to keep from choking sent him close to a faint.

He did not know how long he lay in semiconsciousness before the creak of his cell door opening brought him to alertness. A tall, slender figure entered.

Though Eduardo's first reaction was a quickened heartbeat of fear, he remained still and quiet. Through the slit of his one eye not swollen shut, he watched the shadow of what appeared to be a young man feel his way around the cell to where he lay.

"Senhor Carel?" the young man whispered, kneeling beside Eduardo and peering into his battered face.

"*Si*," Eduardo rasped in response.

"I am a friend. I have brought you some food and drink. I also bring word from Enrique de Leon. He feared being recognized here and so sent me. We have a plan for your escape. I have entered as your servant. My name is David de Sousa, though I'm traveling with the name Paulo de Silva. I am"—here David paused to choose his words—"friends with Isabela de Castro Nuñez, and seek to assist her in reaching her father in Hamburg. I believe you know him . . . Gabril de Castro Nuñez."

David spoke all of this in a quiet rush as he brought a skin of water to Eduardo's parched lips.

Eduardo drank greedily but quickly choked and coughed. David tensed and turned nervously toward the cell door, still ajar. He tore a piece of bread from the small loaf he'd tucked into his tunic and fed pieces to Eduardo, continuing to speak rapidly.

"I spent the last hour with the guards, and brought ale for them to drink. One left before he drank; the other is now safely sleeping, as we doctored the ale with a potion, but it won't last long, so we must unchain you and leave through the fortress door along the river wall. Can you stand?"

David drew a ring of keys from his pouch and began to feel in the dim light of the sputtering candle he'd brought for the locks on the manacles restraining Eduardo's limbs.

After a long minute, Eduardo was free.

He closed and opened his fists gingerly and stretched his legs out from the wall where he sat, flexing his feet. Though every one of his muscles ached, he didn't believe any bones were broken, and after accepting several more pieces of bread and a gulp more of water, he held on to David and attempted to stand.

At first his head swam and he sank back to his knees, dropping his head until the cell stopped spinning.

On the second try, he felt steadier.

As David held the candle between them, Eduardo saw the young man's face more clearly. He was a handsome boy, as tall as Eduardo himself, with chiseled features and deep brown eyes. His young beard was soft but well trimmed.

He was about to ask how David knew he'd been arrested when David began to speak again, urgency speeding his words and movement.

"When I sat with the guards, they were talking about your arrest and about the guards who brought you in. They named the Inquisitors who were to hear your testimony, but they also mentioned that a priest is leading the investigation. The name of the priest is the same as the padre from our church in Abrantes. If he is truly here, we also are in grave danger, as he knows and will easily recognize me and Isabela. He threatened me just before I left Abrantes." David glanced again toward the cell door. His voice became tight. "One of the guards left before they began to drink the ale, and I'm afraid he will get word to the padre that your servant came to assist you. You see why we need to hurry." He urged Eduardo forward.

"Slowly, my boy," Eduardo mumbled, but he managed to shuffle with him.

"But I don't understand how Padre Alvaro knows *you*," David said. "Why were you arrested?"

"I don't know," Eduardo gasped out. "I just don't know."

Leaning heavily on the younger man, he moved as quickly as his battered body would allow into the passage, past the sleeping guard, and toward the hope of escape.

CHAPTER THIRTEEN

Porto, Bayonne, Pinhão, and Benavente

June, 1605

It is not in the stars to hold our destiny but in ourselves.
—WILLIAM SHAKESPEARE

The passageway leading away from Eduardo Carel's cell was long and full of hazards for the injured man, whose every body part radiated pain as David half dragged, half carried him, stumbling over the jagged ground. Eduardo bit his lip to stifle a groan at one point when the boy grabbed his sprained shoulder and they tripped into the rough wall.

At last the corridor descended to a dank landing and a massive iron door with a window grate that admitted the smell of fish and the sea. Eduardo sucked in the fresh air, leaning against the rock wall, as David searched for the key that would open the massive lock that hung from the door's latch. He spoke quietly as he tried one key after another.

"Senhor de Leon booked passage on a caravel that leaves Porto tomorrow for Bayonne. My sisters and I will join him, and he has made arrangements for you as well. We have lodgings near the docks for tonight to give you a chance to rest and recover."

David's glance his way and his unguarded face suggested he thought Eduardo's wounds would take far longer than a night's rest to heal.

Eduardo tried to think—to judge what he was hearing and whether he could trust this boy. *Could this be a trap of some sort? The boy's fear of the priest from Abrantes seemed real—and that priest did come into my cell before, asking about my business in Porto. Was it the same priest?*

Again Eduardo's thoughts became confused, and he slumped farther down the wall.

"Ah, *merda*!" swore David, fumbling through the keys again, the candle on the tiny sconce beside the door flickering.

At last, he found the key that worked and yanked the heavy door open.

"We are close to the river here; God willing, Senhor de Leon is already waiting for us with a skiff to take us to the docks."

Eduardo summoned all his remaining strength and David once again dipped under his arm and held him across the back as they stumbled down the embankment to the river's edge. Behind them, they could hear the first alarms being raised behind the prison walls; David worked to move them faster.

"Other arm," Eduardo gasped out, and the younger man deftly switched to his other, less injured side.

When they reached the water, David set Eduardo onto a tree stump that someone had smoothed into a seat and produced a low whistle that sounded like an evening bird call.

For several minutes nothing happened, and David began to peer up and down the dark riverbank with alternate worried glances back toward the prison, where torchlight now illumined more spots along the walls than before.

Just as David opened his mouth to speak, a small skiff floated silently along the shore toward them, a single man at the oars.

"*Graças a Deus*," David whispered as he held the boat steady and Enrique de Leon helped Eduardo over the gunnel.

Eduardo woke suddenly, heart pounding, to a knocking at the door.

He barely remembered his journey to the bed upon which he now lay. He knew that his two rescuers had taken turns rowing the long distance from the prison to the docks through a waterway crowded with fishing boats, trading ships, and the king's naval boats. Eduardo had been able to do no more than lie low in the bow, old sacking protecting his aching, feverish body from the cedar ribs of the sturdy little craft. Dawn had not been far from reddening the sky when the exhausted men had finally reached a dock and inn that overhung the river's edge. Once settled into a room on the upper floor, Eduardo had collapsed into sleep, only occasionally woken by the slapping of loose shutters and pounding rain that a summer storm had brought in. Even now it continued, tossing the boats in the harbor and making a cacophony of clanging rigging and anchor chains.

Eduardo relaxed as he saw that it was Enrique de Leon, carrying a platter of food, who had knocked and was now entering his room. Behind de Leon stood David de Sousa, seemingly somewhat restored from the previous night's work but still looking weary.

Though still sore and stiff Eduardo was now less feverish, and had greater presence of mind.

"Senhor de Leon," he began, "I cannot begin to thank you and Senhor de Sousa enough for what you have done. I have certainly heard of your remarkable assistance to New Christians and of course of your family's businesses, but I must now add my own deepest gratitude and indebtedness to my admiration. I hope I may someday repay you for my rescue."

De Leon smiled and slightly bowed his head. "I am most happy to have been of service, and to have made your acquaintance. We work toward the same good cause. As you can hear, a storm has moved in and will delay our departure. It may also impede the search for you—"

"But I am in danger as long as I am in Porto, and what is worse, I endanger both you and the young de Sousas," Eduardo interrupted. "You should leave me and make your escape."

De Leon smiled wanly. "We are in no immediate danger, and much as I wish I could send the de Sousa family on their way, the remainder of their journey to Bayonne and beyond is now in *your* hands; I can go no farther with them. So we must do our best to patch you up and send you all on together as soon as the storm breaks."

Eduardo sat up straighter and swung his legs to the side of the bed as de Leon pulled a small table closer with the food and drink. The question that had flitted through his dreams all night now spilled forth.

"What news have you of Isabela de Castro Nuñez, and"—he fought to keep his face impassive—"and perhaps of Ana Martel Gerondi?"

"Of Dama Martel Gerondi I have little news beyond that she left Carcassone with the intention to go to Toulouse, help set up connections to our network there, and hopefully make contact with Isabela at Irouléguy. She was in the care of my son from Girona as far as Carcassonne."

Eduardo closed his eyes and could not withhold the sigh that rose from deep within. When he opened his eyes, he saw that de Leon had cocked his head slightly and was studying him.

"I'm sorry, but beyond that I have no further news," de Leon said. "Of Senhorita de Castro Nuñez, however, I can say more. I myself was detained by the authorities some weeks ago and could not send a message myself, but I managed to get a local schoolmaster to send a message to my sister, who has accompanied the senhorita since they left Abrantes. When I heard of the movement of the Inquisitors to Porto and the rising danger to New Christians there, I sent a message through the schoolmaster that my sister and Isabela should go overland to Irouléguy. God willing, they are on their way over the mountains and into France as we speak."

For the next day and a half, Eduardo Carel stayed hidden in his small room at the top of the inn while the storm raged itself out. He slept, ate what others brought to him, and nursed the wounds on his face, arms, and back. He had had his share of fights as a younger man, but no one had ever beaten him as viciously as had these men. They had asked him again and again about people he'd never heard of—about the nature of his business in Porto.

And he'd *had* business in Porto. He'd made many contacts for the businessmen in Hamburg, and he'd offered to get references from the shipping agents he'd spoken to. And what of this priest? Porto was a significant distance from Abrantes. What had brought this padre to his door, and why had he asked only about people unknown?

Despite having confiscated the papers in his coat pocket, along with the coat itself, his interrogators had, thankfully, missed the slender leather wallet hidden in a long pocket along the inside of his breeches.

Fortunately, he had not yet secured the gold payment due to him from the shipping company, and so he asked Enrique de Leon to take his note to the office, explaining that he was ill and unable to come himself. When de Leon returned with the funds, Eduardo had asked a final favor: for him to go to the market and purchase enough clothing and provisions for the journey to Bayonne, as it would be too dangerous for anyone to try to recover his possessions from his previous lodgings.

At last the evening came when de Leon received word that the winds had shifted, the storm was past, and the ship could finally sail. That night, David joined Eduardo in the inn's common room with two young women, pale and drawn, in clean but worn dresses, with small travel cases at their sides and sturdy cloaks around their shoulders, despite the warm evening.

"May I introduce my sisters, Beatriz and Roshina de Sousa. This is Senhor . . ." David stopped, alarm flashing in his eyes.

"Eduardo Ramos, for now," Eduardo said. "I am most grateful that Senhor de Leon has brought you safely to Porto, and I hope our journey together will be as pleasant and uneventful as possible. And I know you will all join me in thanking Senhor de Leon and bidding him a safe journey."

The girls curtsied and blushed as de Leon kissed each of their hands, and after a moment's hesitation David stepped forward and embraced the man. The group then found their way down to the dock and onto a skiff that shuttled them to their Santa Maria, an old but tidy caravel bobbing in the rough water.

After waving a final goodbye to de Leon, they boarded the ship.

The trip was not pleasant. The caravel, with its two large square sails on the foremasts, triangular lateen sail on the rear mizzen, and shallow keel, worked well for coastal travel and sailed well into the wind. Even so, the wild gusts that had brought the storm and then sent it on its way settled into a steady blow that churned wave after wave, tossing the sturdy boat from peak to trough. It was a first sea voyage for all the de Sousa siblings, and they were wretchedly sick for days.

When at last the winds calmed, David made his way to the deck and found his sisters huddled in their cloaks, peaked faces turned to the sun. He sat on a pile of rope between them, and for the first time they spoke freely of leaving Portugal, of all that had happened to them, of what might have happened to their mother, of the new lands they were going to, and of their possible new lives. Exhausted and worried though he was, David drew each of his sisters into an embrace. As their tears fell on his cloak, he spoke firmly to be heard above the steady wind and the groan of masts and booms.

"You have been so brave and have borne so much," he told them. "Our journey isn't over, but we have safely escaped Portugal. I promise to do my best to find us a new life, a safe and secure life together as a family. Keep faith, and keep your courage."

The girls smiled wanly in return.

Leaving them to enjoy the fresh air and sun, David wished he felt confident in his promise. Just this morning, a man in the hammock near his had spoken of the possibility of an auto-da-fé in Porto, where none had happened in half a century. David had never seen this spectacle of a public sentencing and execution of those convicted by the Inquisitors, but apparently such sentencings and executions by hanging, burning at the stake, or drawing and quartering had become hugely popular entertainments. The man reporting this news to his neighbors in the hold of the Santa Maria had been sorry to miss the event and what would follow—the confiscation of all the Jews' property by the municipality.

David, silent and rigid in his hammock, had thought, *What if the Inquisitors and these spectacles found them in France?* He'd shuddered, and, unable to sleep, risen and spent the remaining nighttime hours walking the decks.

ISABELA'S WAY

No response had come from Isabela to his letter and now he was at sea, physically and at heart. As he walked, however, he thought about Eduardo "Ramos." He noticed that their chaperone seemed to regain strength with each day at sea, perhaps braced by the clear air and increasing distance from narrowly escaped danger. David also saw that the older man was preoccupied, and he wondered if he had someone he loved and wished to protect from peril.

The first three days of Isabela and Dona de Leon's travel from Pinhão required them to cross the Marão mountain range. Blessedly, Dona de Leon had found a carter with two sturdy mules who was making the trip to Benavente in Spain and agreed to take the women along for a modest fee.

An early storm soaked them for a day and a night, but the next day they found lodging in a comfortable inn with clean beds and good food, and from then on weather and company cooperated.

Isabela spent many of the long hours in the cart working on embroidering symbols onto banners, preparing them as instructed. She practiced different combinations of the symbols, not yet understanding exactly what they meant but remaining true to the order in the code sampler Ana Martel Gerondi had sent. The carter had many stories to tell and seemed grateful for an audience. Isabela listened, or she didn't, but on one afternoon he told a story that began to sound familiar and she paused her sewing to pay closer attention.

Long ago in a village here in the mountains there was a young girl. She was most beautiful and the daughter of a wealthy man. Her father had earned a large fortune and took refuge in the mountain town. A young knight fell in love with the girl, but neither the boy's mother nor the girl's father approved of the courtship . . .

Where had Isabela heard this story before? It had been on this journey for certain, but the days and the stories she'd heard were blended and confused in her mind after so many days of travel.

The carter continued.

But the boy was hopelessly in love and could not give up his pursuit of the beautiful girl. He devised a plan . . .

Suddenly Isabela remembered exactly where she had heard the story: at the feet of Dina Mendes, who had come from a mountain town in the north of Portugal very like the landscape they traveled through on this sunny day. Isabela remembered Senhora Mendes's words of comfort about love given and received as a source of strength and courage.

As the carter finished his story of the lovers overcoming challenges, even the challenge of religious difference, Isabela smiled at the memory of Senhora Mendes's kindness and help. And she recalled that on the day she first heard this story, she'd recognized that she loved David. Thinking of all this, the dangers she had escaped receded, even if only for this one idyllic afternoon, with this kind, storytelling man and his comfortable cart.

With newly buoyed spirits, she put away the banners and began to work on a silk handkerchief for the betrothed daughter of Raphael de Mercado. She should already be done with at least part of the trousseau; she'd been spending too much time on the banners.

With this new project, the day seemed brighter, and she noticed a grassy glen with its carpet of wildflowers whose colors popped between the trees like pinecones tossed in a fire. A welcome lightness settled into her center, where nothing but dull weight had sat for weeks, and she began to hum.

When the day's travel came to an end and they walked toward a farmhouse with a sign for rooms, Isabela realized how quiet Dona de Leon had become. Had they proceeded as planned to Porto, she would have been free of responsibility for Isabela now and reunited with her brother. She must be disappointed to have her guardianship so extended in time and distance. And yet perhaps this change could bring her closer to the man whose letter had softened her features and set them into a smile. Isabela wondered if this was the "friend" Dona de Leon had spoken of when she had, with great animation, described her home in the Camargue in the South of France, with wild horses and vast expanses of sea grasses, sea birds, and bands of travelers who spoke a different language, danced, and sang with abandon.

"I'm sorry you've had to extend your journey with me, Dona de Leon," Isabela offered as they sat at the crude wooden table in the farmyard. "But perhaps the rest of this journey will go more easily and you will get home to the Camargue sooner than expected."

Dona de Leon turned to look at Isabela, and an expression of genuine warmth spread across her features, causing Isabela to realize for the first time that her chaperone was actually quite lovely. "Thank you, Isabela, for thinking of me—and yes, I will be happy to return to my home, but let's get you to where you belong first."

Trying to hold on to the joy of the day, Isabela still found herself wondering if she'd ever feel that she belonged anywhere again.

CHAPTER FOURTEEN

Toulouse, Bayonne, Aldudes, and Trouléguy

July, 1605

Lay this unto your breast: old friends,
like old swords still are trusted best.
—JOHN WEBSTER

The day of meetings with traders and selling at the Toulouse market had brought much success to Ana, and she gazed with satisfaction at the fat purse on the table. Her dyes had sold well—much better than expected. She'd not planned to sell as much until she got to the textile center in Lyon.

She lifted her tired legs to the embroidered footstool and leaned back on the upholstered settee. She'd treated herself to finer rooms this time, furnished in the latest, ornate style; sheer curtains billowed over tasseled drapes at the edges of the balcony doors she'd thrown open to let in the breeze.

She surveyed the small, portable pots she'd set some of the woad roots from Jacques de Bernuy into and smiled. These would grow, and the rest she'd put aside to save for use in treating wounds, fevers, and inflammation.

Though pleased with her efforts in Toulouse so far, Ana worried that no news arrived from Eduardo, or from the parties who were supposed to accompany Isabela de Castro Nuñez and David de Sousa to France. So far, Ana had made good use of the wait time, but she never liked uncertainty about her own prospects and plans. *Should I travel to Irouléguy now, before hearing of Isabela's arrival? Should I travel there at all, or wait until Isabela finishes her work there and can make her way to Toulouse?*

Ana poured a glass of wine from a carafe she'd ordered. This Saint Sardos had the soft subtlety and refinement she so enjoyed in French wines, with a touch of fruit that made it wonderful to sip. She leaned back into the settee, letting the warmth of the drink settle into her chest. She had just let her eyelids drop closed when a sharp knock sounded at the door.

An errand boy informed her that a Dr. Francesco Sanches had sent a messenger and wished to call on Ana in the morning. Would she like to send a message in return?

Ana thought for a moment and then replied, "Yes, please tell the messenger that Dr. Sanches may call tomorrow at ten. And will you arrange for some ale in the library at that hour, please?"

The clerk left and Ana returned to her goblet of wine, this time stepping out to the balcony and the relief of cool early evening breezes to enjoy it.

Francesco Sanchez was a physician and philosopher here in Toulouse, though it was rumored that he had been born in Portugal to a Jewish family who had escaped the Inquisition. As a young medical student who had studied first in Italy and then in France, he was best known for his skeptical philosophical work *Quod Nihil Scitur*, which argued that nothing in medicine or any other pursuit of science could really be known and that any conclusions of a scientific nature were suspect. Ana had heard physicians in Girona discourse on this problem but dismissed it as being of little use to her more practical pursuit of healing remedies. What she remembered was that Dr. Sanches had become somewhat of a darling to the Church for his suggestion that truth could be gained through faith. Those in pursuit of scientific knowledge, however, found worth in his further thoughts that observation, experience, and judgment still had value in accruing knowledge, imperfect as it might be.

All this made Ana's head spin, yet now this esteemed man wished to meet with her, and she could not imagine why. How had she even come to his attention? She had never before visited Toulouse; nor, as a woman, was it likely she would have come to his attention from afar, despite her unusual acceptance by the medical community in Girona as a well-educated and skilled healer.

The danger to a woman whose skills as a healer could easily be perverted into charges of heresy or witchcraft must always be part of Ana's awareness. She poured herself more wine and paced from balcony to settee and back again, wondering what Sanches wanted from her.

The next morning dawned dismal and oppressive, with the stillness of an impending storm and humid heat. Vapors of fog mixed with the stench of sewage in the streets. Ana took particular care with her toilette and dress, eschewing her more formal ruff for a simpler linen and lace collar over a gray brocade dress. She arranged her hair loosely at the nape of her neck with a simple headpiece. By ten a.m. she had breakfasted and was sitting in the hotel's library, awaiting her guest.

Francisco Sanches arrived promptly at ten and bowed formally in introduction. He was an imposing man. Though barely taller than she, his substantial body was clothed in voluminous robes with a full, pleated ruff. His face was long and pockmarked, and a pointed beard accentuated his narrow chin. He studied her steadily as she studied him in return.

A maid brought in the ale, and Ana gestured for Dr. Sanches to be seated on a couch while she took a highback chair opposite him. Her subtle upending of a conventional seating arrangement for a man and a woman was intentional. She supposed that having no escort in this meeting, or on this visit to Toulouse at all, for that matter, cast judgment on her from the start—but she could do nothing to remedy that and so proceeded boldly.

"It is a pleasure to make your acquaintance, Dr. Sanches," she began. "We have heard much of you in Girona. I have attended several meetings on the subject of your philosophy of science and medicine."

At this, Dr. Sanches cocked his head to one side and the ghost of a smile played across his thin lips.

"To what do I owe this esteemed visit?" Ana asked.

"Not, I hope, to talk philosophy," he replied, "though perhaps we can engage in that one day as well." When Ana did not respond he continued, "I hoped to invite you to consult in my offices. Your reputation as an herbalist and healer is quite impressive."

Ana stiffened. What possible reputation could have preceded her, and then not as a dye maker but in the dangerous realm of herbal healing? "I cannot imagine that I have any important knowledge to impart to men as esteemed as you and your colleagues, Dr. Sanches," she said, though it pained her to feign this kind of modesty. As she did not know this man, or the source of his interest in her, she could not be too careful.

"Jacques de Bernuy seems to disagree, Madame Martel Gerondi." Dr. Sanches sat back and allowed this information to settle in.

Ana had certainly not expected to hear Jacques de Bernuy's name in this interview, and her surprised expression must have shown that.

"Monsieur Bernuy spoke very highly of your knowledge and experience."

Ana thought quickly. She and Jacques de Bernuy had certainly had a wide-ranging conversation about plants and their dye and medicinal properties. Was it possible that he had spoken to Dr. Sanches of more than her healing skills?

It seemed impossible that after only one meeting, de Bernuy would feel free to discuss their secret and dangerous plan to create a way station for escaping refugees from Portugal in his spacious mansion with others. Unless, of course, both these new acquaintances meant to entrap her. Yet Ana had felt quite certain she could trust de Bernuy after the time she spent with him, and she further trusted her own instincts.

Dr. Sanches seemed to observe these thoughts as they flew through Ana's mind, and just when she reached the end of them he spoke again.

"You may well wonder why I've made the effort to make your acquaintance and suggest a working relationship." He paused and looked over Ana's shoulder to the door of the library, which was firmly shut. "Whatever else you have heard about me, I am sure that the speculation about my religion of origin has also reached your ears. I am in fact what I believe is called a New Christian in your country, and while I did not grow up with the Hebrew religion, my grandfather was a rabbi and a scholar. I have reason to believe that my utility to the royal house and the officials of the Church here in France, along with their interest in me, may soon lose their luster, and even my medical skills may cease to keep revelation of these facts from discrediting and perhaps even endangering my future."

Ana listened intently to this speech, more than surprised at the turn it had taken but still unable to anticipate a connection to herself.

"Dr. Sanches, I still don't understand how the work that I do could benefit the situation you describe."

"I am still in a position of considerable power at court and in the Church's councils, and, more importantly, privy to much information in both places," he said. "I believe such information and influence might be of great value to some of the other work in which you are engaged—work other than your herbal and healing work."

"I see." There was no point in pretending that she did not understand his meaning. She could hardly believe that de Bernuy had revealed their plans, but clearly Dr. Sanches knew enough about them.

"And it is even possible that I may someday be in need of that work." Here, Dr. Sanches emphasized the word *that*. "In such a scenario, you would be in a position to help me and those dear to me. In the meantime, and God willing for a long time, I could be of considerable use to the people you are helping."

Ana struggled to find a way to ask her most pressing question without antagonizing this man, who now had her utterly confused and uncertain.

Before she could try, he said, "You must surely be asking yourself how you can trust me."

The heat in the room added to Ana's discomfort; she drew out her handkerchief to wipe away the perspiration on her face and neck. "Quite," she said.

"I have given thought to what might give you assurances." Dr. Sanches withdrew two documents from his robes and handed her the first.

It had been written in Hamburg nearly a month before, and bore the signature of a doctor there with a Portuguese name. The letter was addressed to Francisco Sanches, on behalf of a patient by the name of Gabril de Castro Nuñez, and requested assistance in finding and helping to conduct Nuñez's daughter Isabela to safety.

"This doctor is an old friend and colleague of mine—we studied together in Italy," Dr. Sanches said. "He has tried to get me to come to Hamburg to practice with him, and if things here continue to worsen, I may do so. As you can see, the letter suggested that I visit Monsieur de Bernuy, and I did so. That is where I learned of you, and, coincidentally, your interest in Mademoiselle de Castro Nuñez. Jacques de Bernuy and I have been friends for many years. I trust him and he apparently trusts you, and that is how I come to be here this morning."

Ana stared at him and expelled a deep breath of relief. It was as if her entire journey since leaving Girona were a puzzle with separate parts, now it felt like a piece had been placed that began to link those parts together.

The doctor handed her the second letter. It was sealed with an unfamiliar stamp. "This arrived at Jacques de Bernuy's only yesterday. He thought you would want to see it right away."

Ana's hand flew to her chest as she opened the letter and cried out, "Eduardo!"

Dated only three days previously, the letter came from Bayonne, and Eduardo's elegant script filled both sides of the page.

My dearest Ana,

I can only hope and pray that this letter finds you safe and close enough to our colleague to receive this news.

Our beleaguered travel party arrived safely in Bayonne just this morning and will remain here until we've had a chance to recover from our various misadventures escaping from Portugal —not the least of which was a wild sail from Porto, which was quite uncomfortable but got us here in less than expected time. I will save the tale of my unpleasant brush with the authorities in Porto for a later communication. And I fervently hope, dear Ana, that such a communication and all further ones will be then and forever in person. Getting to know the fine young man and his sisters, all of whom have grown up too quickly, helps me remember why we do this work, but I fear I am becoming soul weary. I wish only to settle with you, somewhere safe, and live a simple life. May it happen sooner than later.

In the meantime, we have had no further word of my sister and her young charge for nearly a month now. We did hear that they had reached Pinhão and were to travel overland to Irouléguy, where the girl should be safe for a while. I trust you have been successful in finding further havens for her and others through France to the free city of Strasbourg. From there, I know our friend in Hamburg will make arrangements.

I have one unsettling matter to warn you of. There is a priest from Abrantes who seems to have a fixation on our young charges from there. No one quite understands it, but beware. And stay well and safe, dear Ana. I have had no news of you in too long, but know that, as always, I long for you.

*With love,
Eduardo*

Once again, Ana brought her handkerchief to her face, this time to wipe away tears. She looked into Dr. Sanches's gray eyes and saw a new softness there.

"I am fortunate to find such allies here in Toulouse, Dr. Sanches," she said. "I would be happy to work with you."

It had taken nearly two weeks for Isabela and Dona de Leon to reach Aldudes, the settlement in France where the trek through Spain ended. The women crossed a graceful stone bridge into the hamlet, which was bordered by a river to the west, pig farms to the south, and the forested Pyrenees to the north and east, and found their way to the inn where Pedro de Martins was waiting to escort Isabela to the villa of her new employer, Raphael de Mercado.

Suddenly, her odyssey with Dona de Leon drew swiftly to a close, and their separation hit Isabela like a boom of thunder. As reserved and severe as Dona de Leon remained, she had brought Isabela all this way, through danger and with much secrecy—and now, like the only home Isabela had ever known, she would be lost to her, perhaps forever.

"Thank you," Isabela said as she threw her arms around the older woman. "I hope you can return to the Camargue now. May God reward you for all you have done."

Dona de Leon's eyes filled, and she returned Isabela's embrace with a fierce one of her own. Without a further word, she turned to Senhor de Martins, and they exchanged details of the journey to this point and plans moving forward.

After a good supper Isabela retired to her room, where she fell into a long, heavy sleep.

When Isabela awoke the next morning, Dona de Leon had already departed and a sturdy horse and carriage awaited her outside for the half-day ride to Irouléguy.

Isabela's parents had seen to her education in languages, and both her French and Spanish were passable, but neither allowed her to understand the Basque language she had been hearing for days as she traveled north through the Basque Country of Spain and France. Fortunately, Senhor de Martins spoke Spanish and French as well as his native Basque, and with his facilitation they made their way up through mountain villages smoothly, stopping only to rest and water the horses.

Finally they reached a valley, nestled beneath grassy and forested hillsides, with farms and vineyards laid out around a cluster of houses and a small church. Irouléguy.

They passed through the town and up a road that quickly faded to a track and entered pine and beech forests that amazed Isabela with their towering beauty and fresh, pungent scent. The day was clear and cool, and having been awed by a new vista at every turn on the way up the mountainside, she now savored the muted silence of the forest, broken only by the call of distant birds and the jangle of the horse's bridles.

After a half-hour climb the travelers emerged into a wide clearing. Across a flower-studded meadow stood a magnificent chateau, built of stone, with windows set on two stories and square towers rising at both ends of the building. Dormers graced the deeply slanted roof across the face of the building, and gardens at both ends promised more beauty toward the rear.

As they dismounted in the courtyard before a massive wooden door, Isabela tried to smooth her skirts and pull up her bodice. She willed herself to ignore the dust and wrinkles from months of travel and her loose-hanging dress, which made clear how much weight she had lost.

The heavy door swung open and a flurry of maids, footmen, and grooms appeared from all directions to unload her trunk, conduct her into a large hall, and then up an intricately carved staircase to rooms appointed with the finest furnishings she'd ever seen.

As if she'd entered a fairy tale, she was led to a table laden with cheeses, a delicate bread, fresh milk, and plump strawberries. After she sampled this welcome repast, a maid led her down a back staircase to a room with a huge copper tub filled with lavender-scented hot water. The comfort and splendor awed her.

After her bath, the same maid offered her the chance to rest until dinner and the formal greeting of the de Mercados. Isabela gratefully accepted.

In her room, she climbed into the huge bed, draped all the way around with light curtains. The distant lowing of the cows she'd seen on her approach to the chateau and the chirping of birds singing their afternoon song were the only sounds she heard as she fell into a restful sleep.

CHAPTER FIFTEEN

Trouléguy and Toulouse
July, 1605

Attempt the end, and never stand to doubt.
Nothing's so hard but search will find it out.
—Robert Herrick

Isabela awoke to the bustle of skirts, the opening and closing of chests, and the murmur of two women's voices outside her bed curtains. As these were drawn open, late-afternoon light poured in through the open window across the room.

Still drugged with sleep, Isabela tried to focus on the faces peering in at her.

One belonged to a middle-aged woman, her gray streaked hair pulled tightly into a chignon under a ruffled white cap. A spotless white apron covered her gray dress and her pleasant features were arranged into a neutral expression. In contrast, the younger woman had a lush head of curly auburn hair, barely contained in a cap that sat askew, and her smile radiated toward Isabela, who couldn't help smiling in return.

All three women began to speak: Isabela in Portuguese, the younger woman in Spanish, the older one in Basque-accented French. Each stopped, and the older maid took command.

"Welcome, Mademoiselle de Castro Nuñez. It is time to rise and dress for dinner. The Count wishes to see you in the salon in an hour's time. I am Arabelle Asturias, and I am in charge of the household here at Chateau Mercado."

By now Isabela had risen from the bed and stood facing the two maids.

"Good afternoon, Madame Asturias. I am so grateful to be here," she said with a small curtsy, switching to French.

"And this is Sophia Pardo. She will assist you in whatever you might need."

"Señorita Pardo," Isabela said, again with a small curtsy.

Madame Asturias's eyebrows rose in unison. "You may call her Sophia, *mademoiselle*."

Isabela blushed. Having never employed a maid, and having expected to be an employee and not a pampered guest in this house, Isabela realized she had much to learn about where she fit into the hierarchy of Chez Mercado.

"Come, we must dress you," said Madame Asturias.

Isabela clutched her shift—no one since her mother had ever helped her dress—but she obediently followed Madame Asturias to the room's corner, where the trunk she'd brought from Abrantes stood open and partially unpacked. Her clothing had been brushed and pressed and hung on pegs in a giant armoire. Her extra shifts and drawers were nowhere to be seen. In their stead were clean and starched new ones with beautiful lace edging. Hanging next to her own dresses were three additional ones sewn from beautiful brocades and silks.

"Perhaps you would like to choose one of these dresses for tonight." Madame Asturias gestured toward them. "You are very close to the size of Mademoiselle Mercado, and she has offered these to supplement your travel wardrobe. I will leave you to Sophia's assistance."

With that, the housekeeper left the room, and for a moment the two young women regarded each other silently. Then Sophia chose one of the dresses and turned to Isabela.

"Would you like to try this dress, Señorita Isabela?" The girl's face shone with enthusiasm, and she seemed to feel none of the discomfort at being in a service capacity that beset Isabela about being served. "Come, try this on and let us dress your hair."

An hour later, dressed entirely in new clothing, Isabela descended the staircase and entered the main salon, where the Mercado family awaited her. She stopped abruptly just inside the doorway of the immense room. The full complement of Mercado adults and children in this family of eight barely filled a quarter of the elegant space. Isabela stifled a gasp as she took note of silk-covered walls with gilt trim, polished parquet floors, burnished silver sconces, and huge candle-filled candelabras.

A tall, vigorous-looking man of about forty approached her with a warm smile. "Welcome, Isabela. I am Raphael de Mercado. We are so happy you have arrived here safely, and we look forward to your stay. Please meet my wife, Alaia, and my daughter, Miren." Miren Mercado shared her mother's striking beauty: wavy black hair, high color on an unblemished complexion, and slender figure. As each woman approached and curtsied politely, Isabela noted one marked difference: Miren's eyes were soft and brown, while her mother's were as blue and radiant as a summer sky. Isabela was lost in those eyes until Raphael de Mercado continued.

"And these are my other children." Count Mercado introduced five additional children, whose names Isabela barely understood, being either Basque or spoken so quickly that she could do little more than curtsy as each of them did the same or bowed to her.

With introductions complete, the count and Madame Mercado led Isabela to a room off the side of the salon lit by an entire wall of windows. A solid work table, cabinets with rows of small drawers, a dress form, and chairs furnished the well-stocked sewing room.

"This will be your work area, Mademoiselle Nuñez, if it meets your needs," said the count.

Isabela stared wide-eyed at the elegant space. Madame Mercado opened several of the drawers to exhibit cards of silk in a myriad of colors, along with rolls of lace, scissors, pins, and needles. Panels of linen and silk filled the cupboards.

"I am certain I will work very happily here, Monsieur Mercado, thank you," Isabela said. For a moment, all she could think was, *If only Mamãe could see this—. . . what work we could do together in this room.*

With introductions complete, the family moved to a small dining room and Isabela enjoyed a sumptuous first meal in her new home.

The next morning, a new set of clothes appeared in Isabela's room: a dress of heavy cotton and an apron with several pockets. Isabela took this to signal a working day ahead.

She opened her small chest with her sewing supplies and work bag and was reassured to find that all seemed undisturbed. She filled her bag with the items she thought she'd need to start her day and descended to a breakfast of pastry and fresh strawberries.

When Isabela entered the sewing room after breakfast, it already buzzed with activity. Not one but two seamstresses were working on a deep rose—colored silk dress. Seated by the sunlit window, Madame

Mercado had her own hoop in hand and was embroidering an edge on a cutwork doily.

She patted the seat next to her and pointed to a sheaf of papers, a quill, and an ink bottle. "Come, Isabela, sit here, and we will speak about your work. But first, tell me something of yourself. Who are your family, and how was your journey getting to Irouléguy?"

Isabela, taken aback by this personal request, remained momentarily silent.

Apparently sensing her discomfort, Alaia said softly,

"I know you lost your mother and your father is in Hamburg, but tell me about them, and how you learned to do such beautiful work. We all so admired the gloves you embroidered for Miren's intended."

So Isabela did tell, first hesitant and then grateful to describe past happiness, the productive working life of textile trading and skilled embroidery, the broad and interesting circle of friends that had filled her life during her childhood. She chose not to describe the year when it all changed—when the church became a place of fear and uncertainty with the rising threat of the Inquisitors and her father abruptly departed to seek a life for them elsewhere. Of her mother's death she said only that Abrantes had been devastated by the fever that was all too well known across Europe. She then told the story of her journey, focusing more on the adventure and pleasure of her time with Alfonso and Dina Mendes in Castelo de Vide than the confusion and sadness and exhaustion of the escape and uncertainty and danger that she had also experienced.

When she finished, she glanced around the room and noted that Sophia was now seated off to her left, mending a stocking.

Alaia Mercado's beautiful blue eyes rose from her work and fixed on Isabela. "You are a brave girl, called to do much at a young age, but you must understand that you are not alone. There are others, like the Mendeses, like Ana Martel Gerondi, like Simone de Leon . . . and like my husband and I . . . who are also working to save and protect New Christians and conduct them to safety. Those of us who are called to this work must continue to be brave and to contribute wherever and whenever we can."

Her fierce blue gaze returned to her needlework, and Isabela, stunned by this recitation, tried to deduce how Alaia knew the importance of the Mendeses, how she knew anything of Ana Martel Gerondi, and what, beyond securing her services as an embroideress, connected the Mercados to the others.

Isabela turned to Sophia, who now held a linen square, and leaned closer to see what she was embroidering. Her gaze landed on a hamsa, the symbol which she had now sent twice to David. An elaborate tree and bright red pomegranates decorated other parts of the linen.

Why did Sophia know about these symbols, part of a code given to Isabela in utmost secrecy? Who was this girl, and why had Isabela really been brought to Irouléguy?

Two months had passed since Ana Martel Gerondi had arrived in Toulouse and gone to work with Dr. Sanches. She found that he was well trained in the conventional medical practices of the day but had much to learn about the herbal remedies and practices that informed her own work as a healer.

In her first days, she held back from offering more than anise and mint leaves made into a tea for gas and constipation or yarrow and comfrey bandaged onto a simple wound. But when an entire family appeared with coughs, the doctor deferred to Ana, who made poultices of camphor and honey and teas of eucalyptus, rue, and mallow root. She saw the family over several days, and they quickly improved.

As weeks wore on, Dr. Sanches consulted Ana on more serious

wound care, seeking her advice as to when a bandage or poultice sufficed or when surgical procedures were required. When Ana described the new use of maggots on badly infected wounds, Dr. Sanches listened and allowed her to try the flesh eaters on a young boy whose injured leg he thought needed to be amputated. When the wound improved and Ana successfully treated the boy's fever with hyssop, mint, and valerian, both the doctor and the boy's family regarded her with increasing respect.

Ana began to take over the cleaning and stitching of wounds, preparing willow bark teas and stronger spirits for pain relief. She noted when Dr. Sanches chose to assign her patients of her own and when he used her more as an assistant, and soon realized that he protected her from people inclined to regard her skills as magical or worse.

After their first conversation, nothing was spoken of New Christian refugees or the specific plights referred to in the letters he had brought to her until one afternoon in mid-July.

The day was hot and dry, and morning had brought a steady stream of patients to the doctor's rooms. After many hours of work, Ana washed her hands for the final time in a basin of fresh water, removed her dirty apron, and prepared to return to her rooms for dinner.

"Madame Martel Gerondi," the doctor said as his assistants finished sweeping and cleaning instruments. "Would you stay here and dine with me? I've heard some news I wish to share with you."

Something in his mild but guarded tone made Ana turn to him and search his gray eyes for more information, but his look remained steady and unreadable.

"Of course," she said. "I would be happy to join you."

Ana had never before ventured into the private rooms adjoining Francisco Sanches's surgery. A large sitting room, a study, and dining alcove were furnished simply and tastefully. A maid showed her to a settee near a window that looked out into the garden, which she found unexpectedly beautiful. Its architecture was planned but natural looking, with an emphasis on flowers of every sort. The hum of bees and the chirp of birds floated on perfumed air through the terrace door.

Dr. Sanches joined her after changing out of his physician's coat and apron.

"Shall we dine in the garden?" he suggested. "It's such a beautiful day."

Ana agreed, and they were soon seated at a long table under a pergola with a riot of trumpet vine sending orange flowers up one side and early clusters of grapes hanging overhead from a vine on the other. Dinner of pan-fried trout and fresh asparagus came immediately, accompanied by a fine wine and a robust loaf of bread.

They ate in companionable silence for several minutes until Dr. Sanches put down his fork and leaned toward Ana.

"I heard a disturbing conversation yesterday when I was called to the bishop's offices on a matter of business," he said.

Ana finished a bite of the tender trout and waited, giving the doctor her full attention.

"The discussion concerned a young prelate who is expected to visit the bishop soon. He comes from Coimbra in Portugal, apparently at the behest of King Philip of Spain, to counteract the efforts of our recently departed king to make alliances with the Protestants. The intent is to secure control of the queen regent. This prelate is well connected and well-funded in this effort." He paused and drank a substantial draught of wine. "He apparently will be accompanied by a zealous priest who is intent on imposing the dictates of the Inquisition in his area of Portugal and everywhere within reach of the Church."

Ana felt her jaw tighten. Eduardo's letter warned of a priest. *What* was the name? Almeida? Alves? Alvaro! "Who are these Church officials, and what have they to do with us?" she asked, though she dreaded the answer.

"The prelate has only a political cause to uphold, and therefore is unlikely to be of consequence to us—but the priest is another story." Dr. Sanches frowned. "He is from Abrantes, and his zealotry on behalf of the Inquisitors has become well known."

Ana closed her eyes as a shiver ran through her.

"This Padre Alvaro seems dedicated to tracking escapees from Portugal—in particular, two young people from Abrantes who I believe are of your acquaintance."

"But why?" she asked. "Why chase two children across half a continent?"

"I'm afraid you must guess the answer as well as I can, Ana." Dr. Sanches leaned forward, his hands gripping his cup of wine, his gray eyes drilling into Ana's. "The Portuguese have been forced to accept the Inquisition and the sovereignty of King Philip, but the exodus of so many New Christians has caused a financial and skills drain that is disruptive to the country's economy. At the same time, the increase in persecution has required the creation of many paths of escape. I suspect this Padre Alvaro is on to the development of one such system—the one of which the two young people of your acquaintance and responsibility have been beneficiaries." The doctor's voice became softer but more urgent. "His presence and potential meddling put them at risk of capture and prosecution, along with anyone who assists them." He remained hunched forward for a long moment—then he sat back in his chair and simply stared at Ana.

She suddenly felt as if ants were crawling up her arms, under her shift, and down her legs. The enormity of the doctor's words washed over her in waves of mounting fear. *I must get to Isabela, and we must set out for Lyon.*

"When do these churchmen arrive?" she asked. "I must leave at once to warn Isabela and move her toward Lyon and then Strasbourg."

She moved her chair back as if preparing to rise, but Dr. Sanches raised his hand.

"I have another idea," he said. "As you know, I believe nothing can be known in an ultimate sense, but we should not abandon all attempts to gain what knowledge we can."

Ana could scarcely understand his attempt to engage her in a discussion of his famous philosophical theories now, of all times, but he quickly continued.

"I visited the bishop yesterday for the purpose of treating a young man—he said the boy was a nephew—and the youth requires follow-up in a few days. I told the bishop I would be sending an assistant. I think you should go. I am sorry to say this, but as a woman, you will be less likely to engender any hesitation on the part of the household to speak freely, and it may even be possible for you to report to the bishop himself and hear some information of value while you are there."

This was a calculating side of Dr. Sanches that Ana had seen before and did not like; however, she needed to work in concert with him for everyone's safety.

As often happened, he appeared to read her mind. "As you will see, the nature of the young man's symptoms suggest his having engaged in sexual acts that I am certain the bishop would not want rumored about. Your being in possession of such information might be of some benefit. None of my other assistants are privy to the importance of gaining this kind of information and leverage. That is why I'm asking this of you, in full knowledge of the risks you will take, including delaying in your reaching Senhorita de Castro Nuñez."

Her many weeks of work with Dr. Sanches had caused Ana's guarded trust of him to slowly grow, but this proposed plan tested that trust. He gazed at her intently, and she knew she hadn't much time to decide.

"I will do this on the condition that you send word immediately to Irouléguy that I will arrive within a fortnight to take Isabela."

Dr. Sanches smiled at her. "I sent word this morning."

CHAPTER SIXTEEN

Irouléguy and Hamburg
August, 1605

*A spark of impenetrable darkness flashed
within the concealed of the concealed.*
—The Zohar

August heat scorched the hillsides above Irouléguy and penetrated the thick stone walls of Chateau Mercado. A week of wearying work was nearly complete. On Friday, the dressmaking and embroidery came to an end by four in the afternoon, and Saturday never involved more than a half-day if any of the week's projects were incomplete. Sunday was a day of rest.

Arms stretched straight from her shoulders, Isabela flexed her tired hands, clenching and relaxing her fingers. She then gently swung her arms in a twist to release the tension in her back from long hours of sitting. She had found a corner of the terrace outside the sewing room that was shaded by a beech tree whose leaves of deep purple, pink, and white were unlike any Isabela had seen in all her travels. The additional mercy of a breeze rising from the valley below cooled her bare arms and, having pulled her cap off, she lifted her heavy curls from her neck to allow the air to tease perspiration from its nape.

From below came the rushing noise of a mountain stream that

farther down became a small waterfall. In her time at the chateau she had not yet followed the path down as far as the cascade, though the Mercado children spoke of escapades in the pools above and below the falls. Perhaps tomorrow afternoon she could venture in that direction. Perhaps Sophia would come with her.

Sophia had proved a welcome friend, talented embroideress, and helpful ally in Isabela's adjustment to the household. They spoke in a mixture of French and Spanish. Isabela had noticed that as talkative and friendly as Sophia was, she spoke little of her family or background, often deftly changing the topic when Isabela tried to ask any questions.

The work on Miren's trousseau was more extensive than anything Isabela could have imagined. Yards and yards of silks in the jewel tones that best suited the young woman had become a dozen dresses, all of them copied from the latest Parisian styles. Those intended for evening wear had lace collars and Venetian glass beads sewn onto the bodices with gold thread. The day dresses were less ornate but still decorated with embroidered cuffs, collars, and bodice edgings. In the more sober colors befitting Miren's fiancé, the tailors had made frock coats, breeches, waistcoats, along with fine linen shirts, before handing the garments off to the embroiderers to embellish. For the household, Sophia and Isabela had embroidered pillowcases, hand towels, bedsheet edgings, and duvet covers until their eyes could hardly focus.

Madame Mercado was kind but exacting. Isabela had never worked so hard in her life. She was treated graciously and amply provided for, but no mention of when the trousseau would be complete came from the mistress or anyone else. Nor did word of a plan for Isabela to leave Irouléguy or reconnect with her father or David reach her. She found herself from time to time staring out the terrace doors into the summer heat and wishing her mother were next to her, working with these beautiful fabrics and fine threads. At night, with the casements thrown wide open in her bedchamber, Isabela searched the tapestry of stars for hints that her father or David gazed at the same round moon or shooting stars streaking across the inky blackness.

In this way, more than a month had passed.

Now Isabela, sitting on the stone bench under the beech tree, opened *Les amours de Poliphile et de Mellonimphe*, one of a new type of story the French called an *amour*, which she had borrowed from the Mercado library. Isabela had been given free rein to explore and read what she would, and while she'd begun her searching in the hopes of improving her French, she now indulged herself for love of the varied genres the count had acquired.

When Isabela next looked up from her book, the sun had sunk behind the chateau. As she rose, replacing her cap and gathering her shawl, movement off the far end of the terrace caught her eye. Sophia, carrying what looked like a market basket, hurried down the path toward a lower terrace where the cook kept a kitchen garden and the groundskeepers stored their tools and carts. Isabela loved to wander in the orderly rows of lavender, marigolds, and zinnias, the round barrels containing cascades of mint, and the surrounding sections of lettuce, carrots, onions, garlic, and seasonal vegetables.

What could Sophia be doing down there at this hour? Surely Cook is already far into preparing supper.

Isabela crossed the terrace and stepped onto the path to follow her friend, but Sophia darted so quickly that she had rounded a curve into a copse of trees before Isabela could so much as call out to her. This she found odd. Though energetic enough in talking and laughing, Sophia did not, in Isabela's experience, do anything swiftly.

Isabela arrived in the garden to find it deserted, with no sign of Sophia. Birds sang their full-throated evening songs, the trees behind her shook their leaves in the stiffening breeze, and the remaining sunlight fell in golden pools. Isabela listened for sounds of footsteps but heard instead a low hum that rose and lowered somewhere between a chant and a song. Looking for the source, she rounded the gardener's shed and cocked her head to one side. The sound was coming from the woods at the other side of the clearing.

She hesitated, thinking she ought to return to the chateau and prepare for dinner, yet she was curious. *What is that sound, and where did Sophia disappear to?*

As soon as Isabela entered the wood, the path widened. Some twenty yards in, another footpath cut to the right. The droning sound became louder, though it was still muffled, and Isabela followed it to a tiny and windowless but well-built hut of fieldstone and logs, roofed with thatch. She could hear the chanting more clearly now.

She rounded the corner of the building to find a door that faced the far side of the woods. The uncleared access, recently trampled, confirmed her sense that intruders weren't welcome.

As she crept closer to the door, she noted that a wide metal grate stretched above the lintel and the low chanting became more distinct the closer she came. The voices were men's voices, the chants in a language Isabela didn't recognize.

While some light still filtered through the trees, twilight would quickly yield to darkness. Unnerved by this realization, Isabela turned away from the strange little house—and nearly collided with Sophia, who appeared as if by magic from the trees.

"Oh!" Isabela cried, first surprised and then relieved to see her friend. "What are you doing here?"

The chanting stopped abruptly, and the door swung open behind Isabela. She turned to see a handsome man of medium height wearing a tunic with a fringed scarf and black silk brimless hat—Pedro de Martins. He wore a scarf that featured designs of a six-sided star, a candelabra, and the shape of a hand, intricately decorated.

On seeing Isabela, Senhor de Martins casually removed his scarf, folded it into a pouch in his tunic, and shifted his sharp gaze to Sophia in the fading light.

"Isabela de Castro Nuñez, may I introduce you to Señor Pedro de Martins," Sophia said, shifting from one foot to the other.

"We are acquainted, Señorita Pardo," said Senhor de Martins. "And Senhorita de Castro Nuñez, I hope to see you later at dinner and in the next days. I have much to share with you, but I don't wish to detain you at this late hour."

"Yes," Sophia said. "Señor Martins, if you will return my basket, I will accompany Señorita Isabela back to the chateau so she can prepare for dinner."

Darkness descended rapidly, Sophia capably led the way back through the forest, past the lower garden, and up the path to the chateau.

Isabela picked up her skirts and hurried after her. "Who were the men with Senhor de Martins?" she gasped out, stumbling. "What do you have in that basket? What is so secret? *Sophia?*"

Sophia finally stopped and turned back to Isabela. "The men you heard are Jews, and they were praying to greet the Sabbath. They must meet in secret, as it is dangerous to do so openly. I bring them candlesticks to light the sabbath candles, and a special challah bread which Cook helps me bake on Friday." At Isabela's questioning look, she asked, "You know about the Jewish sabbath, don't you?"

Catching her breath, Isabela said, "Not really . . . I didn't know many Jews in Abrantes."

Sophia stared at her friend with an expression of bafflement.

"What—"

"Well, we must hurry and not be late for dinner," Sophia said quickly, and carried on toward the chateau.

ISABELA'S WAY

When Pedro de Martins appeared at dinner, he was dressed in conventional clothing and said nothing at all to Isabela until after the meal, when the children had been sent to bed and the adults had retired to the terrace.

On the terrace, torches relieved the dark and small tables were set with sweetmeats and bottles of cordials. Senhor de Martins steered Isabela to her favorite bench at the far end and offered her a glass of sweet wine.

"I have come today from Toulouse with a message from a friend," he began.

Isabela's heart leaped in her chest, wishing more than believing that he had word from David.

"Dama Martel Gerondi has been working there these past two months and plans to journey here soon to take you away and travel with you toward Germany, in the hopes you can meet with your father there."

Isabela's hand flew to her mouth. All she could say was, "Oh!"

"Unfortunately," Senhor de Martins said quietly and quickly, "there is also imminent danger. Two emissaries from the Church in Portugal are due to visit the bishop in Toulouse. One of them is known to you, and his fervor to impose the Inquisition on every country in Europe and his suspicions about your escape and your work pose a serious threat,"

Isabela looked wide-eyed at Pedro. "Who is this person? And what of my work? What possible interest could anyone have in my work on a noblewoman's trousseau?"

Senhor de Martins sighed and fingered the buttons on his coat. "The priest is Padre Alvaro, and it isn't your work here for the Mercados that is in question."

Isabela tried to think, but the mention of Padre Alvaro and Senhor de Martins's other explanations flitted in and out of her mind like swallows in a belfry. And then the conversation with Alfonso Mendes in his study at Castelo de Vide returned to her: *New Christians and hidden Jews . . . We are trying to establish safe passage to Amsterdam, Venice, and Hamburg . . . Your father and Dama Martel Gerondi are part of it . . . Your embroidered cloths will be a signal . . . symbols of safety or harm.*"

Isabela saw her dawning recognition reflected in her companion's watchful eyes.

"I think you understand," he said. "And so we ask that you create two banners for the Mercados: one to signify safety at the chateau, and one to warn of danger. I believe you have learned the necessary symbols. They will fly with the count's pennants to alert approaching travelers. As soon as Dama Martel Gerondi arrives, you will depart with her and continue this work as you make your way to safety. Do you understand?"

Isabela looked out over the congenial group of family and friends she had come to know and care for, and who had provided her with a home, work, and payment. Turning back to Senhor de Martins, she asked in a hushed voice, "Are the Mercados secret Jews?"

"Not at all," he replied. "They are good Christians who have put themselves and their children at risk to save lives." He let this sink into Isabela's thoughts. "But *I* am," he continued. "What you heard tonight in the forest was a service to greet the Jewish sabbath. We must meet only in secret in these dangerous times. But perhaps one day Jewish practice will come back into your life."

What does he mean "back" into my life?

Before Isabela could ask, Raphael Mercado summoned Senhor de Martins into the chateau, and Isabela was left alone to contemplate all she had learned.

ISABELA'S WAY

Gabril de Castro Nuñez found the climate in Hamburg challenging. August in Abrantes was the hottest month, with scorching days of burning sun and little rain to provide relief. In Hamburg, August temperatures rarely allowed for shedding a coat, and while the unrelenting showers of July had abated, there were still few purely sunny days. The confluence of rivers with plentiful water, however, brought greenery to the forests and gardens of the area, which amazed him first with their lush scents of pines and then wide swaths of floral beauty.

He had spent months negotiating for the opportunity to travel to Venice, first with the Wirtschaftsrat who oversaw the thriving businesses in the city and then with contacts in Venice, where as an agent of the burghers he planned to broker deals for trade in glass, grain, salt, and silk. The shipping connections between Portugal and Hamburg also fell in his purview. Finally, all the permissions and contacts were in place—all except the arrangement that would bring him together again with Isabela.

Making his way along the Monkedamm on this rare day of sun and warmth, Gabril rehearsed his arguments to the Kehillah, the group that had now successfully advocated for the nascent Jewish community on a number of issues and was clandestinely working to bring more refugees to the city. Each time Gabril entered the office, the head of the group groaned, knowing what was coming: Gabril was going to press for departure. This time, however, he had a letter signed by four traders in Venice, requesting that he come to complete negotiations for lucrative contracts. He was under pressure to close these deals; surely the Kehillah would recognize the importance his establishment of this trade signified for Jewish businessmen.

As soon as Gabril entered the office today, he noticed a change.

Typically, a single assistant sat in the anteroom and the head of the committee worked quietly behind his office door. Today the doors were thrown open, half a dozen people bustled amongst the tables and desks, and a cacophony of voices filled the space.

From the center of this chaos, the head man appeared and quickly drew Gabril into his room, shooing out the other workers and closing the door.

"Your timing is impeccable, Senhor Nuñez. I would have sent for you within the hour. The time for you to travel has come, and you must go now."

"What has happened?" Gabril asked. "What have you heard?"

"The final locations for the network are mostly in place, and the pressure to move people quickly has increased with the intensification of the Inquisition in Portugal and efforts to reintroduce the Inquisitors to France in places where their work had subsided." He gestured to a chair. "Sit down, Gabril."

Gabril obeyed, and the head man continued.

"Due to the efforts of some clergy, suspicion around the escape of your daughter and the young de Sousa boy has made it necessary to move them more quickly than we planned. I finally heard from Eduardo. He experienced a harrowing imprisonment in Porto, but through the good offices of Enrique de Leon and David de Sousa he escaped and conducted the de Sousas to Bayonne. They all needed some rest and recuperation so have paused there for the time being, but they should be on the move shortly. Eduardo heard that your daughter made it safely to Irouléguy and has been working there. Jacques de Bernuy confirms that Ana Martel Gerondi is in Toulouse, waiting for word that it is time to move Isabela and continue her journey. We have sent that word. And Jacques also confirms that your doctor's letter to his friend in Toulouse successfully brought that friend into the network. As you know, these communications are sporadic and risky, but a large bundle came in this morning. And so you see that the time has finally come for you to work your way to Lyon. Are your business arrangements ready?"

With a broad smile, Gabril answered, "Altogether ready."

The two men set to work, arranging travel details, exchanging contacts, reviewing the business deals in Venice, and finally going over the plan for Isabela and Ana's itinerary.

"We have safe houses from Toulouse to Montpelier in place, but those north to Lyon and then Strasbourg remain unconfirmed," the head man said. "If for any reason they need to hide, our contact in the Camargue is prepared to shelter them."

After more than an hour, the two men shook hands.

"I wish you all the good Lord's protection on your journey, Gabril," the head man said.

Gabril was already on the street and walking speedily to his rooms before a stab of fear punctured his elation at finally journeying to Isabela. *What danger surrounds her now?*

CHAPTER SEVENTEEN

Toulouse and Bayonne
August, 1605

Go, the Lord said to me, and lead the people on their way.
—DEUTERONOMY 10:11

*A*na checked her medicine chest one more time in the vestibule of the bishop's residence. Cooler than in the afternoon air outside, it was still stifling indoors. Even the stone walls of the entryway seemed to radiate heat. She wiped her forehead with a clean linen cloth and reviewed the packets and bottles—slippery bark, cherry bark, fleabane, and dried winterberry for infection, meadow saffron and valerian for pain and the treatment of sexual diseases, milkweed for the swelling of hands and feet, and tincture of pasqueflower, which she had to use sparingly, as it could dangerously slow the rate of the heart.

Just as she finished repacking her case, a young novitiate appeared and motioned Ana to follow her down a corridor and up a staircase to the private chambers. After gently knocking at a door, she stood aside and allowed Ana to enter a spacious room with an enormous curtained bed at its center.

The floor was strewn with rushes, sweet meadow, and rosemary, all of which only slightly mediated an oppressive heat and the overpowering scent of unwashed body and sickness that stopped Ana with a fetid gust. The tightly closed bed curtains hid the patient, and a young nurse, startled awake by Ana's entry, jumped to her feet and began to rearrange items on the bedside table.

Ana immediately instructed the nurse to open the window shutters and the room door while she drew back the bed curtains. Blinking up at her in the sudden light lay a boy of not more than fourteen years. His fair hair was plastered to his broad forehead and his bedclothes were soaked with sweat. Small ulcers crowded the corners of his full lips and the hairless skin of his broad chest, visible at the open neck of his nightshirt, revealed an angry red rash.

"Good afternoon," Ana began in French. "I am Madame Martel Gerondi, and I am here to care for you on behalf of Dr. Sanches. What is your name?"

The boy looked up at her, his eyes still seeming to adjust to the light, and said in a raspy voice, "Antoine."

"Yes, all right Antoine, Dr. Sanches tells me you are suffering from these sores, and I see the rash on your chest—is there anything more that bothers you?"

The boy's eyes, now wide open, were a near violet blue and quickly filled with tears. "I am so tired and weak, and everything hurts, especially at night, and the sores . . ." Here his voice faded and he turned his head. "Are in other places too."

Ana put her hand gently on the boy's shoulder. "I will try to make you more comfortable, but first let's get you clean and get some fresh bedclothes and some fresh air, shall we?"

Tears spilled over Antoine's long lashes as he choked out a simple "Merci, madame."

For the next hour Ana gave quiet orders to the nurse, a young and inexperienced novitiate who was only too happy to be sent off for warm water, fresh beer, and clean bed and wash linens. Ana scrutinized the tinctures and salves on the bedside table and put aside the mercury ointment, purgatives, lancets, and glass cups—all evidence of previous treatment attempts. She then turned back to the boy, helped him out of his nightshirt, and gently washed him, taking care to preserve what modesty she could for him with the use of a sheet.

All the while, she asked the boy simple questions about where he was from, who his family were, what he studied, and what he liked to do, working hard to keep her voice and expression relaxed and pleasant while her stomach roiled at the rash and sores all over his body. She noted that when he spoke of his family, he did not mention being the bishop's nephew, and she did not ask if that were the case.

Blessedly, a late-afternoon breeze suddenly blew into the room, breaking the stifling heat. Ana applied poultices of milkweed over Antoine's many sores and then prepared two draughts—one of meadow saffron and valerian, one of slippery bark and fleabane—and a tincture of dried pasqueflower. This last remedy she gave to Antoine in a small dropper, and then she mixed honey into the draughts, whose bitter taste might make them difficult to drink.

"I will ask you to drink these preparations over the next hours, and I hope you will sleep well and be much more comfortable once you do," she said.

"Am I going to die?" Antoine asked, his eyes squeezed shut.

Before Ana could answer, hurried footsteps sounded in the hall and two clergymen rounded into the room and came to an abrupt halt before the bed.

The larger man, heavy and florid, perspiring from the heat and hurry, wore the chasuble of a bishop, and it appeared he had come directly from mass.

"Madame Martel Gerondi?" he fairly barked.

Ana bowed her head. "Your Excellency."

The bishop neither responded nor introduced the other man; instead, he walked past Ana to the bedside and gazed down at Antoine.

"How do you fare today, my son?" he asked.

"Better, Your Excellency," came the weak voice from the bed.

The bishop turned back to Ana. "Why are the windows and doors and bed curtains open? And what are these potions?"

Ana drew herself up to her full height—as tall as the bishop and taller than the cleric behind him, a simple priest by the look of his robes—and said, "I was asked by Dr. Sanches to continue his treatment of this boy, and I am following his prescribed plan." She and Dr. Sanches had rehearsed this explanation in anticipation of this exact questioning.

"And you agree with this plan?" the bishop shot back.

This was a dangerous question, but Ana knew not to suggest by a pause in answering that she understood the danger. She was well aware how easily a woman healer could be seen as a witch. "Dr. Sanches and I are in agreement in our treatment approaches," she said firmly.

"You speak very confidently as a healer, not a doctor. Do you not believe in expelling the vapors of sickness and preventing the intrusion of evil spirits from the outside?" This came from the other cleric, who now stepped to the bedside and addressed Ana in a knife-like voice. His sharp brown eyes drilled into hers with an aggression that brought heat to her cheeks and perspiration to her forehead beyond the heat of the afternoon.

"My task here is to soothe and address the boy's symptoms," Ana replied steadily, "and I leave the welfare of his spirit to his religious advisors." She immediately regretted the pique that showed in her tone and was further discomfited by the scowl that appeared on the priest's face in response to it.

The bishop moved closer to the boy and said gently, "Father Alvaro visits us from Portugal and will stay for a fortnight to conduct business for the Church. He will come to you before bedtime and pray for your recovery." He turned back Ana. "You will stop by my study before you take your leave, Madame Martel Gerondi."

After patting the boy's shoulder, the bishop left the room with the priest following close behind him.

Antoine drew a deep breath and closed his eyes. After Ana summoned the nurse and gave her instructions, she finished arranging the herbs and tinctures needed for the poultices and draughts. Then, promising to return the next day, she asked to be taken to the bishop's study, leaving the sleeping boy to rest.

Ana was ushered into a stately room with tall ceilings, an entire wall of bookshelves, and an intricately carved desk at its center. Two ornately carved chairs with tapestry cushions sat before the desk; Father Alvaro already occupied one of them.

The bishop rose from a small altar across the room and settled behind the desk into a highback chair. A platter with cheeses, brown bread, and cut peaches lay between the two men. Ana was not asked to sit.

"Madame Martel Gerondi, how is it that you come to Toulouse at this time?" the bishop asked. "I understand you traveled here from Girona. You are far from home. And your French is excellent. How is that?"

Unprepared for such personal questioning and wondering who had supplied this information or why any of it interested the bishop, Ana considered her answer carefully. "My primary occupation is as a dye maker, and I came to Toulouse to secure high-quality woad before taking my dyes to market in Lyon. My late husband did a good bit of business in Provence, and I often accompanied him. He too spoke French quite frequently."

The bishop's eyebrows rose. "A dye maker, and yet you have worked these past months with Dr. Sanches in his medical practice."

Ana waited for a question to emerge, but none came. Trying to remain still in what had become an uncomfortably long standing posture, she simply stated, "Yes." Whatever trap these men were trying to set, she would not willingly fall into it.

"And when do you intend to depart for . . . Lyon, I think you said?" This time it was Father Alvaro who spoke.

"I promised Dr. Sanches that I would see the bishop's . . . nephew on a path to recovery, if possible, before I leave," said Ana.

Her slight pause before saying the word "nephew" caused a frown to crease the bishop's forehead. "I thank you for your endeavors, *madame*, and I wish you well on your further journeys," he said. "But do you travel alone? These are dangerous times, especially for a woman traveling alone."

"I have been fortunate to secure protectors to travel with me throughout my journey, Your Excellency. As to your nephew," she continued quickly, "as I know Dr. Sanches told you, the pox has taken hold quite firmly. I have left the doctor's instructions for his treatments, which should keep him more comfortable and able to rest better. He is young and strong and has a chance to recover."

"A chance?" the bishop asked, his face softening into concern for the first time.

Ana took a chance and said in a sober voice, "It's a serious disease, Your Excellency. We don't see it often in a boy so young. But as I said, he appears to be strong and in good health otherwise, so we can only hope."

"And pray," said Father Alvaro, who looked at Ana intently.
"Yes Father, and pray," she said.

David stood on the right bank of the Adour River in Bayonne and breathed deeply of the scent drifting out of the open door of a small shop in front of him. The shop produced chocolate, a delicacy new to both David and the French. Cacao beans brought from the New World were boiled with water, then mixed with cream and sugar, and drunk as an elixir. He had smelled it in passing by the shops that made it many times but had not yet tasted it, as it was very expensive. The New Christians who had settled along this bank of the river in Bayonne had established several thriving chocolate shops to serve the wealthy.

David had now been in this bustling port town for nearly two months. His first weeks had been spent securing rooms for himself and his sisters, helping Eduardo Carel recover from his injuries, and finding work at the docks for their livelihood. As soon as the shipping agent who hired him learned that he could read and write Portuguese, he'd brought David into the office to keep accounts and read manifests. David also had passable Spanish, but no French, so Eduardo had set him to learning the new language well enough to use on their further travels. He'd also found the de Sousa sisters work in the home of a well-to-do New Christian family. Almost immediately, Beatriz had caught the eye of one of the family's many sons, and David was gratified to see that the boy's attentions brought color to Beatriz's cheeks and light into her long-listless eyes.

And so for now they had all settled in, waiting for the right time to move forward. David wondered when that time would come.

Now he walked through the Saint-Esprit district, with its rows of stone houses and busy shops and chatter in Portuguese, Spanish, and

French everywhere around him. He felt safer and more secure here than he had in months, and he walked with a buoyant step toward the meeting Eduardo had asked for at a small bistro near his rooms.

On Saturday, the Jewish sabbath, the quiet in this neighborhood contrasted sharply with the bustle elsewhere in the city. But today was Sunday; the streets were full, few residents ventured toward a church, and some were working in their shops. Bayonne could surely provide a good life for New Christians, even if they were still supposed to practice Catholicism in public—but David's thoughts were not on religious practice. He had no wish to settle anywhere without Isabela.

Word of her was scant, but he knew she had reached Chateau Mercado in Irouléguy, which was at most three days distant from Bayonne, and he could barely obey Eduardo's orders that they wait to journey toward her.

When he entered the brasserie, which was little more than the ground floor of the proprietor's house at the center of a long row of homes in the Jewish quarter, David found Eduardo Carel seated at a small table just inside the door. The man's recovery was nearly complete; the watchful intelligence of his blue eyes, his well-trimmed beard, his upright posture, well-made clothing, and imposing height once more commanded attention, interest, and respect. Only an occasional wince when lifting something heavy or after a long walk betrayed his still-compromised bones and muscles.

Eduardo directed David to sit and ordered him a cider, the local fermented drink made from apples for which David was slowly acquiring a taste. A plate of cheese and olives sat between the two men, and they ate, exchanged news, and drank for some time before Eduardo turned to the topic David waited for.

"I have had a message from Toulouse," he began.

David's jaw clenched at the serious tone of Eduardo's voice. *Why*

Toulouse and not Irouléguy? Has Isabela moved even farther away? Why did we wait to go to her?

"It is time for me to tell you more of the work that I do, and what you and I must do moving forward," Eduardo continued.

"Enrique de Leon explained about the network in Portugal, and I assume you are part of the same effort," David said.

"Yes," Eduardo said, "but what we do changes once we leave Portugal and move through France and into Germany or Italy or on to Amsterdam. The greatest danger still exists in Spain and Portugal, and there our effort is simply to help people escape those countries. Once we bring people to France, some settle here, in places like Bayonne, where Jews and New Christians have established communities that allow us to live in relative peace, while others move on to cities like Venice and Hamburg and Amsterdam, where we hope our futures will be even more secure and where our people can in some instances even practice our religion openly. That requires us to develop a system of safe places along travel routes that protect our people and maintain their hidden identities."

David shifted in his chair, his knee beginning a nervous bobbing under the table.

"It is time for us to leave Bayonne," Eduardo said. "There is danger in Toulouse, so we must bypass that city, where we thought to find safe haven, and make our way directly to Lyon."

"But what about Isabela in Irouléguy?" David demanded. "Is she safe? And what is this danger of which you speak?"

"Ana Martel Gerondi will soon be on her way from Toulouse to Irouléguy, and from there begin the journey with Isabela to Lyon. The danger is in the form of Padre Alvaro, with whom I know you have great familiarity."

David paled at the mention of the padre. He launched forward, his hands slamming onto the table.

"He's a dangerous man," he whispered hoarsely. "He has threatened me and my family."

"I have heard as much, and that is why it is time to move. But you have some important decisions to make. My desire is to try to reach Irouléguy when Ana Martel Gerondi is there and travel as a group. But there is another consideration." Eduardo shifted in his chair and stared into his cup of cider. When he looked back up at David, his eyes were troubled. "You—actually, *we*—have to decide what is best for your sisters."

David slumped over the table, his head in his hands. "I know. I have been thinking about them also."

A look of what seemed to be relief spread across Eduardo's features, and he spoke quickly. "I know you feel responsible for your sisters and want to personally ensure their safety and security, but this next portion of our journey may involve some danger. They seem to be doing well in their work in the house of the Mirandas. And if I am not mistaken, the oldest Miranda boy has designs on Beatriz. They are an honorable family, and I do not think Beatriz and Roshina wish to be separated. The Mirandas have already expressed to me that they would welcome both girls into their household for as long as it would take us to establish where it is safe for you and perhaps Isabela to settle, once she is reunited with her father."

David nodded his head at this recitation, though the weight of a stone settled in the pit of his stomach as the direction of Eduardo's argument became clear. "You want me to leave my sisters here," he said, his voice leaden. "They will impede our journey moving forward."

"And staying will protect them from what could be a perilous journey," Eduardo emphasized. "This entire effort is new and untried. There have already been obstacles, and there will be more. We need people like you to help establish and maintain the connections so vital to our efforts, but the work is not without danger."

"And yet you risk taking Isabela through that danger," David challenged.

Eduardo sighed. "Yes, Isabela has an important part to play in this whole process. Through her skill at embroidery and her growing reputation, she provides signals of safety or danger at houses along the escape route."

"Does she know the risk you have exposed her to?" David demanded. "She is a fourteen-year-old girl!"

"At first we thought it best that she not know fully the purposes of her work. We thought the less she knew, the better, in case she was caught and interrogated. But some of the people she met along her journey felt she had a right to know and to understand the gravity of what we've asked her to do. So yes, she is now aware."

David's anger flared, "Does her father know? Did he agree to compromising her in this way?"

Eduardo placed a hand on David's shoulder. "It's a complicated set of decisions we have all had to make—but I trust that they will, with God's help, bring him and Isabela together again."

David scowled and turned away from the attempt at comfort. *Perhaps with God's will and some simpler decisions, Isabela and I will be together again.*

CHAPTER EIGHTEEN

Hamburg, Venice, and Villecomtal-sur-Arros

August, 1605

Be strong and courageous. Do not fear or be in dread of them for it is the LORD your God who goes with you.
—DEUTERONOMY 31:6

Gabril knew now that he had not fully understand the peril that faced his daughter when he'd agreed to become a part of the escape network to bring refugees from Portugal to Hamburg.

After his meeting at the Kehilla, he had swiftly made preparation for the journey to Venice—settling accounts, packing a small trunk, and arranging travel all in one day.

The arduous two-week trip overland by coach had proved easier with good weather, and even the harder ride over the Alps by horse and mule offered few obstacles. He'd had long hours to reflect on all the challenges and losses that had brought him to this lonely journey, but he'd also felt for the first time in months that he moved toward reunion with Isabela and perhaps a new, more settled life.

When he finally arrived in Venice, he'd been grateful to exchange the jolts and bruises of road travel for the sway of gondolas. Due to all his advance preparation, he'd been able to swiftly conduct the business of concluding contracts and other trade arrangements for his colleagues in Hamburg, and after a week's time he'd turned his attention toward the journey to reach Isabela.

Yet another week had passed since then, and only now had he received word from the Kehillah in Hamburg—a forwarded letter from Eduardo Carel, dated nearly a month earlier:

Dear Gabril,

By now you must know that I successfully reached Bayonne with the young de Sousas and have spent some time here recovering from injuries I sustained as a guest of the Inquisitors in Porto. I am also hoping you are aware that Isabela has been employed at Chateau Mercado in Irouléguy, where she has distinguished herself with her embroidery skills and hard work.

Ana Martel Gerondi bided her time in Toulouse, intending to allow Isabela to finish her obligation in Irouléguy, but recently the arrival of a priest from Abrantes in Toulouse and his inquiries about the transport of refugees across the country, as well as his knowledge of your daughter and the de Sousas, has worried Ana enough that she will quickly remove Isabela to Lyon, if not all the way to Strasbourg. I fervently hope you will make your way to France to conduct her into Germany if it is still your wish to settle in Hamburg.

David has been very insistent that he reunite with Isabela. To his credit, but also perhaps a liability, he is angry that Isabela may be in peril because of her work on our behalf.

ISABELA'S WAY

He and I plan to depart for Irouléguy within a day or two. His sisters are settled here in Bayonne and will remain here, at least until David finds a better place for them.

As you know, my fervent wish is to once again see Ana. I am weary still from the effects of my imprisonment and perhaps also from exhaustion at confronting so much evil in our midst.

I wish you strength for your journey, as I do for my own, and pray to whatever God remains in the world that we may once again live in peace.

Yours,
Eduardo

Gabril tossed the letter aside and paced the small room in the Locanda, his housing since his arrival in Venice. His relief that Eduardo and Ana were close to reaching Isabela was mitigated by the alarming news of possible danger to her. He had agreed to send her to Raphael de Mercado to work on the daughter's trousseau, but what further work had Eduardo written about? Was the network using Isabela's skills in a way that endangered her? He had not, would not, have agreed to that.

Within the hour, he had packed his trunk and departed for Strasbourg.

The August heat vanished from one day to the next as a north wind rose and blew rain and chill over the mountains to Irouléguy. In four days, Eduardo and David traveled across the coastal plain from Bayonne and into the hills that preceded the mountains of the Basque

Pyrenees. David had never before seen real mountains, and he marveled at the towering trees, changing vistas, and variety of plants he saw along the way.

David might have pushed on in order to reach Isabela sooner had he not recognized that Eduardo had not regained full strength; the older man was clearly fatigued by the end of each day of travel. Seeing this, he tempered his eagerness and agreed to spending one final night at a snug inn before, after an ample breakfast, beginning the last half-day's journey to the Mercado chateau.

After two hours of rocky switchback roads, the chateau appeared to them, perched on the mountainside above. Stone and metal glinted in the sunlight, and David thought he'd never seen such a beautiful building. As they approached, two stone pillars defined the intersection where the track leading up to the chateau, now invisible in the forested access, departed from the main road. Atop one of the pillars flew the banner of the house, and atop the other was hoisted a beautiful banner with an embroidered design of different symbols, bordered in the colors of the Mercados.

David turned in, quickening his pace, but Eduardo called out sharply, "Stop! It isn't safe."

"What?" David asked.

"That banner, the one on the right. Do you see the ten points sewn in black? The unlit candle, the purple rose, and the upside-down lion? Those all signal danger. This is Isabela's work. The chateau is compromised somehow. We can't approach it. We have to leave."

"We can't leave! What if she's in danger?" David turned into the track but stopped when a voice behind him spoke.

"She isn't there. They've been taken."

Both Eduardo and David whipped around.

A long cut split the craggy forehead of the man in front of them. He looked quite different from before, with his torn and disheveled clothing reinforcing the expression of despair in his wild eyes, but David recognized Pedro de Martins from their meetings in Abrantes.

"Senhor de Martins! Who took them? What happened?" David demanded.

Pedro looked to Eduardo and then back to David, who nodded quickly. "This is Eduardo Carel. He's a friend."

"Monsieur de Martin, I have heard of your good work, and I thank you for it," Eduardo said. "Can you tell us what happened?"

"There isn't time," de Martins said. "I must find the doctor. There are injured people, and you must follow Madame Martel Gerondi and Isabela."

"They took Ana too?" Eduardo cried.

"Yes," de Martins said grimly. "Come with me and I will see to it that you get fresh horses—but hurry! I'll explain as we go."

The three men set off toward the village of Irouléguy, David's pace too fast for the other two men. As David reluctantly slowed, de Martins began to tell the story of the previous day between gasps of breath.

"The count and his family left four days ago to visit the countess's family in Saint-Jean-Pied-de-Port, so only a few men and basic staff remained at the chateau. Two days ago, Madame Martel Gerondi arrived with news of danger in Toulouse. This priest from Abrantes has created a stir about Jews and New Christians' clandestine activities. Madame Martel Gerondi wanted Isabela to prepare to leave immediately, but I told her I had to send word to the Count de Mercado. He is charged with responsibility for the mademoiselle, and I am responsible to him." Here, de Martins stopped speaking, lowered his head, and slowed his step, breathing heavily.

"I understand," Eduardo said. "It was your duty."

De Martins looked up at him with an expression of gratitude and continued. "Early this morning, before most of the household woke, a band of men broke into the kitchen, beat the cook, and made their way from room to room until they found Isabela, Madame Martel Gerondi, and one of the maids, Sophia, all sleeping. They bound them up and forced them down the stairs. The kitchen maid ran to my quarters and woke me. I got up to the chateau as fast as I could. I found Sophia trying to fight them off. I fought too but they . . ." De Martins's voice choked, and tears ran down his face. "I couldn't protect her. She is my . . . We are . . . But it was too late. There were too many of them, and they told me they would kill the women if I tried to stop them."

"But who are they, and what do they want?" David asked.

"A rough lot," de Martins said with a look of disgust. "They didn't look like officials of any sort, and all they said is, 'There's good money to be had for witches in Toulouse.' But I have to get help. There's so much blood."

The three men came to a path on the outskirts of Irouléguy; de Martins turned onto it and led David and Eduardo to a small cottage with a large corral and many horses beside it. He knocked at the door and then slumped onto the bench next to it. When a young man emerged, he struggled back to his feet and arranged for three horses.

Once David and Eduardo had tied their bags to their saddles, they listened to de Martins's instructions for the fastest route toward Toulouse.

"Will you be able to make it to find a doctor?" Eduardo asked.

"I will—now go," de Martins said. "And quickly!"

David let Eduardo, the more experienced horseman, set the pace as they urged the horses down the road descending from the mountains. They couldn't go too quickly, given both the ruts and rocks, but they also needed to make up for the head start the kidnappers had—if they were even following the right route.

ISABELA'S WAY

They rode in grim silence for the first hour, each man with his own thoughts. Finally, David said, "If we find them, . . ." He sat up straighter in his saddle. "*When* we find them, how will we free them? We have no weapons beyond our knives, and we are no doubt outnumbered."

"Have you ever used a sword?" Eduardo asked.

"I have," David said. "My father taught me. But other than contests at festivals, I haven't had much use for one."

"When we get to Lescar we will arm ourselves. But our best weapon will be surprise. I don't think they will expect to be followed. Ana and Isabela had no news of our arrival, nor did the count, and they left Monsieur de Martins injured. If we can keep our pace, we should be traveling faster than they and will hopefully overtake them well before Toulouse. Circumstances will dictate what happens then."

David recognized the logic of this explanation, but it was of little comfort. He had never been a fighter. More often, he had followed his father's leadership style of mediation and fair judgment. But he would do whatever was required to save Isabela.

As the road left the last of the foothills and leveled out, Eduardo picked up speed and David had to concentrate on remaining seated on his horse. He was grateful for the distraction from his dark thoughts.

A night and a day passed with no sign or clues to the whereabouts of the women and their abductors. Eduardo and David stopped only long enough in Lescar to purchase swords and food supplies, and to take a few hours of sleep for themselves and their horses. Eduardo, with his flawless French, subtly inquired as to the possible whereabouts of a party of men and women, but neither the innkeeper, the shopkeeper, nor the stable boys had seen Ana and Isabela.

Disheartened but with renewed resolve to push forward, they continued toward Toulouse. The weather was favorable, and they made good progress over the improving road.

By the time evening fell, the two men had exhausted themselves and the horses. They came upon the village of Villecomtal-sur-Arros, barely a small collection of cottages amidst surrounding farms, as the last of the sun slipped beyond the horizon. The Aros River was cool and clear, and at the edge of town they stopped to let the horses drink before continuing on.

Making their way slowly along the road, they encountered an old man tending a kitchen garden near the road,

"Monsieur," Eduardo said, "we are looking for a place to rest and perhaps a meal."

"Ah, *oui*, it is a day for that, it seems," the man answered.

Eduardo and David straightened as one in their saddles.

"Is the village full, then?" Eduardo asked, careful to keep his tone casual.

"No, no," the man answered. "But I didn't fancy the last ones that asked. A rough crew, and something about them I didn't like."

Eduardo tensed. Finally, a hint they were on the right path.

The farmer looked up at them and seemed to come to a decision. "I have room in the barn for the two of you and your horses. There's a dry, decent loft, water, and hay. I'm not much of a cook, but since my wife died I get my bread and cheese from my neighbor and make a good enough stew."

"Thank you, *monsieur*, we will gratefully stay—but can you tell me more about the party you mentioned?" Eduardo pressed, dismounting his horse. "Were there women in the group?"

The farmer studied Eduardo, who met his gaze directly.

"I didn't see any women, but a couple of the men stayed back with a wagon—more of a cart, really—and there were at least two people in the back making a good bit of noise. Three of the men had ridden right on up to my cottage to inquire about lodging and food, so I was a good distance from the road and couldn't see well. When I sent them on their way, they moved the cart and the other men up the road before I could see any more."

"May I ask where you sent them?" Eduardo asked, unable to keep the ferocity out of his voice as he asked this.

The farmer stepped back and once again scrutinized Eduardo, and then David. "Why do you ask?"

"We are in search of a band of men who kidnapped two women dear to us who are in great peril," Eduardo said, deciding honesty was his best course. "I have no reason to hope that we can prove to you that we are men of good character, except that you judged them to be the opposite, and you have accepted us into your household. So I rely on your good judgment going forward."

The old man nodded. "I sent them to a neighboring farm—a larger place with many family men residing in several houses and with a larger barn. It's as close to an inn as we have in these parts, and I thought that bunch would be able to handle the trouble if there were any. I don't know that they were allowed to stay there, but it's not been even an hour since they were here, so they are not far ahead. If you want to rest your horses, we've cut a trail between our properties that bypasses the road and gets you there more quickly. Come and eat something first, and I'll show you the way."

This the famished pair agreed to immediately.

The sun hovered on the western horizon as David and Eduardo reached the neighboring farm on the path the old man had shown them. Approaching from the rear, they could see a large barn and several outbuildings. A fenced pasture closest to the path held a dozen horses.

Eduardo signaled to David to follow and began to work his way silently along the back of the pasture fence and toward the outbuildings. No one appeared in the gathering dusk, and the horses seemed more interested in their fodder than the silent, creeping men at the end of their field.

The first building was little more than a shed containing feed and tools, and the second shed was empty. David and Eduardo stole toward the next building, and the next. By now, darkness was complete. With no moon and scattered clouds darkening and then revealing the starlit sky, they finally reached the barn.

Rather than approach the front, where a guard would likely be posted, they circled to the rear, where the hayloft door stood at twice a man's height from the ground. A crude ladder was built onto the side of the barn. Eduardo gestured for David to climb it.

At the top of the ladder, David stood on the ledge and put his ear to the loft door. Hearing nothing, he drew his knife and attempted to pry open the huge wooden door, to no avail. He looked up and saw the latch securing it. It was too high for him to reach, but he slid his sword upward until the metal met the latch and then tapped away until it rose, allowing him to open the far side of the door and slip into the loft.

He took a moment to allow his eyes to adjust to the pitch dark. Behind him, he heard Eduardo enter and pull the door closed without entirely latching it.

Crouching, David felt his way across the loft with hands extended, listening for any sound. On his right he felt stacks of hay. The barn was vast, and below he heard the occasional stir of cows and horses and smelled their earthy scents. When he reached the edge of the loft, the floor beneath him creaked loudly and he fell to his knees and peered over into the barn below.

A lantern shone to the side of the entrance at the opposite end of the barn, and David could see a man slumped over in a chair at the edge of the lantern's light, immediately next to a closed door.

Eduardo pulled David back and whispered to him, "I'll work my way around to the left. You move directly to the door, and if he wakes, I'll distract him. If there's enough noise to attract the others, your job is to get to Ana and Isabela, get them out of here—up and out of the hayloft, if necessary—and take them back to the old man. I trust he'll hide us until morning. No matter what happens to me, get them out. Do you understand?"

"Yes," David whispered, then slipped down the ladder to the floor below.

He crept across the barn to the closed door, sword in hand, and with agonizing care lifted the latch and pushed the door slowly so it would not creak.

But it did creak, and as David entered the room and saw Ana and Isabela, bound, gagged, and huddled together on the floor, he heard the shout of the wakened guard and Eduardo's challenge from across the barn.

The guard paid no attention to Eduardo but charged in behind David, dagger raised.

With all the death from disease and the evil of the Inquisition that David had seen in his young life, he'd never thought that he could kill a man, but when the moment came, he did not think but acted. He swept his sword in a sharp arc, slicing the knife out of the guard's hand, and then brought the sword back across the man's neck, knocking him to the ground before he could utter a sound.

Without looking back at the man, he hurried across the room, freed the two women, and pulled Isabela to her feet. Clutching her to his chest, he whispered, "Are you hurt? Can you walk?" Turning to Ana, he asked, "Can you?"

In the next moment, Eduardo had Ana in his arms. After giving her a ferocious embrace, he stepped back to look at her in the dim lantern light.

"We are all right," Ana gasped out.

"Then we must go now," Eduardo said.

CHAPTER NINETEEN

Villecomtal-sur-Arros and Muret

August, 1605

Those who are pained by the suffering of good people—their iniquities are removed from the world.
—THE ZOHAR

Though the August evening offered only the slightest chill, Isabela shook as David led her to the old man's farmhouse. No one followed the party of four as they made their escape; somehow, no one had been woken by David's scuffle with the guard in the barn.

David's arm around her shoulder and his other hand under her elbow allowed Isabela to rest her head on his chest, and her feet to barely skim the forest path. Their escorts followed them, murmuring to one another.

"It was awful, David," Isabela began. "Those horrible men just attacked, and—"

"Shhh," he whispered into her hair. "Let's get to safety and get you something to eat and drink, and then you can tell us everything."

In a short while they reached the house. The old man greeted them immediately and ushered them into the large kitchen where a fire in the hearth warmed a brick and tile box built to one side and the aroma of stew welcomed the tired group.

He withdrew an iron pot from the box and set out mugs of ale.

"But they're still so close," Isabela said with a shudder as they all seated themselves at the large kitchen table and the old man dished stew into bowls.

"As kidnappers, they would be unwise to pursue, especially not knowing how many rescuers are involved," Eduardo said. "I rather think they will focus on how to avoid or explain themselves to whoever hired them." He took a sip of ale and stared at Ana. "Who are these men? Did you hear who they work for? Is it Padre Alvaro?"

Isabela sat upright in her chair. "Padre Alvaro? What has he to do with all of this?"

Ana sank her elbows to the table and cradled her head in her hands. She said nothing for a long moment.

"Ana," Eduardo coaxed, "I know all this is painful, but you must see that it's important for us to understand if we are to help keep you both safe."

With all eyes turned to her, Ana told the whole story—starting with her work with Jacques de Bernuy and then continuing with Francesco Sanches, her assignment to care for the boy Antoine, and her challenging interaction with Padre Alvaro. She seemed convinced that Alvaro was the source of danger.

"I believe he sees me as a threat—would like to cast me as witch and heretic," she said. "Those men said as much when they had had enough to drink. I am less certain of his interest in Isabela and David."

"He knows of this network you've made her part of," David hissed.

Isabela glanced across the room to the hearth, but the old man had left.

"She is as much at risk as you now," David said. "He was suspicious of my work to assist people escaping Abrantes; before I left, he threatened my family."

"I heard of that possibility but did not know it to be true," Ana said, her forehead creasing into a frown.

"The plan to stop in Toulouse is too dangerous," Eduardo said. "We must travel to Lyon and then to Strasbourg, where hopefully Isabela's father will meet us. From there he can take her to safety in Hamburg."

Isabela placed both her hands on the table and leaned in. "You all speak of me as if I were a child or sitting elsewhere, rather than right here." Her voice remained low but strong. "Who formed this network? How exactly is my father involved, and who is communicating with him? And it is clear to me now that this effort has imperiled people who sheltered and protected me and who became my friends. What right had you to make that choice on my behalf?" She sent reproachful looks at each of them.

Eduardo cleared his throat, but Ana placed a hand on his arm and spoke instead.

"I first met you because your father wished to bring you and your mother to Hamburg and he recognized the danger of returning himself or asking you to come alone," she said. "Eduardo asked me to help—not only you but the many others who are at risk because of their Jewish roots. At the same time, we have been working to establish a string of secure havens and a way to signal safety or danger. Your skill as an embroideress has made you valuable to that effort." She looked into Isabela's eyes. "It's also been important that you were brought up a Catholic. Nothing in your behavior would suggest you were anything otherwise, and with your blond hair and blue eyes . . ."

"But I *am* Catholic," Isabela said in a strangled whisper. The moment she spoke, and just as three pair of eyes lowered to avoid hers, a tumble of thoughts crowded into her confused head. *The letter with the* document in unknown script in Pai's trunk in Abrantes, the hidden Friday night candle lighting, my parents' nervousness at church, Padre Alvaro's close attention to my every move, Sophia's surprise at the little knowledge I possess about Jewish ritual . . .

Isabela swung her attention to David and repeated, "I am Catholic"—less assertively this time, but daring him to refute her.

Before David could respond, Eduardo Carel cleared his throat again. "It's true you were raised a New Christian. It's not my place to tell you this, but under these circumstances, I'm certain your father would permit me. All four of your grandparents were born Jews and forced to convert. Your parents have kept their faith alive but secret. For your safety, they raised you Catholic. The purpose of your father's journey to Hamburg was to establish a means of support in a city that will allow your family to practice Judaism in your own home—and perhaps, eventually, even publicly."

Isabela, absently pulling on a curl that had escaped her cap, stared across the room into the embers left from the fire. Suddenly she could not keep her eyelids open for the fury of thoughts exploding in her head. Leaning back in her chair, she tried to breathe deeply, to address the anger, shock, and fear in some manageable order.

"You've been too young . . ." Eduardo continued

Isabela's eyes flew open and she spun toward Carel. "Too young? Who do you think nursed my mother, and then buried her, and then worked with her patrons to make my own living? Old enough to be useful and be put into danger, but too young to know what I need to know to make my own decisions, is that it?" She spat the last words before slumping back into her chair.

"Isabela," David said in a choked voice.

She turned to him, and the savage look on her face silenced him. Ana stood and drew herself up to her full, imposing height. "I am sorry that this has come in a rush to you, Isabela, but we are all still in danger and need to leave as soon as possible, for our safety and that of our host. We can discuss all this later, but right now I suggest we establish a plan and then retire. If you are all willing, I will prepare some hot water and a tincture of chamomile, valerian, and elderberry that will help us all sleep more easily."

As if a wind had suddenly left off slapping a bed sheet on a laundry rope, the warring emotions drained from Isabela's head and chest. She nodded her agreement silently.

Eduardo suggested they hire a messenger to travel to Irouléguy and arrange for Pedro de Martins to send the women's belongings to Muret, a town outside Toulouse. It was a long day's ride from this farm but off the major road to the city. Though it would delay their progress, both women agreed that replacing their chests and baskets of silks and needles, herbs, and dyes, not to mention their clothing, would require an even longer delay.

David agreed to sleep close to Isabela and Ana, and Eduardo said he would make his bed near the barn door, in case unwanted visitors came in the night. He would speak to the farmer in the morning and ask him to visit his neighbor to learn if the men had left. All agreed to allow themselves four hours of sleep and a good breakfast before departing.

With draughts of the hot concoction consumed, the weary group made their way to the barn.

Minutes after Ana laid her blankets next to Isabela, the girl's steady breathing and David's gentle snore confirmed their swift lapse into sleep. After stepping carefully around them, she descended the ladder from the hayloft to the floor of the small barn, where she knew she would find Eduardo still awake.

Wordlessly, she slipped under the rough blanket and into his fierce embrace. Months of vigilance and tension melted in the warmth of his body next to hers, but immediately tears of rage and shame followed, defying her will to suppress them.

"What is it, Ana?" he asked, lifting her chin so he could look into her face.

She thought she would tell him these were tears of relief and joy to be with him again. She was both relieved and joyful, it was true, but the assault at Irouléguy ruled her tightly controlled emotions. She had lied for and about Eduardo, but never to him. "Those men who attacked us in Irouléguy— . . . they were brutal." Though she whispered, her throat constricted such that she was barely audible. "I feel soiled."

She could feel Eduardo stiffen even as his arms tightened around her.

"Are you hurt?" he asked. "Did they . . ."

Ana squeezed her eyes shut. "They tried," she said, struggling to keep her whisper steady. She would not lie, but she would not recreate for this man whom she loved the scene that haunted her still: her fighting off two of the kidnappers while a third attacked Sophia with the scissors she had tried to defend herself with, with Isabela lying hidden under the bed just feet away.

When Ana first heard the shouting and screaming, she'd instructed Isabela to stay hidden. After Sophia was injured, one of the men had torn Ana's drawers down, and he'd been struggling to mount her when Pedro de Martins burst in. The ensuing fight had left Pedro, Sophia, and one of the gardeners bleeding, and when Isabela had heard the men threatening to cut Sophia's throat if they didn't direct them to Isabela, the girl had defied Ana's instructions, crawled out from under the bed, and offered herself in exchange for Sophia.

Ana nestled further into Eduardo's arms, weeping softly, allowing her brave front to collapse for these few moments.

Eventually, she slept.

The rooster's crow found Ana in the kitchen, helping the old farmer prepare breakfast. Soon Isabela and David appeared, sleepy-eyed but smiling shyly at each other. Ana's raised eyebrow went unnoticed.

Clouds roiled overhead as the farmer departed for his neighbor's property to learn of the kidnappers. He returned shortly with news that the kidnappers had departed in the night, with no mention of a murder.

The dark sky gave way to rain, thunder, and lightning as the foursome departed Villecomtal-sur-Arros, having first dispatched a messenger to Irouléguy. The day-long journey to Muret was dismal. The men's overcoats gave some protection, but Ana and Isabela had none of their own clothing, and though the farmer had generously offered them any remaining clothing of his wife's, only Isabela could fit into the extra skirt and kirtle she found—neither of which offered protection from the storm. Both women were soaked through by the time the party arrived at the inn in Muret.

The travelers ate a late supper in their wet clothes. Ana and Isabela finished first and retired to their room as soon as they were done.

Ana frowned at how Isabela shivered as they slipped into bed, but hoped a good night's sleep would put her to rights.

The men remained in the tavern, eating their supper in companionable silence until Eduardo withdrew a small book from his bag and began reading.

David leaned over and noted the symbols and unusual letters on the open page. "What language are you reading?"

Eduardo pulled the book closer and glanced around the room, which was empty of other customers. He regarded David for a long moment. "I find it helpful in these trying times to concentrate on more elevated thoughts . . .— to find meaning and connection from our world to realms above our world. This is a book of the Kabbalah, a Jewish mystical and philosophical study of spirituality and symbolism and connection to the divine. I find it comforting and meaningful."

David studied his hands, clasped in his lap, and then looked back up at Eduardo. "Isn't it dangerous to possess such a book?"

"Yes," Eduardo said. "Dangerous, but also nourishing and consolatory. One wants to rise above the present to remain hopeful about the future."

"Are you a practicing Jew?" David asked quietly. "Is this mystical study an intellectual interest, or a religious one?"

Eduardo gazed into the fire. "Some of both. Judaism is a religion of study and community ritual. In the absence of the ability to do either freely, I find that discovering meaning through prayer, meditation, and the study of numbers and Hebrew letters in the sacred texts represents a path to the divine. This practice allows me to connect in a deep and private way. It gives me support for the work I do—which, as you say, is dangerous, and also lonely."

David nodded as he absorbed these words. "I don't know what to think about being Jewish. My mother forbade any discussion of it and became so fiercely devout in her Catholic faith that I never thought of our Jewish past. Since my father died and I took over his work as head of the New Christian community, I've learned how many versions of New Christians there are—and how tentative our acceptance is."

After moments of silence, Eduardo asked with a gentle smile, "Is there a question of me in this?"

David did not hesitate. "I want to make a life with Isabela, wherever we may end up, and now she is shocked and angry that she never knew of her Jewish past. How should we think of ourselves? Are we Jews or Christians?"

Eduardo leaned back in his chair and joined his fingertips in front of his chest. "That, my young friend, is a question for Isabela and you to decide."

Isabela woke the next morning with a wet cough and a head cold. Ana placed an ear to her chest and frowned.

"Your thorough soaking yesterday did you no good," she said. "I only wish I had my herbal chest. I did get some garlic clove and cinnamon and eucalyptus from the cook to brew a tea. A bit of honey will soothe your throat. It's just as well we have to wait a day or two for our belongings. You should rest."

Three days passed before a wagon arrived with the chests and satchels full of Ana's and Isabela's possessions, as well as a bounty of food. The driver produced a letter from Raphael de Mercado, addressed to Isabela.

Still ill, Isabela sat up in bed and read the letter Ana brought to her.

Dear Isabela,

We returned to Irouléguy to find the catastrophe that you experienced four days ago. We were devastated that you and Madame Martel Gerondi were exposed to such a horror but are so grateful that Messieurs Carel and de Sousa were able to rescue you and conduct you to safety. Thankfully, both Monsieur de Martins and our own Sophia are recovering well, and our other staff also fare well.

We send your possessions as well as provisions for your further journey. Please keep us advised of your safe travels, and we only wish you could attend Miren's wedding and see the public display of your fine work in her gown and those of her attendants. Her trousseau is magnificent, in great part due to your skill and hard work.

We wish you all good fortune in your future, and please recommend us to your father and to Madame Martel Gerondi and Messieurs Carel and de Sousa.

All good wishes,
Raphael and Alaia Mercado

Ana applied an onion poultice to Isabela's chest. While she steamed eucalyptus to further ease Isabela's breathing, Isabela wrote a reply to the Mercados, thanking them for their delivery, wishing Miren well for her wedding, and asking that special greetings go to Sophia, with gratitude for her recovery and deep regret that Isabela's presence had exposed her to such consequences.

Ana sat quietly at Isabela's bedside as she finished her letter, then took it to the innkeeper to post. Upon returning to their room, she found Isabela lying on her side, her cheeks stained with tears. Gone was the fierce young woman of three nights ago; in her place was a little girl, overwhelmed and lost.

"My poor girl," she said, stroking Isabela's tangled curls. "It's been a lot this past week. Have courage. We will soon be on our way to Lyon, and then, with good fortune, on to your father in Strasbourg."

Isabela studied her face. "You are so strong," she said. "I don't know how to think about all that has happened."

"Don't think now, Isabela," Ana replied. "We have a plan, and it will be arduous, but all to a good end. You are among people who care for you and will protect you."

"But I can't help thinking of Sophia. We hear she is recovering, but it's my fault this happened." A new round of sobs shook Isabela.

"You are good to care for your friend, but it's not your fault. I am the one they were most interested in capturing, and your friends in Irouléguy are well aware of the danger they embraced in agreeing to help our network. And I have learned something else too, Isabela: you are no longer a child but a brave and talented young woman. I promise not to keep secrets from you, and to include you in decisions from now on."

With that, Ana leaned down and pulled her young friend into a long hug.

CHAPTER TWENTY

Muret, Toulouse, and Carcassone

August, 1605

The best laid schemes o' mice an' men / Gang aft a-gley.
—Robert Burns

The journey to Lyon would take nearly a week. Eduardo—Isabela was still adjusting to thinking of him this way, but Ana had insisted that they refer to each other by first name—had determined that they should head south first, giving Toulouse a wide berth, and then turn east toward the southern coastal plain. For several days they would in large part retrace Ana Martel Gerondi's steps to Carcassone from three months previous. From there they would travel to Montpelier and then gradually turn north to follow the Rhône River valley to Lyon.

The August days remained warm but no longer scorching, and the relentless summer sun gave way to occasional days of thunderstorms. Everywhere along the route, Eduardo pointed out to his companions evidence of Good King Henry of France's efforts to improve roads, build bridges, and bring commerce to the country. Farms, quarries, mills, and small towns with cottage industries appeared along their way.

Eduardo further informed them of King Henry's work to eradicate the religious skirmishes that had plagued the country for years. He told them of the Edict at Nantes, which granted religious freedom to both the Protestant Huguenots and Catholics, and nominally to other religions, and a lively discussion of the presence of clergy in favor of Inquisitors in Toulouse brought the question of safety for Jews into a late-night conversation at a tavern. The many hours on horseback in inns and taverns along the route also gave David time to ask Eduardo more about the tenets of Judaism, the mystical branch of Kabbalah, and the meaning behind many of the symbols Isabela had learned to embroider.

In quiet moments, Isabela thought much about her father, wondering if she really knew this man, whom she had not seen now for more than six months. When he left she had been a good Catholic girl, learning her mother's embroidery art, secure in her sheltered life in Abrantes, only vaguely aware that her father's many journeys as a textile merchant could result in a move for the family.

Now, she tried to understand how the loss of her mother and her home, and the unsettling knowledge that her parents considered themselves, and therefore her, hidden Jews should influence her own sense of herself. She had conducted a business, lived on her own, moved in her feelings for David from friend and supporter to loved one.

She kept a polite distance from David after the group left Muret, first because the slow recovery from the ague had left her weak, and then because she did not know where to start with all her conflicting thoughts and feelings. She used the time, at Ana's request, to embroider several sets of banners with symbols of safety or danger to leave with network houses along the way.

The silence between the two young people came to an end on the third day of travel, when David rode his horse up alongside Isabela, who was taking a turn riding on the wagon. A passing shower had ceased and the sun shone weakly through striations of lingering clouds.

"Did you stay dry under the canvas?" he asked her. "Are you feeling well?"

Isabela squinted up at his backlit figure. "Yes, thank you. Dry and well."

"I've thought much about the night in Villecomtal-sur-Arros."

Isabela's body tensed, but she remained silent.

He grasped the wagon side and leaned forward, bringing his face closer to hers. "I killed a man. You were shocked by revelations about your family. This journey has challenged us both and is likely to continue to do so. I want to talk to you about our future . . . our future together." The wagon hit a rut and tilted, nearly unseating David, who straightened in his saddle and fell behind.

Isabela turned back, met his eyes, and nodded slowly.

At the front of the party, Eduardo came to a halt. Far ahead, high above the road, stood the walled city of Carcassone, its stone turrets and ramparts burnished gold in the late afternoon sunlight.

Isabela stood in the wagon and stared at the wonder. Both Ana and David dismounted and stood at the wagon's sides.

"It's like a dream," Isabela said.

David stood open-mouthed, also staring at the city, but Ana looked up at her and smiled.

"Yes, it is beautiful. And we will go to the market tomorrow and get provisions. I'm sure we'll find a bounty of silks, and many herbs to replenish our stores. We won't do better until we arrive in Lyon."

"We will enter the city tomorrow," Eduardo announced, "but for now there is a farm up this track where we may stay for the night."

Though Isabela wished for a good meal and bed at an inn, she dutifully sat back in the wagon, and was pleasantly surprised to arrive just a few minutes later at a large farmhouse with well-kept outbuildings, a healthy herd of cattle, and large gardens and fields.

Ana selected a pair of Isabela's banners and presented them to the couple, who welcomed them inside.

"I'll help our hosts prepare supper," Ana said quietly to Isabela after they'd deposited their belongings in the room where they would sleep that night. "Why don't you take a walk and stretch your legs?"

Having sat or ridden most of the day, Isabela gratefully accepted the offer. She slipped out the door and set off in the early-evening light along a pasture fence.

Moments later, she heard footsteps behind her. She turned to see David hurrying to join her. She waited and felt her heart beat faster. As he reached her, she resumed walking and instinctively linked her arm with his.

They walked arm in arm until she'd gathered the thoughts she'd been trying to put in order since he'd spoken to her earlier in the afternoon.

"I know you want to talk about our future, and so do I," she began. "But I need to say some things about myself first."

David slowed his long stride, letting Isabela set the pace of their walk as well as their conversation.

"As you said, a lot has happened since we left Abrantes, and it has changed the way I think about myself, my family, and my future." David's arm stiffened in hers and he slowed, but Isabela gently pulled him forward. "I feel as if I hardly know my father, the man we are journeying to meet. I've missed him so much, but now I wonder who he really is, and even why I would want to go with him to Hamburg."

David stopped and looked into her eyes. "Isabela, you can't mean that. All he's ever tried to do—"

"Don't tell me what I do or do not mean. I know what I mean, even if you don't like it." Isabela's voice rose and became harsher than she intended as she said this. Softening her voice, she added, "He and my mother lied to me all my life about who we are. I know they thought it was for my own good, but it makes me wonder what else I think I know about them, about myself, that isn't true or real."

Taking David's arm again, she resumed their walk at a measured pace, as if their rhythmic footfalls might help her calibrate her thoughts.

"I don't like being tricked into doing this work for other refugees, but I do understand how important it is, and I want to continue. I just won't be treated like a child who needs more protection than anyone else." Now it was she who stopped and looked up at David with a wry smile. "And my feelings for you are not the feelings of a child."

David, whose expression had moved from consternation to thoughtfulness, now broke into a grin with a hint of a blush around his trimmed beard.

"One more thing," she said as she pulled him back into a walk. "I don't know how to fit this whole idea of being a Jew into my life. I want to learn more about what it means to me and to whatever world I find myself in in the future." She drew a deep breath, then blew it out. "All of this is going to take time to figure out." Stopping once again, she took both of David's hands in hers and looked intently at him. "I have dreamed of nothing more fervently than being together again and living a life with you, and I do love you. I just need you to see that I have also changed and grown older. I know you have too."

With that, she stood on her toes, took his face into her hands, and drew him into a long kiss.

Ana, standing at the kitchen window, had thrown open the shutters to let in the evening breeze. She watched the two young people, arm in arm, walk along the fence line, stop, start, stop again, walk more, and then linger in a kiss. She smiled; their young love pulled at her heartstrings, though she knew their path ahead would not be smooth.

"The fools!" said Padre Alvaro, pacing back and forth in the bishop's study. "Send them to do a simple task, and they bungle it."

The bishop sat rigidly behind his massive desk. "Perhaps you were hasty in securing the services of . . . unofficial forces." His soft voice belied the icy stare he was directing at the padre. "Doing so without my knowledge or permission was also unwise, at best."

At this, the padre ceased his pacing and faced the bishop. "I didn't want to bother you, Your Excellency, with a minor matter such as this. Surely Your Excellency wishes to suppress the practice of witchcraft and the transport of heretic Jews through Toulouse."

"Do you refer to Madame Martel Gerondi when you speak of witchcraft?" the bishop asked, again in a soft voice, but this time through a clenched jaw.

Unheeding, the padre answered, "But of course. Your own physician questioned her methods in the treatment of your . . . nephew." He raised an eyebrow as he spoke these last words. "Surely it is the duty of the Church to root out evil and heretical practices."

The bishop rose, his gaze fixed on the padre. "My physician had no quarrel with the outcome of Madame Martel Gerondi's care of my nephew. He fares far better than he did previously. And your concern for the duties of the Church is admirable, Padre Alvaro, but perhaps you have, in your zeal, forgotten your vows of humility and obedience to higher authority. I strongly suggest that you return to your parish, where your service to your congregation has been missing these last weeks. The Church in France is perfectly capable of protecting our flock from dangerous outside influences. And we are possibly in a very different time with regard to the work of the Inquisitors than you in Portugal. Toulouse always welcomes our brethren from elsewhere to share what we each have to offer, but I believe you have worn out your welcome."

Padre Alvaro stared wide-eyed at the bishop, a flush rising to his cheeks. He bowed stiffly. "Yes, Your Excellency."

Padre Alvaro turned abruptly and left the room without even noticing Jacques de Bernuy's presence.

Hunched over account books at a desk under the window, Jacques kept his head down, allowing only a slight smile in reaction to all he had heard. He continued to work as the bishop sighed heavily and took his own seat across the room.

"I trust you will find a way to communicate these events to Madame Martel Gerondi, Monsieur de Bernuy?" inquired the bishop.

Though startled at the directness of this request, Jacques replied, "Of course, Your Excellency."

Ana, Eduardo, David, and Isabela made their way up the steep hill road to Carcassone, which was crowded with a frieze of wagons, carts, and foot traffic on the brilliant August morning. They joined the throng bound for market, the largest in the area because of the huge garrison posted in the city. Having left most of their possessions at the farmhouse, the foursome had only lists of needed provisions, along with a few of Ana's new dyes to sell and a set of Isabela's banners to distribute.

Isabela and David were more awed when they entered the city gates than they had been at their first distant sight of the fortress the previous day. They gaped up at the towering fortifications and massive citadel. Ana allowed them a few moments to gawk before reminding them of the task at hand.

"Come," she said briskly. "We have much to do."

Remembering well her recent visit to the market, she led the way to the market lane, and soon the four travelers were busy shopping.

Ana returned to the merchant who had purchased dyes on her previous trip and sold him the new blue and purple dyes she'd made from Jacques de Bernuy's woad. She moved on to an herbalist whose wide selection allowed her to replenish the supplies that her work in Toulouse had diminished.

As she prepared to leave, a skirmish broke out just in front of the shop. A soldier pulled at the arm of an old woman, while a younger woman held to her other side.

"Please, sir," cried the young woman. "She is no witch. She is old and off in the head. She means no harm."

Ana recognized the old woman who had accosted her when she'd last been in Carcassone. "*Monsieur,*" she said, moving between the girl and her grandmother, "this woman is no witch; she is demented."

Just as Ana spoke, the old woman, now appearing even more deranged than when Ana had last seen her, turned toward her and once again stared at the elaborate filigreed cross pendant that hung on Ana's breast. Already agitated, the sight seemed to derange the woman further, and with impossible speed she turned to the soldier, unsheathed his dagger, and slashed at Ana, first slicing across her collar bone and then driving the point of the knife into her shoulder.

Ana fell back amidst the screams of the granddaughter, shouts of the soldier, and general commotion in the crowded lane. Blood began to pour from Ana's wounds and a wave of pain dizzied her.

Just as she began to fall, a strong set of arms clasped her from behind, holding her up.

"I'm here," David said into her ear, "but the others are elsewhere in the market. We need to get you out of the street."

"Take me back into the apothecary," Ana gasped out.

David half led, half carried Ana into the shop, where only the apothecary's assistant remained. The young man blanched at the blood now staining the entire left side of Ana's bodice. David felt faint himself, but he sat her on a bench and turned to the assistant. "We need a physician," he said slowly, carefully thinking of each French word.

Ana slumped to the side; David caught her by her good arm before she could slide off the bench. She was very pale and her eyelids fluttered open, then closed again. In fitful whispers she said, "Tell him I need a poultice of comfrey for the wounds and a tincture of poppy seed for the pain. Also, clean linen and a linen towel and hot water. I should lie down flat." Her head dropped heavily forward, but she tried to lift it again.

The bench was too short to lay her down there. In the workroom behind the counter, David saw a large table. "Clear that off," he told the assistant, pointing.

"But the master doesn't—"

"Clear it now," David commanded. "I will talk to your master."

Ana was nearly as tall as David, but he was strong enough to lift her into his arms and carry her through to the table, where he sat her down gently. He removed his cloak and made a pillow of it for her before lowering her down. As he laid her back she winced and became even more pale, occasioning another moment of dizziness in David.

Once settled, she began to give him instructions even as, with her right hand, she began to untie her cloak and unlace her bodice. "Make sure the water is as hot as you can stand it. Pull my bodice and my dress and my shift away from the wounds; cut them off if you have to. Wet the towel and clean around the edges of the wound and then apply pressure. We have to first staunch the bleeding. If I faint, hold the pressure until the bleeding slows."

"Shouldn't we wait for the doctor?" David asked, his stomach roiling. "Or Eduardo?"

"No. You must do this now, David. You can do this." She drew shallow, quick breaths.

The boy appeared with a bowl of water, a towel, and linen strips, and then disappeared among the rows of shelves. He soon returned with a tincture, drops of which he measured into a cup of ale. "The tincture of poppy," he said, handing it to David.

Ana's eyes fluttered open and she tried to lift her head. David placed his hand under it and brought the cup to her colorless lips.

After drinking, she said, "This will make me sleep. Follow my direction no matter what anyone says. Find Eduardo and Isabela and take me back to the farmhouse as soon as possible." Panting, she dropped her head back against David's cloak.

She remained conscious for a few minutes longer, groaning each time David had to move her injured arm or shoulder, but finally she fell into a stupor.

Once he knew she no longer had conscious pain, David found it easier to clean and treat the wounds as Ana had instructed, though it felt like an impossibly long time that he applied pressure to the wounds before they ceased bleeding. With the help of the assistant, he prepared the poultices and gently bound them to Ana's shoulder and chest. He marveled at the creamy whiteness of her soft skin, having never before seen the bare torso of a grown woman. Out of respect for her modesty, he quickly covered her with her shredded shift, untied bodice, and cloak once the poultices were set.

He instructed the assistant to stand outside the shop and look for people matching the descriptions he gave of Isabela and Eduardo. Meanwhile, he sat by Ana's side, watching to make certain she still breathed.

It took him a long while to realize that his own body shivered with nerves and exhaustion.

CHAPTER TWENTY-ONE

Carcassone and The Camargue

August, 1605

Come live with me, and be my love,
And we will some new pleasures prove
—JOHN DONNE

Almost an hour passed before the apothecary assistant spotted Eduardo and Isabela and rushed them into the shop, where Ana was still lying insensible on the long table and David was slumped on a stool at her side, his head in his hands.

He jolted to his feet as Eduardo cried, "Ana!"

She did not move, and David explained in a disjointed rush what he'd seen and what he'd done, finishing with Ana's order to move her back to the farmhouse with all speed.

Isabela sank to the stool, dropping her parcels to the floor, while Eduardo grasped Ana's limp hand in his own.

"I did exactly what Ana instructed, but the blood was everywhere and the wound in her shoulder is deep," David said.

Eduardo nodded. "You did well." Stroking her pale cheek, he tried again, "Ana, can you hear me? Can you open your eyes?"

While she continued to breathe, she did not rouse.

Eduardo stood just as the door to the shop flew open and three men strode into the small public space.

"Master," the assistant cried.

The apothecary hurried into his workroom and surveyed Ana's lifeless body, the bloody linens and bowl of water, his terrified assistant, and the three strangers. Before he could say a word, Eduardo introduced himself, David, and Isabela and gave a short summary of their situation.

"We are in need of a cart to transport Madame Martel Gerondi to our lodgings," he said. "We are most grateful for the assistance of your young man here, and we will gladly compensate you for the equipment and medicines used."

The other two men had made their way into the work room, and now one of them spoke.

"I am the gendarme who witnessed the incident. And this is Dr. Cordot, who will tend to the *madame*."

The doctor stepped forward, but David intercepted him. "Madame Martel Gerondi gave me very firm instructions before taking a poppy tincture, and she asked, once I finished, that she be taken back to our lodgings."

The physician's eyebrows rose and he cocked his head to one side in an expression of mild annoyance.

David gathered his nerve and continued. "She is herself an experienced healer . . . but I am not. Perhaps you could inspect my work?"

At this, Dr. Cordot's mouth twitched into what might have been a smile. David stepped back and the doctor leaned over Ana. After pulling back the cloak, examining the poultice and bandaging, and asking David several terse questions, he re-covered her.

"What dosage of poppy tincture was administered?" he asked the apothecary's assistant.

"Three drops, sir, exactly as she requested, sir," the frazzled boy replied.

He turned back to David. "Well done, young man. Madame seems to have directed her care with some presence of mind, especially considering these wounds. You must watch for fever and reapply the poultice each day."

David's shoulders relaxed in relief.

"The old woman will be no more trouble," the gendarme said with apparent satisfaction. "She'll hang as a witch and a murderer."

Isabela gasped, but Eduardo put a hand on her shoulder and she quieted herself. He then turned to the apothecary and made arrangements for a cart and paid him for his services.

Midway in the arduous trip down from Carcassone and back to the farmhouse, Ana woke. Isabela, at her side, did her best to minimize the effects of the cart's jolts and sways, as each shift seemed to elicit another groan from Ana. The farmer and his wife assisted in carrying Ana to her room, and Isabela spent a sleepless night at her side. By morning, Ana began to shiver and sweat, moving in and out of delirium.

David knocked at their bedroom door early. Isabela let him in and eventually accepted his insistence that she get some sleep and allow him to tend to Ana.

Taking Isabela's place on the bedside stool, David frowned at Ana's pale visage, the sheen of sweat on her brow, and the shivers that disturbed the stillness of her sleep. He applied a cool, wet cloth to her forehead, as Isabela had instructed.

After several minutes, Ana woke. Seeing David next to her, she attempted a smile that emerged more as a grimace.

"Ah, it's my surgeon," she said in a raspy voice.

"Only the hands that carried out orders." He smiled.

"Thank you, David." She reached her hand to hold his. "But I think your work as a physician is not finished—I have fever. I need you to prepare a draught to bring it down, and to tend to the wounds."

"But Isabela is here—"

"Yes, and you must work together, but she needs sleep—and somehow I think you have the touch of a healer, so help me, please." She closed her eyes and rested for a moment. "In my chest of herbs, you will find angelica, valerian, hyssop, mint, willow bark, and meadowsweet. Bring them to me, and I will instruct you how to make teas and tinctures for fever."

She continued to give instructions for new poultices for her wounds, and draughts for pain. "If you bring the herbs," she finished, "I can give instructions for a tea that will ease my pain and help me to sleep as well."

David, worried at her increasing pallor and tremors, hurried to do her bidding. With the help of the farmer's wife, he prepared the teas and tinctures and poultices, fumbling with utensils and mixing bowls but heeding Ana's advice closely.

After delivering a hyssop valerian tea to her, he returned to the hearth worktable. He was there, working on a poultice, when Eduardo entered the room and took him aside.

"I'm afraid we must move," Eduardo said. "The news in Carcassone is disturbing. It seems Ana's defense of that deranged woman, along with her purchase of healing herbs, has stirred suspicion. The granddaughter is saying Ana put a spell on the woman, inciting her to violence. I'm sure it's an effort to save the poor miserable creature and the gendarme will be embarrassed to have let it all happen, but I don't think it's safe to stay."

"Ana has taken fever. I don't think she can move." David's heart beat faster as he spoke. He had always deferred to Eduardo, but Ana's trust in him had struck a chord and given him courage to speak his mind.

Eduardo's eyes narrowed with concern. "Thank you for caring for her. Come, let's ask her when it will be safe to move."

David colored and, laden with salves, tinctures and fresh linen, followed Eduardo to Ana's room.

In three days' time, the travelers moved past Carcassone, taking a longer route south of the main road to avoid discovery and allow for a slower pace. Ana lay on a bed of rough blankets in the wagon, and Eduardo and David took turns leading one horse while Isabela rode on a second one, either just behind the wagon or, when the road's width allowed, at its side.

Eduardo was consumed with worry for Ana; though she now remained awake more than asleep, she was still quite ill. Her fever abated, then reemerged, and she continued to give David and Isabela instructions for her care, asking them daily to describe the wounds she could not see for herself.

Late in the afternoon on their first day of travel, she summoned Eduardo to her side.

She grasped his hand, her hollow-eyed face marked by red spots on each cheek. "I'm not improving, Eduardo. My wounds fester, and the fever weakens me further. I fear . . ."

Eduardo squeezed her hand. "We must find a physician. We are less than a day from Bezier."

"No," she said. "I want to go to the Camargue. I know of a good surgeon in Montpellier who teaches medicine. If he can help me, we can hide there until I recover. I cannot travel all the way to Lyon like this. Otherwise, you must leave me and continue on without me."

"No!" he said. "Not again—I won't be separated!" He rubbed a hand over his face. "I thought David and Isabela carried out your instructions properly."

She laid her head back down on the blankets, her drawn face signaling her exhaustion. "They have done their best, but rooms in a farmhouse and the bed of a wagon are no surgery. I need someone with expert skills now if I am to . . ." She expelled a tremulous breath. "If I am to recover."

And so the travelers detoured to the outskirts of Montpellier, a town roiled in recent months by fighting between Catholic forces and the Huguenots, who had been given freedom there and now fought fiercely to protect it.

Eduardo secured lodgings at a small inn and waited until just before nightfall to enter the city and locate the physician.

He came at morning's first light, and he frowned as he removed Ana's bandages. Though she'd shut her eyes tightly, tears squeezed from them as she prepared for what she knew he would say.

"These are grave wounds, and they have festered. Your friends have tended them conscientiously, but I'm afraid it's not been enough." He felt Ana's pulse, which beat faint and fast. He looked at Eduardo. "I'd like to take her to my surgery." Looking back at Ana, he said, "I want to cleanse these wounds again, and perhaps apply maggots."

"Will it be safe with all the disorder?" Eduardo asked.

The doctor sighed. "I hope so. We haven't yet had a problem at the school."

In short order, Ana was propped in the doctor's carriage, feverish and stuporous, dosed on boiled willow bark tea. Isabela and David stood close together as the carriage rolled away, worry pinching both their faces. Eduardo, soon to follow the carriage, instructed them to remain at the inn, to make preparations for the journey to the Camargue, and pray for Ana's recovery.

In less than an hour, he was gone.

Isabela watched as Eduardo's horse became a mere speck on the horizon. She began to turn back toward the inn but stopped, keeping her face angled into the gentle morning breeze. A faint scent of salt tickled her nose and left a trace on her lips.

"We must be close to the sea," she said softly, suddenly aware that she and David were alone for the first time since they'd left Abrantes. "I can smell it on the breeze."

David stood next to her and breathed in deeply. "Hmm," he murmured, closing his eyes.

Isabela faced him then and truly looked at him as she hadn't in the last weeks. He seemed even taller, though also thinner. The sinews in his arms and shoulders and neck stood out, testimony to the physical demands of his months of travel. All boyish softness had left his face. He needed a haircut and a beard trim, but she still found him immensely attractive. As he opened his eyes to look at her, the warm brown she knew so well also held a new depth that made him seem older.

"It's Friday," she said. "My mother always lighted candles in secret on Friday evening. I've learned it's a way to greet the Sabbath. My friend Sophia in Irouléguy gave me a small set of candlesticks. I'd like to light them at supper tonight and pray for Ana. Is that all right with you?"

David pulled her into an embrace. "I would like that," he said.

"Eduardo has been teaching me about the beliefs and the symbols of mystical Jewish study, and I find it fascinating." He grasped her shoulders and stepped back so he could look directly into her eyes. "I don't know any longer exactly what I believe in, Isabela. But I do know I want you to be my wife, and I want to make a family with you—so we must decide together about our religion. Will you explore with me?"

Isabela reached a hand to David's face and, with a giggle, asked, "David de Sousa, did you just make a marriage proposal?"

His eyes widened; then he broke into a broad grin. "Yes, Senhorita de Castro Nuñez. I believe I did."

Isabela, suddenly feeling the weight of the moment, grew somber. "Then if we ever find my father, God willing, you may ask him for my hand."

Dawn broke over the salt marsh, igniting the morning mists to a pale pink that matched the hue of flamingos stepping delicately through the shallows to eat and feed their chicks. Simone de Leon stood by the door of Claudio's cottage and greeted the first rays of sunlight with face lifted and eyes shut, breathing in the fresh cool air, before moving to the rain barrel and dipping the water bucket into it.

She placed the bucket on the table next to the door, shed her blouse, and washed. A welcome shiver passed over her chest as the breeze began to dry her.

Her gentle sigh changed to a gasp as Claudio stepped out of the cottage and reached around her back to cup her breasts in his strong hands. Leaning back into him, she drew deep breaths and wrapped her hands around his forearms, every nerve in her body thrilling.

"Good morning, *querida*," he said into her hair. "I must move a herd of horses this morning. Will you come with me?"

Simone turned and pulled his golden curls down to engage him in a deep kiss, then pushed him back. "Yes, it's a good day to practice."

Since her return to the Camargue, she had begun to work the horses with Claudio, and she'd found that she had both the sensibility and the interest needed to manage the beautiful beasts. Claudio had worked with her for weeks to tame a small mare, and now Simone flew across the marshes on the bare back of the strong white steed, her thighs one with the rippling muscles of the horse's flanks.

The morning's work challenged both horses and riders. Claudio and Simone worked together to separate the main stallion and drive him forward, then circle back to push the rest of the herd in his direction. That accomplished, they worked for another couple of hours to move strays back into the group, and by noon the small herd of forty horses was settled into a fresh grazing area with a stream running along the edge, a good distance away from where they'd started.

Horses and riders were mud-spattered and sweaty, and before returning to their cottage Claudio and Simone bathed in the stream. After exiting the water, they lounged naked in the grass and the warm sun until the pull of a midday meal at the cottage brought them back to their wet clothing.

As they dressed, the horses' heads rose as one, ears forward, necks turning toward the track below that led from the road to the cottage. Barely visible to human eyes, a lone rider made his way toward the house.

Claudio finished dressing and stood for a moment watching as Simone tied the laces of her bodice. "A Roma horse," he said, frowning slightly. "I'm not expecting anyone."

He rode ahead of Simone down the gentle slope toward the hillock on which the cottage stood. She moved more slowly, letting her sure-footed mare find her way as the rocky path gave way to marsh grass and swales of brackish water.

By the time she arrived, Claudio and the visitor were inside. Simone dismounted, brought feed and water for the horses, and quietly entered the cottage.

Claudio and a man Simone did not recognize, dressed in the white shirt, loose pants, brown cape, and slouch hat of a Roma, were seated at the table.

The man stood and bowed slightly as Claudio introduced him.

"This man brings a message from the doctor in Montpellier. Ana Martel Gerondi is wounded and seriously ill. She needs to shelter here to recover. Her young friends of your acquaintance, along with a gentleman protector, will accompany her here shortly."

Simone sat heavily. A jolt of fear dropped like a stone in her chest. *Isabela?* Months had passed since she had been forced to think of the plight of those escaping Portugal, and only in the last weeks had she finally received news that her brother and nephew had returned safely to their home in Figueres. Living in peace and quiet here in the Camargue with Claudio, the horses and the birds allowed her to breathe freely, to rest deeply, to dwell in her love for Claudio and their life together. She had no wish to return to a life of threat and danger, even if for a good cause.

She sighed. "Of course."

"There is more," Claudio continued. "There was trouble in Carcassone, and unrest in Montpellier."

"Will they be bringing danger to us?" Simone asked. As soon as the question left her lips, she regretted its peevish tone. "You cannot answer that," she said quickly, and rose to prepare the midday meal. "Please ask our guest to join us."

Claudio, switching from Spanish to Romani, invited the messenger to eat with them and instructing him to afterward return to Montpellier with assurances that Dama Martel Gerondi and her party would be sheltered.

Simone distracted herself with the task of preparing food as Claudio brought out a flask of wine to serve their guest.

Four days later, the Roma man returned with a small caravan of horses and a large wagon. The party moved slowly in the afternoon heat. Watching them approach, Simone quickly picked out Isabela riding behind the wagon, her horse between those of two men.

Claudio rode out to meet the party and lead them up the steep hill to the cottage.

Simone had spent the last two days preparing an extra pallet in the cottage and three more in the shelter behind it. She had baked fresh bread and prepared a fish stew laden with potatoes, carrots, rosemary, and thyme from the garden. Sea lavender and the last yellow iris of the season, which for the last two months had grown in wild profusion around the cottage, decorated the table. All was ready for the visitors, yet Simone remained nervous. Even the constancy of the sea breeze didn't soothe away the clammy perspiration from her forehead and underarms.

When finally the travelers halted in the dooryard of the cottage and Simone saw one careworn face and bedraggled body after another dismount and stand uncertainly by the wagon, her unease vanished. She was most struck by Isabela, whom she had left as a young girl, travel-weary but pretty and with the freshness of girlhood and innocence still about her. Now she saw a young woman: thinner, perhaps taller, and with a straightforward gaze and upright posture that betokened a confidence and worldliness she had not possessed a few short months earlier.

As soon as Isabela caught sight of Simone, she strode forward and threw her arms around her.

David de Sousa and Eduardo Carel were quickly introduced. Simone paused, thinking she had met Señor Carel sometime in the past, but she had no time to ponder this as all attention turned to the wagon, where a tall figure lay wrapped in blankets, despite the heat of the afternoon. Simone stepped closer. Ana Martel Gerondi's deathly pale face contrasted sharply with the tumble of long black curls that lay tangled around it.

Simone turned first to Isabela, but before she could say a word Señor Carel stepped forward, every part of his tall body and intense face, anchored by ice blue eyes, demanding her full attention.

"Señora de Leon, first I humbly thank you for offering us refuge. I am indebted to your brother, who similarly helped Señor de Sousa and me in our efforts to find our way out of Portugal. Our friend . . ." Here he stopped, took a deep breath, and gazed down at Ana. "Our friend, Dama Martel Gerondi, who I believe you know is part of our rescue network, was badly injured in an attack in Carcassone, and the wound became infected. We have just come from a surgery in Montpellier, but our physician said we cannot travel further until Dama Martel Gerondi regains some strength, and it was too dangerous to stay in Montpellier with the unrest there. She has lost a great deal of blood and has battled the purulence for days. She is so weak."

At this, Señor Carel's voice broke and he stepped back, lowering his fierce eyes.

Thinking again that she'd seen those eyes before, Simone began to give orders.

Under her direction, the group set to work. While Eduardo worked to make a sling of the blanket underneath Ana and, avoiding her wounded shoulder, carry her into the cottage, Claudio brought buckets of water for the travelers to wash with. Simone herself went to heat a tea of willowbark, hyssop, and mint for fever and pain.

Isabela worked by Simone's side until Ana was settled and the meal laid on the table, though Simone could see that she too was exhausted. She touched the girl's shoulder gently.

"Thank you for your help, but surely you too are weary from your journey. I look forward to hearing all that has happened—but now, go and wash, come eat, and then rest. Tell the others to do the same. I will keep close watch on Dama Martel Gerondi."

CHAPTER TWENTY-TWO

Lyon and The Camargue

August, 1605

Heal me, O Lord, and I shall be healed; save me, and I shall be saved.
—JEREMIAH 17:14

Gabril de Castro Nuñez stood on the Pont de la Guillotiére and surveyed the beauty of Lyon in the distance. The August twilight lit the Cathédrale Saint-Jean-Baptiste's roof and spires and made a golden carpet of the pasture between the bridge and the town. He let out a sigh of pleasure at the sight, and then resumed walking.

As he made his way across the field, Gabril reviewed the plan sent to him by the Kehillah in Hamburg to facilitate the movement of refugees from Portugal through France and into the German nation. He was to confirm the extension of safe houses north from Avignon to Lyon, and then even farther north to Strasbourg.

Two rivers flowed through the heart of Lyon, making it a hub of commerce in the Rhône valley and offering possibilities to transport refugees passing through to points north.

Apart from his assigned tasks for the Kehillah, Gabril was thrilled to visit this thriving center of the silk trade again. As a young man, just before assuming the mantle of his father's textile business, he had made the journey to Lyon to buy fabric and thread. On that first foray as a buyer, he had traveled by himself to Toulouse and then Lyon, soaking up all the aspects of this capitol of silk, from worm to loom, along the way. With his eye for artistry and his head for business, he'd made many profitable purchases and established solid contacts that had supported his family's business in subsequent years.

Gabril quickened his pace in the late-afternoon heat, grateful for the gentle breeze coming off the Saône River. His destination was a silk merchant, Alberto Dumond, on Rue Mourguet, just across the river and in the center of ateliers and the warren of covered passageways that connected them to the weaving workshops at the edges of the city. Gabril was fascinated with these secret *traboules*, as they were called locally, used to protect the deliveries of delicate silks from the elements of nature but also from thieves. Perhaps they could be equally useful to shuttle refugees in and out of the city. He meant to explore that possibility.

The Le Soierie Dumond looked much the same as it had more than a decade before. Gabril stood for a moment on the paving stones of the tidy street, looking up and down the lane as the last shoppers hurried home in the twilight, before stepping into the shop.

Unlike many of the other stores in the silk district, Atelier Dumond was both a retail business and a workshop. The rhythmic thump of the loom's beaters and the occasional voices of the weavers tossing orders to their assistants still flowed from the back of the shop, where spools of brilliantly colored threads were arranged in orderly rows on wooden racks.

At the front of the shop, in light now dimming, a gorgeous array of silk fabric—displayed on shelves and tables and draped on mannequins—featured a wide array of colors and woven patterns. All else for the moment forgotten, Gabril stood in the doorway and feasted his eyes on the beautiful display.

A stocky man of middle age appeared from the back of the shop. "May I be of assistance?"

"Monsieur Dumond, if I am not mistaken?" Gabril replied, and allowed the man to observe him for a moment. Though he was fluent in French, he knew his Portuguese accent was detectable. "It has been entirely too long since we have seen each other in person. I am Gabril de Castro Nuñez."

Alberto Dumond's face broke into a quick smile—but it disappeared as fast as it had come. He glanced behind Gabril to the street and out the shop windows. "How do you do, Monsieur Nuñez," he said, extending a handshake and simultaneously steering Gabril toward the tiny office off the showroom.

He closed the door and gestured for Gabril to sit at a small table. "I hardly recognize you, Gabril," he said. "It has been a long time." This time, Alberto's smile was broad and extended all the way to his large brown eyes. "It's good to see you, but I'm afraid we must be far more careful than I'd hoped with regard to the part of your association with us that has nothing to do with silk."

Gabril's own smile faded and he sat back in his chair, waiting for the other man to continue.

"I've had an unexpected visit from a cleric friend who got wind of a concern in the bishop's council regarding a suspected network to move Iberian New Christians and Jews through Lyon toward Italy and the German nation."

"Did he tell you how that concern arose?" Gabril asked.

"He did. Apparently there is a treatise making the circuit of Church officials, written by a priest from Abrantes, Portugal, accusing the French Church of ignoring the infiltration of our cities and towns with Jews and New Christians in name only. He insists that they are heretical in their beliefs, avaricious, and a danger to both our governments and our faith. He was apparently rebuffed by the bishop in Toulouse but seeks to make his case in Lyon. He mentions in particular, . . ." Alberto sighed. "He seeks a young girl and a young man from Abrantes who he believes are part of this network, along with their protectress, a healer and dye maker whom he accuses of witchcraft." Alberto allowed this information to sink in, then said, "Needless to say, I was quite alarmed at this information, which I believe my friend shared with me as a warning."

Feeling the blood drain from his head, Gabril gripped the arms of his chair. "Padre Alvaro?"

"Yes," Alberto said, "I believe that was the name. I have had word from Jacques de Bernuy relating the Bishop of Toulouse's expulsion of the good padre from that city. He wished to communicate those facts to Ana Martel Gerondi, but I'm afraid we have been out of contact with her since their party left Carcassone. A party of four, it seems; a man older than the de Sousa boy is also said to be with them."

The two men stared at each other for a long moment.

"This implicates my daughter," Gabril finally said. "I must find her and take her to safety in Hamburg." He thought for a moment. "I truly hope the man you mentioned is my friend, Eduardo Carel. He is to be trusted and has his own interest in conducting the group to safety. But even so, I must find them!"

Alberto sighed again. "I understand. But I'm afraid at this moment, *they* must find *you*. I've sent a message to the last safe farmhouse that we know that sheltered them near Carcassonne, and I expect to hear back within the day. In the meantime, you should conduct your business in silks with all normal appearance. But be careful, Gabril. Creating suspicion will help no one. I've arranged for you to stay at a comfortable pension with good food and wine." He reached across the table and grasped Gabril's arm. "I promise to send word as soon as I hear anything. Come back tomorrow, and we will talk silk."

The two men rose and clasped hands, fear and fatigue causing both to hold the other a moment longer than necessary. After a final squeeze, Gabril turned and left the shop, stepping into the gathering darkness and the night sounds of distant church bells and closing shutters.

Two days passed at the cottage in the Camargue, and still Ana drifted in and out of consciousness, fevered sweats alternating with restless sleep. Isabela and Simone took turns keeping vigil at her bedside, spooning broth into her, and tending to garden and household tasks, while David and Eduardo assisted Claudio in the fall roundup of horses.

When Ana slept, Isabela returned to her embroidery, preparing signal banners for the network houses and inns and collars, cuffs, and caps for the messengers and hosts. The symbols for safety and danger and the signs identifying their wearers as trusted members of the network now came easily to her, and she enjoyed incorporating them into designs using the new fabrics and threads she'd purchased in Carcassonne.

Late on the second day, after Simone had administered a tincture of poppy to ease Ana into a restful sleep, the remaining five members of their group sat around the table outdoors in the approaching evening cool. Eduardo moved in and out of the cottage, haunted worry now a fixture on his gaunt face.

After his third check on Ana, Simone spoke.

"Senor Carel, I am no healer, but I believe Senora Martel Gerondi has sustained herself through this trial and is beginning to recover. Perhaps she is not entirely out of danger, but today she was present enough to give us detailed instructions for her care, so you must have hope."

She smiled as she spoke, and Eduardo was not the only one who took comfort from her words.

"Thank you again, Senora de Leon, for your kindness and all your assistance. We are deeply indebted to you and to Claudio." He looked between her and Isabela. "Do you have a sense of how long it might be before Ana can be moved? I must get a message to my friends in Lyon, where we were expected by now, to let them know what has happened and when we might arrive." He looked in Claudio's direction as he said this last bit.

"We are a day's ride from the Rhône, where a boatman can take you to Arles," Claudio said. "I have a trusted friend there who would get a message first to Avignon and then to Lyon. At best it will be a two-day ride. If you await an answer, I expect it will be a week before you return here." He looked to Simone. "Will the senora be well enough to move in a week?"

All eyes turned to Simone, but it was Isabela who spoke.

"It is possible, but we cannot know for certain. We will know more in a week's time, and we will wait until she is strong enough." Her statement contained no question, only a pronouncement, and she met her older companions' gazes with a fierceness that brooked no opposition.

"I will depart tomorrow for Arles, then," said Eduardo.

"I will go with you," David offered. "You have done so much for me and my family."

"No, David," Eduardo said firmly. "You can best serve by staying here to help. Claudio tells me you've become quite the horseman and have been helpful. And I believe a certain young lady has no wish to be separated from you again."

Isabela blushed and nodded her agreement, her eyes fixed on David.

The next morning, Eduardo rose just before sunrise and made preparations for his journey. Isabela wrapped bread and cheese and a hard sausage into a small satchel and filled a goatskin with wine, then gathered a number of banners and clothing items for Eduardo to send to Lyon.

As sunlight began to pour into the cottage through the east window, Eduardo sat at Ana's bedside and stroked her black curls. Her eyes fluttered open, and her gaze was as clear as it had been in weeks.

She reached up and took his hand in hers. "I'm so sorry I have been such a worry."

Eduardo clasped her hand in both of his and drew it to his lips. "Don't. I'm just so grateful that you've come back to us." He smiled, but then became serious again. "I must go to Arles and send word to Lyon. We have been out of contact for too long, and they will all be worried for our safety. I will try to learn of Gabril's whereabouts as well. I should only be gone a week." He kissed her hand again, and his heart lurched as he saw tears fill her beautiful green eyes, now appearing even larger in her thinned face. "I have no more wish to leave you than you have for me to go, but I must. We've come this far, and we need to complete our mission. Your task is to regain your strength and dream up a plan for where we will go and what we will do when we have safely delivered Isabela—and, I suppose, David—to Gabril."

Ana reached up to touch Eduardo's face and began to sit up, only to fall back onto her pallet.

"Shh," said Eduardo. "Rest, and let the others care for you. I love you, *querida*."

A single tear tracked down Ana's cheek, but she forced a smile and squeezed Eduardo's hand. He rose and made his way out to the horse Claudio had readied for him.

Claudio watched as his tall new friend rode down the hill to the narrow track that would lead him to the broader lane through the grassy marsh and out of the Camargue toward the Rhône and Arles. He sent a short prayer up to the heavens for the other man's safekeeping and swift return to the cottage.

In the days that followed, Ana gained strength, ate more, and, though she had to lean heavily upon Isabela or Simone, periodically made her way to a chair outdoors for brief periods of fresh air and morning sun. It was David who most often changed her bandages and applied the poultices and salves per her instructions, and finally her wound began to heal.

One morning, only four days after Eduardo's departure, Isabela saw a horseman riding up the hill. She flew back to the cottage, eager to hear what news he might be carrying with him.

Simone and Claudio fed the messenger and settled him with a mug of ale before asking for his news. His message came not from Eduardo but from the farmhouse near Carcassonne where they had sheltered the previous week.

"Just after you left, a messenger came to the farmhouse near Carcassone," he reported. "Alberto Dumond in Lyon requested information as to your whereabouts and when you might arrive in Lyon. A second message came two days later, informing us that

Monsieur de Castro Nuñez had arrived in Lyon and was desperate for word of his daughter."

Isabela's hands flew to her mouth. Was her father really so close?

"Monsieur Dumond also warns of danger from a priest who seems committed to the idea that a network of heretics has established a corps of sympathetic safe houses through the South of France to get refugees to Venice and Hamburg. He has written a treatise and is attempting to convince the bishop in Lyon to take action, having failed at the same effort in Toulouse."

Isabela met David's eyes and saw the same panicked recognition that she felt in herself. *Padre Alvaro.*

"Monsieur Dumond advises that you leave for Lyon in all haste, though as discreetly as possible. He sends with me this list of places to stay on your route, though again, caution will be necessary." He pulled a parchment from his satchel and handed it to Claudio, who passed it immediately to David.

Ana, who had now been out of bed for over an hour, slumped back in her chair and covered her face with one hand.

"We cannot leave just yet," David said firmly, "though we are most grateful for your messages," he said, turning to the messenger.

Speaking to the others, David continued, "Ana is not yet strong enough for travel, and Eduardo has gone to Arles to send communications to Lyon. He won't return for several days."

Ana looked up and began to speak as if to protest, but David shook his head and said, "We will travel together." Turning back to the messenger, he said "We greatly appreciate the information as to friendly sanctuaries."

The man nodded, then rose with a sigh to make his return trip. "I wish you safe passage."

When the messenger was gone, Isabela went to the garden to finish harvesting beans and cabbage Simone needed for a soup. David soon followed and found her seated on a bench, her basket half empty. She looked up at him and made no effort to hide her tears.

"Isabela, what is it?" He sat beside her and put an arm around her shoulders.

"I've waited so long to hear word of my father, and now that I know he is so close, I'm excited, but also a little frightened." She stared down at her lap. "Is that terrible of me?" Raising her gaze to his, she searched his eyes. "It's been so long since I've seen or heard from him and I'm not the same girl he left with my mother. What will he think of me or expect from me?"

"Oh, Isa," David said, pulling her closer. "He can only be so proud of who you've become and all that you've conquered. He has marshaled all of these people to help us come this far. I know all he wants is to see you safe with him in a better life. Of course you aren't the same. And neither is he. But he loves you, and you are all he has left of his family." His voice caught. "You are fortunate to have him."

She wrapped her arms around him and returned his embrace. "You are right. I am."

Two days later, Claudio brought the last of the herd in for winter pasturing on the grasslands. A cool breeze set the seedheads dancing, and cottony clouds played hide-and-seek with the sun. Just as he finished settling the herd, a tiny speck of horse and rider drew his attention far to the east. When the traveler came close enough, he could see that the rider was Eduardo, and that he was leading a second horse—a sturdy draft animal pulling a wagon.

Claudio rode out to join him, and by the time the two men arrived at the cottage, the other inhabitants all stood in the dooryard to greet them. Ana's cheeks bore the faintest healthy flush, and she returned Eduardo's embrace with more strength than she'd shown in weeks.

They all sat to dine on Simone's hearty soup, and Eduardo related what his journey had accomplished. His passage to the river and securing of a boat had gone easily, and he'd quickly found Claudio's contact in Arles. His host had been generous and fed him well. He'd managed to send a lengthy message to Lyon detailing the attack in Carcassonne, the need for Ana to recover in the Camargue, and the plan to travel to Lyon as soon as possible. He had sent the bundle of banners and other embroidered items with the written messages.

In turn, Claudio told of the news the messenger had brought, including the warnings about the priest's effort to expose the refugee network and implicate Isabela, David, and Ana.

They all spoke late into the evening, long after Ana gave up in exhaustion and went to sleep. By the time their last candle burned low, a plan for their passage to Lyon was in place. They would leave in five days.

CHAPTER TWENTY-THREE

Lyon

September, 1605

He threatens many that hath injured one.
—BEN JONSON

Tired and hungry after a long day conducting business in the silk market of Le Croix-Rousse, Gabril hurried down Rue Mourguet in the fading light toward his pension. He had hired a cart for the hour's passage through Lyon's crowded streets and across the bridge into the fifth arrondissement. He asked to be let out ten minutes from his destination—to make certain he wasn't followed, and to purchase a flagon of wine before returning to his rooms.

Weeks of work connecting silk manufacturers with his fledgling association of import/export merchants in Hamburg had borne ample fruit. Combined with what he had accomplished in Venice, he could easily justify the expense of his trip to Italy and France. His letters were posted and the receipt of the first funds for facilitating the transactions should have been cause for celebration, but Gabril had ducked out of the toasts after a polite first glass, eager to see if a letter or message awaited him.

Eduardo's letter and package had come to Alberto Dumond ten days before, along with further disturbing news of Padre Alvaro from

Jacques de Bernuy. Contrary to the orders of the Toulouse bishop, it was rumored, the padre had not returned to Portugal but was now in Lyon, agitating for Church officials to use their Inquisitorial powers to root out the efforts of the suspected refugee network. As a result of this new worry, Alberto no longer wished to meet Gabril at his atelier; instead, he arranged to send messages to the pension or met him at out-of-the-way bistros.

As the days passed and he waited for further word, Gabril had become more and more distraught. As he traveled through throngs of townspeople during his visits to the silk producers and traders, he found himself looking at the faces of young girls and realizing with a shock that after nearly a year apart from his daughter, he might not recognize the young woman she had become.

Gabril turned the corner into the alley leading to his pension. He never saw the man who stepped out of the neighboring doorway and knocked him to the ground with a crack of a knife hilt to his head. He had lost consciousness by the time a second man bound his hands and feet, and gagged him. The two men dragged him to a waiting cart and in moments disappeared, as though no one had been in the street at all.

The journey from the Camargue began with retracing Eduardo's steps to Arles, then continuing to follow the Rhône River to Avignon, Bollene, Valence, and finally to Vernaison. Using the catalog of houses and inns given them by the messenger, the four travelers were able to make good headway toward Lyon in a short time, stopping only to eat, ask for the occasional direction, and allow Ana a midafternoon rest each day. Along the way, Isabela left gifts of embroidery for their hosts, as well as the requisite banners signaling continued safety or warning at each stop.

ISABELA'S WAY

In this way, they arrived at the small recommended inn in Vernaison, a long morning's walk from Lyon, just four days after their departure from the Camargue.

Once Ana and Isabela were settled in their room, Eduardo beckoned David to the innkeeper's private quarters. The man they met there was young, with thin brown hair and a short but well-built body. Without a word, he handed a letter to Eduardo, who blanched as he read its contents, and then passed it to David.

Monsieur Carel,

If you have followed the advice of our guides, I pray you will arrive in Vernaison and receive this letter. On Monday last, Gabril de Castro Nuñez disappeared with no trace. It is now Wednesday and I have had no word from or about him. I know that he concluded his business with the silk merchants and was only awaiting your arrival with his daughter, which he expected by now.

You will be acquainted with the danger brought by the priest Alvaro from Abrantes, and I must suspect his involvement, though my efforts to confirm this through my acquaintances in the Church have not been successful.

I do not know how to advise you, sir, except to beg you to keep the de Castro Nuñez girl safely away until we learn of her father's fate. I believe I may be under surveillance myself and have sent this missive through circuitous means to avoid your detection and mine. Please be as circumspect in your communications, as I trust you know that neither of us is of help to our cause unless we remain alive and free of chains.

With sorrow to bear this news, and with the promise of more whenever I learn something,

I remain your servant,
Alberto Dumond

David felt the weight of a boulder press him into his seat. He could barely breathe. Still no one spoke, and the silence seemed to go on—until, suddenly, all three men began to speak at once.

"You can remain here."

"Isabela will be crushed by this. We mustn't tell her."

"I will leave for Lyon tonight."

At this statement of Eduardo's, the two other men stopped and looked at him.

"But where would you go? We don't know where Senhor Nuñez is or who is holding him. If Alberto Dumond is being watched, surely we can't go to him." David made these pronouncements tentatively.

"We do know he is in danger." Eduardo closed his eyes. "If he is still alive at all, and the priest has him, he won't keep him alive for long. I have to find him. I have to know what he's using Gabril for. I suspect it's to draw in accomplices and justify his ranting efforts over these last months." He gripped David's shoulder. "I know you will want to come with me, and I wish I could have your help, but someone must stay and protect Ana and Isabela."

David shook his head. "But—"

"Monsieur Carel," the innkeeper interjected. "I would be honored to watch over Madam Martel Gerondi and Mademoiselle de Castro Nuñez. I promise you I will guard them as my own. They will be safe and well cared for here until you return."

"Thank you," David said, and looked into Eduardo's eyes. "I will not allow you to do this alone. I would never forgive myself if Isabela lost her father because I stood by and did nothing."

Eduardo spent only a moment considering his words and the innkeeper's offer before reaching for the innkeeper's hand and shaking it firmly. "You do us a great service, sir. Now I must write a note to Ana and Isabela, and then we must depart."

"I will saddle fresh horses and my wife will pack a food bag, as you may arrive too late to find food when you get there." The innkeeper scribbled a few lines on a scrap of parchment and handed it to Eduardo. "Here is the address of a trusted friend. I will meet you in the stables shortly with the supplies."

Eduardo scrawled a note while David collected their things.

In twenty minutes' time, they were riding for Lyon.

Ana paced the small room on the inn's upper floor, her mouth set in a grim line. She clutched Eduardo's note in one hand, the other hand holding on to chair, table, and bed frame as she circled the small space.

Isabela sat listless in the single chair, head in hands, elbows on the table, her shoulders' gentle shaking the only evidence of her soundless weeping.

A wave of regret doused Ana's anger; she paused and put an arm around her young friend. "I'm sorry, Isabela. I'm sorry this is happening, and I'm sorry my injury delayed our journey. If we had come earlier—"

"No, Ana." Isabela's head snapped up. "You and Eduardo did everything to help us get to my father. And you've put yourselves in danger because of it. I just can't believe we got this close and now I don't know what has happened to my father and if . . ." She dissolved back into tears.

"And now we've been left here, with no idea where they've gone or what they plan to do, and without a single word to us." Ana fairly spat the words out, fists clenched, shoulders tensed.

She sat abruptly on the bed and spoke more calmly. "We'll just have to make a plan of our own."

Isabela turned to her in surprise. "What kind of plan?"

Gabril's first awareness came with a dull ache at the back of his head when he tried to move. He lay on his left cheek, strain in his shoulder urging him to move. The position of his tied hands, behind him, prevented his rolling onto his back. When he attempted to sit up the dull ache became a searing jolt of pain, and so he lay still, adjusting his position as best as possible to ease the discomfort.

A window he couldn't see behind him allowed what he guessed to be morning light to pour into the room. He was on a floor—a fine wooden floor, by the looks of the parquet and polish—and across the room an elegant carpet spread before a stately stone hearth. No fire warmed the room, and he shivered with cold.

He tried to understand what happened and where he was, but pain and confusion overcame him and he slipped back out of consciousness.

Gabril awoke again to find himself slumped against the back of a settee, his hands unbound. He opened his eyes and tried to focus on the hunk of bread and tankard of ale set before him on a table. He was terribly thirsty and was reaching for the tankard when a voice stopped him.

"Good morning, Senhor Nuñez. I am pleased you've rejoined us."

The man's voice was familiar, the greeting spoken in colloquial Portuguese.

A shooting pain from head to neck froze Gabril when he tried to turn to locate the face associated with the voice.

"You are a hard man to locate, and your daughter and friends even harder," the voice continued.

Gabril gasped as the man came around the settee and he recognized Padre Alvaro.

"Please, *senhor*, help yourself to a little breakfast. You've had a hard night. It's been quite a while since we've seen each other," he went on, his voice smooth as silk. "I was so sorry for the loss of your wife, may God commend her soul. I tried to give your daughter some business, as she was all on her own; I must say, she inherited her mother's skill with needle and thread."

At this mention of Isabela, Gabril's heart pounded in his chest, but he said nothing. He resolved to wait for the padre, whom he knew to be a wily man, to reveal what he would.

With as much casual indifference as he could muster, he reached for the tankard and sipped some ale.

"I'm afraid she repaid my generosity by leaving Abrantes—and, along with the de Sousa boy, taking a number of other New Christians with her, depriving the municipality of their tax contributions and the many services they've provided to the town. I am given to understand that many among these New Christians are not Christian at all but rather Jews, heretics who disregard the tenets of the Church. And it appears that people of like mind, specifically a Christian traitor named Ana Martel Gerondi, have assisted these heretics by creating a network designed to help them leave Portugal."

Gabril took another sip of ale, trying to remain stone-faced even as his pulse raced.

"Given the length of your absence and the disappearance of your daughter, I suspect you have no intention of returning to Portugal, and I begin to wonder if you too might be involved in this illegal and dangerous trafficking of heretics."

A long silence ensued. It seemed Padre Alvaro had finished his speech.

Gabril placed the tankard on the table. "It is true I miss my daughter and wish to see her, but I am here in Lyon on business at the silk market—business I have only just finished. As far as I am aware, my daughter is in Irouléguy, where she is helping to embroider the trousseau for the daughter of the house and improve her French at the same time."

Padre Alvaro studied Gabril. "That would mean you are sadly misinformed, *senhor*, though I believe you are in fact very well informed. But we shall see. I suspect your friends will come looking for you, and then I will have you all conveniently in one place. I shall ask to convene an Inquisitorial tribunal, and we will see how your heretical little group fares." He fingered the heavy silver cross that hung on his cassock. "While we wait, I suggest you make yourself comfortable. Avail yourself of the library if you wish." He extended his hand toward the far wall, where in the brightening light Gabril could see shelves of books. "We have made certain you will be easy enough to find, and no one will worry about entering one of the finer addresses in Lyon. But rest assured, you are very well guarded."

Padre Alvaro turned abruptly and knocked sharply at the door.

As a guard opened the door and the padre swept out of the room, Gabril leaned back against the settee and tried to think past the throbbing pain in his head.

ISABELA'S WAY

The only rest Eduardo and David had found during the night had been on two hard benches in the common room of a rough inn on the outskirts of Lyon. Tired and hungry, the two made their way toward Rue Mourguet and the last known address of Gabril de Castro Nuñez.

Morning sun ignited the stone façade of the buildings on the open square at the end of the still-darkened cobblestone street, a heavenly, golden light that lifted David's spirits some.

Eduardo stopped before they reached the square.

"Cross the square and take the road straight ahead. Before you reach Rue Mourguet, there should be a cafe to your left. Take a seat so you can see the alleyway to the right that leads to Gabril's rooms. Observe anyone who goes in and out, but don't approach. I expect that even in your hat and farmer tunic, the priest would recognize you. I will go to Dumond and learn what I can. When I come back perhaps I will investigate the alley and the rooms." He clapped David on the shoulder. "Be careful, my boy. Caution, not bravado, will win the day. We don't want to have come this far and lose you. I would have Satan to pay with Ana and Isabela if anything were to happen to you."

They entered the square, and the fierce September sunlight momentarily blinded David. As Eduardo turned to the left, he walked straight ahead, praying for the warm light to be a harbinger of good fortune in the day ahead.

"I won't be left as useless," Ana snapped, turning her flashing green eyes on Isabela.

Isabela was struck dumb at the force of the older woman's outburst. As they stared at each other, Isabela felt her own anguish rise and pour out of the cauldron of pent-up frustration and fear. "He is my father," she choked out.

"Right," said Ana.

She instructed Isabela to bind her arm to her torso to stabilize the shoulder wound, and promised they would stop if she tired. Moving quietly, they packed only what they could carry on the horses—including Ana's case of herbs and salves.

In the end, the two women simply rode their horses out of the inn's small barn early enough in the morning that no one stirred to stop them.

They followed the main road to Lyon, stopping only to board their horses at a stable at the edge of the city before continuing onward on foot.

Isabela stood back in wonder as she regarded the fine house before her.

Without hesitation, Ana lifted the heavy knocker of the imposing door and let it drop before leaning with her good arm against the door frame.

Isabela came forward and slipped her arm around Ana just as the door opened and a liveried servant looked at the two women with suspicion.

Isabela cast her eyes down. They were dusty, unkempt from the short night and the ride.

Ana was pale but spoke clearly and confidently. "I should like to see Madame Dumond. She is not expecting me, but please tell her it is Ana Martel Gerondi."

"Madame Martel Gerondi is weak and must rest," Isabela added. "May we please come in while you convey our message to your mistress?"

The servant eyed the two women for a moment, but relented.

With a sigh, he conducted them into the entry hall, seated them on an ornately carved bench, and summoned a parlor maid to stay with them while he sought out Madame Dumond.

Ana closed her eyes and leaned her head back while Isabela marveled at the furnishings of the hall. The floors were a mosaic of multi-colored marble tiles bordered by parquetry, all polished to a gleam. Opposite their bench, a massive gilt-framed mirror covered the wall above a demilune console table, upon which a Chinese vase held a profusion of lavender and tall sprays of white, bell-shaped flowers that Isabela had never seen before. The blooms scented the air, and early-morning light from the leaded window above the door reflected off the mirror to ignite all the colors. Isabela had thought that the Mercados' villa was the most beautiful she had ever seen, but this home was even finer.

She had just leaned forward to peer farther down the hall when a diminutive woman appeared at the top of the stairs. Upon catching sight of Ana and Isabela, she fairly flew down the steps in a flurry of turquoise taffeta and lace.

"Oh Ana," she cried. "Look at you. Let's get you to a more comfortable spot." She turned to Isabela as she helped Ana to her feet. "*Bonjour mademoiselle*, I am Marie Dumond. And you are?"

"Isabela de Castro Nuñez, Madame Dumond." Isabela stood and gave a brief curtsy.

"Come," the tiny woman commanded. "We must help Ana upstairs."

Ana roused herself as Isabela, Marie, and a housemaid fairly carried her up the stairs.

"Marie, Eduardo is walking into a trap, with Gabril as the bait," she said, her voice hoarse with fatigue. "I need your help."

Isabela nearly dropped the arm she held. "What are you saying?" she gasped.

Before Ana could answer, Madame Dumond said sharply, "We must tend to her first. Isabela, help me undress her. Eliza, fetch hot water and towels and . . ." She looked at Isabela. "Did Madame Martel Gerondi bring her herbs?"

Isabela nodded mutely.

"And Madame Martel Gerondi's herb case."

CHAPTER TWENTY-FOUR

Lyon

September, 1605

There is no greater hell than to be a prisoner of fear.
—Ben Jonson

"Who built all these passageways?" David huffed as he and Eduardo sprinted through the second *traboule*, clambering up a circular staircase and then down a steep flight of stone steps.

They arrived at a heavy door. Before unbolting it, Eduardo explained, "Hundreds of years ago, they were built to make it easier to reach the river and fetch water rather than winding around the streets. Now the weavers use them to take their silk to market. They offer protection on more than one level—from the weather, and also from thieves."

Eduardo opened the door and scanned the empty street up and down before waving David through. When he closed the door behind them, David marveled at how it fit back into the face of the building with no trace of its presence, its stone matching the building exactly.

They emerged into the center of the Croix-Rousse district, where all the silk weavers had their production houses. Eduardo pulled ahead with his long-legged stride, and David hurried to catch up to him.

Halfway up the street, Eduardo stopped and felt around the wall of a building until he located the door of the next *traboule*. This one was broader and, thankfully, lit by moonlight allowed in by a window in the roof.

Moving swiftly, the two men entered and exited two more passageways before finding themselves near the footbridge over the Saône that would take them to the Vieux Lyon, where Dumond believed Gabril was being held.

A damp chill blew off the river, making David shiver, and the overpowering smell of human waste and unwashed bodies hit him as they made their way past quayside bodies huddled around small fires or simply lying at the side of narrow lanes that ran up from the riverbank.

On Place de la Bellaine, Marie Dumond rang the massive bell at the outer gate of an elegant home. Dark had fallen, and only the street lamp lit the cloaked figure holding a parcel and her carriage, which waited on the other side of the broad road.

When a porter opened the gate, Marie entered a courtyard laden with the perfume of the last of the season's roses. In front of her, a profusion of bougainvillea draped the copper archway leading to the entrance of the house.

"I will see that Madam receives your parcel," said the porter.

"No, I must deliver it myself—apothecary's orders," Marie replied. "I have specific instructions."

The porter hesitated, but then conducted her to the private quarters of the woman of the house, Madame de Valoise.

ISABELA'S WAY

Twenty minutes later, her business accomplished, Marie departed the mansion. She paused at the outer gate, removed a length of cloth from her satchel, and hung it by its cord from an iron hook in the adjacent wall. She then retired to her carriage, instructed the driver to move forward several houses, and waited.

Gabril finished the thin soup and hunk of cheese brought to him for his supper and set aside a novel, *Amadis de Gaula*, which he had read before in Portuguese and was now struggling to read in French. He closed his eyes, savoring the warmth of the fire, newly rebuilt with a fresh load of wood brought with his dinner. He barely remembered the story of the star-crossed love of Amadis and the princess Oriana and only read on of their fantastical misadventures to distract himself from his predicament.

His love and life with Mariem and then Isabela had been deeply fortunate and fulfilling until the assertions of the Inquisition and the pestilence turned it all into a waking nightmare. He pounded his clenched fist on the broad wood of the armchair, trying to think clearly past the lingering pain at the back of his skull. He couldn't just sit here, the bait set to trap Isabela and the others. Thus far, he had held fast to his story that he knew nothing of Isabela's whereabouts, but less than an hour ago the padre had paced in front of the hearth, badgering him with questions about Eduardo and Ana, most of which he truly could not answer though he feigned even more ignorance than he possessed. Padre Alvaro seemed to be running out of patience, and Gabril running out of time to formulate a plan.

He knew for certain that the library was well guarded, solidly locked from the outside. Though no longer shackled or bound, he remained weak and dizzy. Still, he tried to think.

David de Sousa crept along the stone wall, his fingers searching for the slight protrusion that would signal an entrance to a *traboule*. He tried to remember the ingenious sequence of pressure and pulling that would release the stone and reveal a hidden latch to gain entrance to the passageway. If Eduardo's information was correct, this *traboule* ran between the western wall of the building he believed held Gabril and the neighboring house.

He glanced up and down the street and saw only a lone carriage several houses away. It took several more minutes before he found the right stone and several tries before he managed to release it. After looking once more toward the entrance gate a dozen meters away and seeing no one, he threw the latch up and pulled at the door, which swung open with remarkable ease given the stone's weight. He stepped around and through the door and was turning to pull it shut when something small and swift slipped past him and into the passage.

The door swung shut and David froze in the pitch dark, the sound of his own heavy breathing reverberating off the stone walls.

"Monsieur de Sousa, I hope," came a soft woman's voice in slightly accented French.

David waited, but nothing more than a rustling and the striking of a flint disrupted the silence, followed by the soft glow of a tiny oil lamp. In its light David was astonished to see a tiny woman, dressed in a fine cloak, holding the lamp in one hand and a fine dagger pointed directly at him in the other.

His hand clapped to his side and onto the handle of his own knife, but before he could grasp it the woman spoke calmly but forcefully.

"Don't. I mean you no harm, but don't be misled by my size. I can defend myself readily."

Still barely able to believe his eyes and ears, David slowly dropped his hand to his side and considered the woman in front of him. She was at least ten years older than he, with sharp though pleasing features and dark eyes that firmly held his gaze. Brown ringlets spilled out of her hood and framed her face. She wore several gold rings set with jewels on her gloved hands.

"I was hoping to intercept you before you entered, but this meeting will have to suffice," she said. "I am Marie Dumond. I am a friend of Ana Martel Girondi and also of Gabril de Castro Nuñez."

Relief flooded through David. "Have you word from Isabela or Ana?"

"Yes, they are both safe at my home for the moment, but you are not safe here. Monsieur de Castro Nuñez is well guarded here, and you are expected to try to rescue him. It is a trap, and he is the bait."

"We know that, Madame Dumond, but Señor Carel believes we can free him. He has a plan."

"With all due respect to Monsieur Carel, that is exactly what Padre Alvaro expects. He knows you and will recognize you immediately." She handed the lantern to David and carefully sheathed her dagger in the folds of her cloak. "As unlikely as it may seem, Monsieur de Sousa, you must allow the women to conduct this rescue. This house has been commandeered by the padre, but I am good friends with the lady of the house, Madame Valoise, and I delivered a potent sedative to her in the guise of an apothecary's assistant. Shortly she will administer it in the evening ale to all the guards and, with any luck, to the good padre. Madame Martel Gerondi will be summoned to address the illness of the guards. She will bring Isabela with her, and you two will stay in the *traboule*. In all the confusion in the house, I will conduct Monsieur de Castro Nuñez into the passageway and my carriage will meet us at the other end of the *traboule*. With more luck, we will transport the five of you to Strasbourg before daylight."

David stared at her with widened eyes, trying to take in all this information.

"I will show you the secret exit from the library where Monsieur de Castro Nuñez is held. But then you must intercept Monsieur Carel, for if he intercedes our plan will be disrupted."

With that, Madame Dumond reclaimed the lantern, turned on her heel, and made haste down the passage, with David dutifully following her.

Rest and good nourishment had greatly improved Ana's condition, but she still had not regained full strength. The plan she, Marie, and Isabela had devised would require her to present herself in her usual formidable fashion, however, and so she prepared carefully. She chose the finest of the gowns Marie had secured for her and carefully dressed her hair with elaborate braiding that framed her face. She chose a black lace headdress and an embroidered cloak to complete her outfit. Then she rested and awaited the appointed time in the evening to appear at the Valoises' villa.

When the message came, Ana rose and joined Isabela in the front hall. She barely recognized her young friend. Isabela's golden curls were pulled tightly into a chignon, a deep hood hid her face, and a black velvet cape flowed from her shoulders, obscuring her slight figure.

The Valoise carriage drove the two women through the dark streets and let them off in front of the maison. As soon as they alighted, Isabela grasped Ana's arm.

"It's one of my banners," she whispered, pointing to the side of the entrance gate. "Those are the symbols for danger."

"I expect Madame Dumond placed that there in case she was unable to intercept David and Eduardo. I wish we'd gotten word of them." Ana straightened her shoulders and rang the bell for the porter. "Remember to stand against the wall just between the two houses and wait to be admitted to the *traboule*," she instructed in a low voice. "Someone will come to you as soon as I am admitted to the house."

Isabela clutched her friend tightly. "I'm scared."

"I know," Ana said. "But we have to be brave . . . again."

Isabela nodded, then turned and walked swiftly along the wall. Moments after she disappeared into the darkness, the porter opened the gate and conducted Ana across the courtyard and into the house. She allowed herself to marvel at the splendor of the entry hall for only a moment before turning to the porter.

"I am to attend Madame Valoise in the conservatory, where I believe she has established an infirmary."

The porter shook his head. "Père Alvaro has ordered anyone entering the house to be brought to him right away. You must wait for his return."

Ana drew herself to her full, imposing height and looked sternly at the porter. "I am here to avert the immediate need for the good father, but I cannot help the poor fellows if I can't get to them."

The porter shook his head but led Ana to the back of the hall and into the conservatory. Lamps were lit around the glass room and cots surrounded the central fountain. Above, the vaulted glass ceiling let in the faint light of a thousand stars in the clear night sky above the town. Only maids and a finely dressed woman attended the five lifeless men sprawled on the cots. Padre Alvaro was nowhere to be seen, and Ana breathed a sigh of relief as Madame Valoise caught sight of her and approached.

"My god, I am happy to see you," she said by way of greeting. Her handsome face was drawn and pale, but she was nearly as tall as Ana and stood erect. "Everything has worked out as planned, except that the priest took no ale this evening and the de Sousa boy has been unable to intercept Monsieur Carel."

Ana closed her eyes and took in a sharp breath. "We must proceed quickly regardless, don't you agree?"

"Yes," Madame Valoise answered.

Ana reached into her bag and withdrew a large vial of liquid. "Are they all breathing?"

Madame Valoise nodded. "They are, but some only shallowly."

"As soon as we have gone, made a weak tea of mint and three drops of this to help reverse the effects of the poppy and henbane." Ana reached out a hand and laid it gently on the other woman's arm. "I am sorry to have put you and your family at risk. I expect these guards will awake with nothing more than a headache, but still—"

"It is Père Alvaro who has endangered not only us but many others with his fanaticism," Madame Valoise interrupted angrily. "He has put my husband and many others in the silk and weavers' guilds in a difficult position, as the Church is an important customer and influential with many of our other clients." She lowered her voice, glancing at the motionless figures and leaning in toward Ana. "What scares me the most is that I fear this priest and these ruffians are acting outside the Church's oversight even as they assert its authority."

"You are most likely correct, Madame Valoise." Ana grimaced. "Where is Père Alvaro right now, do you know?"

"He took my husband out to dine and meet with other town fathers, I believe in an attempt to persuade them to his effort."

"Then, indeed, we must move quickly."

The two women returned to the main hall, and Madame Valoise led the way to the library.

ISABELA'S WAY

Gabril de Castro Nuñez would never quite be able to reconstruct the order of events of that September evening with any accuracy. It seemed to him that it all happened in an instant. He was startled out of a doze by the simultaneous crash of a shattering window pane behind him and the entry into the library from the hall of two tall women he'd never seen before. He tried to leap to his feet but, dizzy with pain, he immediately slumped back against the settee. The bookcase wall opposite the hearth moved and Gabril closed his eyes, thinking he would faint.

Behind him, he heard, "Gabril, it's Eduardo. I've unlatched the shutter, can you reach the window fastener?"

Just as Gabril tried to open his eyes again, one of the women flew toward the window.

"Eduardo, thank God!" She unfastened the window latch and swept the broken glass from the ledge.

Just then, the other woman moved to the library wall, and in a moment an entire section of the wall moved into the room, revealing a dark passageway. The woman disappeared into the darkness and returned seconds later leading a young man dressed in ragged farm clothes with unkempt hair and several days' growth of beard.

"Senhor de Castro Nuñez, it is a relief to reach you and see you safe," the young man said in perfect Portuguese.

Gabril looked with incomprehension at him for a long moment.

"I'm David de Sousa," David finally said.

Gabril's bewilderment changed to astonishment as he gazed first at David, then at Eduardo, and then back to David. He tried again to find his legs to stand. "Isabela," he said. "Where is she?"

David was about to answer when the library door banged open and Padre Alvaro burst in. A distinguished-looking man followed directly behind him and demanded, "Where is my wife?"

Padre Alvaro returned to the door and shouted, "Guard!"

Huddled in the darkness of the *traboule*, Isabela, Madame Valoise, and Madame Dumond listened to the shouts coming from the Valoise library through the opening of the secret bookshelf door.

"David de Sousa," said Padre Alvaro, "what a pleasure to find you drawn into this conspiracy. I will enjoy seeing you convicted, along with your whore of a mother."

Isabela stifled a gasp at this.

David didn't respond; Isabela only heard the scuffle of feet, the sluicing sound of a sword's metal withdrawing from a scabbard, and then the urgent voice of Eduardo Carel saying, "Don't, David."

David held the padre at sword point even as the cleric sneered.

"Oh, but he should know. His mother rebuffed my advances at first, but she relented when her children's safety was at stake. Not to mention that of the young Senhorita de Castro Nuñez."

David brought the sword to the padre's neck, ready to slit his throat, but Eduardo shoved the priest to the floor and pulled his hands behind him.

Ana's cool but commanding voice rose above the commotion.

"Gentlemen! Restrain Padre Alvaro, but leave his punishment to the Church. I have messaged Jacques de Bernuy, who will acquaint the Bishop of Toulouse with the facts of the padre's violation of orders, and I expect the church elders have had quite enough of his troublemaking. Perhaps, Monsieur Valoise, you and your wife will have complaints as to the way your hospitality has been abused?"

Hearing Ana's words, David's boiling blood cooled somewhat.

He stepped away from the padre and was sheathing his sword as an unfamiliar woman entered the library, followed by Isabela and Madame Dumond.

"Papai," Isabela cried and flew to the settee, where Gabril sat in stunned silence.

Eduardo finished tying the padre's hands behind his back. He pulled him to his feet and stuffed a cloth into his mouth before pushing him into the hall, where David saw him also binding his feet before hurrying back into the room and over to Ana's side as she sank into a chair by the hearth.

The woman David had not yet met—Madame Valoise, he quickly surmised—updated her husband on all that had happened over the course of the day and night. When she was done, Madame Dumond spoke up.

"We must help our friends through the *traboule* and into their carriage. The padre is restrained, but their safety is far from assured in Lyon tonight. Come."

Isabela rose and helped her father to his feet. David ran to help. With one of Gabril's arms around his shoulder and the other around Isabela's, they made their way slowly into the *traboule*, where Madame Dumond stood with a lighted lantern. Eduardo half led, half carried Ana into the passageway. The Valoises wished the group godspeed and, after seeing them disappear into the darkness, secured the secret bookcase doorway, restoring their library to its normal appearance.

EPILOGUE

Hamburg

October, 1606

My face in thine eye, thine in mine appeares,
And true plaine hearts doe in the faces rest
—JOHN DONNE

Isabela pulled her new fine wool cloak tightly around her neck as she emerged onto the Monkedammfleet canal and into the sharp breeze that blew off the Elbe River. Tall warehouses lined both sides of the canal, shielding her somewhat from the cool October breeze.

Autumn here was very different than autumn in Abrantes. More than the cooler temperatures, Isabela found it difficult to negotiate the constant wind and rain in this bustling city. As the canal led to the river, the wind grew nearly to a gale, and twice Isabela sheltered in a doorway to catch her breath and steady herself. The passages built right into the face of the buildings narrowed nearly to the width of a single cart between entrances, and the busy streets made it take longer than usual to reach her destination.

Stepping around scaffolding and piles of brick and stone—the city exploded with new construction—Isabela finally turned away from the river and into the town center. She smiled to herself, realizing that these surroundings had become familiar, she now navigated the narrow curving streets between the canals and passageways with more ease, and people were even beginning to recognize her in the market.

Within a few minutes she arrived at St. Jacobi, where today the Hamburg council would meet. The other three parishes were sending their council members, along with the dozens of citizen representatives that comprised the Kollegium, Hamburg's entire governing body, and the august group would officially confirm the appointment of the first four non-Lutheran brokers to the Bourse of Hamburg. One of those new members of the stock exchange was Gabril de Castro Nuñez, and Isabela's employer, Frau Jesurun, had given her the morning off so she could attend the ceremony with David.

The Jesuruns were an old Portuguese Jewish family that had come to Hamburg and established their textile business as soon as Jews were allowed to conduct business in the city. They were the first contacts Gabril had made when he'd come to sell his textiles. Not only did they manufacture and import fabrics but they had now also begun to employ dressmakers and tailors to create fine clothing for the wealthy burghers of the city. When Isabela submitted samples of her embroidery, Frau Jesurun had hired her immediately. She now worked with the tailors and dressmakers on clothing design in a dedicated workroom on the second floor of the Jesurun mansion—a lovely space with windows that admitted morning light and fresh air. She had quickly established a sizable roster of clients.

As Isabela stood in the square in front of the church, she saw David approach from the other direction. She smiled as she noted how handsome he looked in his dark cloak, his medical bag at his side. In the year since they'd arrived, David had studied with the prominent physician Rodrigo de Castro and was already beginning to treat patients. He no longer had to send funds to his sisters, as they were both married and happy in Bayonne.

ISABELA'S WAY

Inside her cloak Isabela reached up to feel the pendant at her neck. A sapphire surrounded by seven pearls encased in gold filigree hung from a heavy gold chain. David had given it to her as a betrothal gift. When he clasped it around her neck, he'd explained that the sapphire was Isabela's birthstone and represented fidelity and good fortune, and that the number seven was the most important number in Jewish mysticism, representing spiritual wholeness and completion, and so he'd asked the jeweler to add seven pearls. In addition to his study of medicine, David had set himself to studying religious texts and mysticism with scholars in his new community.

David reached Isabela and, smiling, took her arm. They entered the church and found seats close to the front.

"For his international work on behalf of the Hansiatic City of Hamburg, bringing new economic opportunity we ask Herr Gabriel Castro-Nuñez to come forward . . ."

Isabela watched her father rise and walk to the dais. He stood tall, elegantly dressed in fine black breeches and a doublet she had embroidered with the castle and lions from the city's coat of arms. As the head of the city council enumerated his achievements and contributions, Isabela marveled that the work that brought this honor had covered for the dangerous work of bringing their countrymen out of Portugal and to this new life.

Just as the ribboned medallion was pinned to her father's doublet, sunlight streamed through the eastern windows, casting splashes of color across the stone floor and, for a moment, lighting his figure in a warm glow.

If only Mamãe could see him now, Isabela thought, missing her mother as she had so often in this new life.

As her father resumed his seat on the dais and the ceremony continued, her thoughts strayed to the letter she'd just received from Ana. She and Eduardo had settled in the Principality of Catalonia, north of

Girona, in the small town of Besalú. A tight-knit community of New Christians lived and prospered there, secretly practicing their Jewish traditions and even studying the mystical tenets of Kabbalah.

Ana's words from her last letter floated into Isabela's thoughts:

I am so pleased to read from your beautiful missive of your betrothal to David. As our sages tell us, love is the single most necessary ingredient for human happiness and the purest expression of the soul. It has been my privilege to watch your love grow and share in it.

Eduardo and I live a quiet life here. I have sold my property in Girona and bought a small farm outside the town here in the north. My herbs have been reestablished well on the hillside where we live, and I still make dyes and do a bit of healing when asked. Eduardo teaches mathematics at the local school but also gives himself to his fascination with numerology and mysticism. We are happy and at peace after all the long years of separation and danger.

You will be pleased to hear that we have had word from the Camargue and our friends there are safe and content, though our visit there cost them more scrutiny than I would have wished. Against all odds of age and convention, Simone has borne a daughter, and she has named her Isabela!

I treasure the collar you embroidered for me more than I can say in words, for each time I don it I feel the beauty in you touching me. I hope you think of your stitches gracing the bodies of friends, helping show the way for strangers, "for we were once strangers in the land of Egypt."

Give our love and best wishes to your father, to dear David, and to our other friends in Hamburg. Tell David how proud I am that he has chosen to study the healing arts. He has the instinct.

We wish you the blessings of a long and happy life in your new home, and remember to count your blessings, as I do each day. We have both been given chances for a better life. With God's help, we will use them wisely.

And do write to me, Isabela. I so wish to hear it all.

Isabela found David's hand next to hers and grasped it. *Helping show the way . . .*

Isabela's Way
List of Characters

Isabela de Castro Nuñez — The main character, a fourteen-year-old embroideress. Her mother, Mariem, has died of the plague in their hometown of Abrantes, Portugal, and her father, Gabril, is in Hamburg looking to reestablish his family in a place safer for New Christians, also known as Conversos. She is shy and tentative at the beginning of the story, but as she gradually learns the purpose of her embroidery assignments as she travels far from home to escape the Inquisition, she becomes stronger and more confident.

Gabril de Castro Nunez — Isabela's father, a textile merchant.

David de Sousa — Eighteen years old, David is Isabela's friend, supporter, and eventual husband. He is in charge of the New Christian (converted Jews) community in Abrantes until he learns they must all escape. He is responsible for his mother and sisters and must take a different path of escape from Isabela.

Beatriz and Rosinha de Sousa — David's sisters.

Adriana Gomez de Sousa — David's mother.

Ana Martel Gerondi — Protectress and guide to Isabela and David. Along with Isabela's father, Gabril, and her lover, Eduardo, she is part of a secret escape network to conduct persecuted Conversos from Portugal to Hamburg Germany. She is a dye maker and herbal healer.

Eduardo Carel — Colleague of Gabril de Castro Nuñez and the lover of Ana Martel Gerondi.

Padre Alvaro — Priest in Abrantes dedicated to imposing the Inquisition and pursuing Isabela and David.

Alfonso Mendes and Dina Mendes — Faith keepers, mystics, advisors to Ana Martel Gerondi, part of the escape network, providers of embroidery codes.

The Leon Family — Christian guides for escaping Jews and New Christians. Simone leads Isabela, her brother Enrique leads David, and Enrique's son, Diego, leads Ana Martel Gerondi on their different routes to France.

Dr. Francisco Sanches — Physician, Ana's employer in Toulouse, and a member of the escape network.

Jacques de Bernuy — Dye dealer and provider of a safe house for the escape network.

The Mercados — Raphael and Alaia, wealthy landowners in Irouléguy who hire Isabela to embroider their daughter Miren's trousseau.

Sophia Pardo — The Mercados's housemaid and a hidden Jew.

Pedro de Martins — Courier and member of the escape network.

Claudio — Simone de Leon's lover. He lives in the Camargue and tends the famed wild white horses there.

Alberto Dumond—silk merchant and member of network in Lyon.

Acknowledgments

The idea for *Isabela's Way* came to me on day three of a warrior-woman bike ride from Portugal to the Alhambra in Granada, Spain, in 2011. Many family and medical events had conspired to find me doing this trip solo, and it was lonely but fabulous. I have Pedro Martins and guides Luis and Jorge to thank for creating an itinerary that included the standing stones of a Celtic burial site on a hilltop near Crato, Portugal. On the way down, Isabela came to me, but with *Even in Darkness* unfinished and *Hard Cider* already in the wings, I told her to wait.

She did.

When it was her turn, I researched and traveled heavily to create the authenticity, sights, sounds, and smells that bring my fiction alive for me. For assistance in my 2017 research trip, I thank Heritage Private Tours, dear friend and poet Mimi Zollars Sapparrart, and Mimi's wonderful husband, Pascal. Thanks also to Douglas Leach, who fed me royally in Macanet, Figueres, Spain and led me to Girona and its Jewish historical treasures.

The pandemic disrupted further travel for a few years, but a return trip in 2022 allowed me to complete my research by following my characters' paths to Hamburg. Thank you to Karen Ensign for indulging my research needs while creating a perfect travel itinerary through Spain, France, and Germany, and to my husband, Barry, for accompanying me on that journey.

The generosity, careful reading, and continuous support of my writing partners, Patty Hoffman and Diane Davidson, has kept me going through all phases of the creation of this book. They are a priceless gift.

My thanks go to early readers Pamela Grath, David Moses, of blessed memory, Dan Voorhees, and Kathe Langberg, whose input and editing made this a better book.

I cannot possibly list all the resources that informed my understanding of life in early-seventeenth-century Europe, the history of Jews, the impact of the Inquisition, and the work of embroiderers during that time. But certain books had early or outsize influence. My thanks go to Mary Morris for *Gateway to the Moon*, Rachel Kadish for *The Weight of Ink*, Melodie Winawer for *The Scribe of Siena*, and Clare Hunter for *Threads of Life: A History of the World Through the Eye of a Needle*. Many thanks to Genie Milgrom, Rebeca D'Harlingue, Esther Erman, Rivka Amado, Jenni Ogden, Michelle Cameron, Elayne Klasson, Kathy Watson, Florence Kraut, and Ruth Behar for their reading of the manuscript and kind endorsements.

For the genealogical research that led me to find my ancestor who was born in Abrantes, Portugal, in 1586 and died in Hamburg, Germany, in 1655, I have first to thank my great-grandfather, Anton Nathusius, whose meticulously drawn family tree of my great-grandmother's Sephardic Jewish family started me on the trail. Ancestry.com and my fellow researchers there also have my gratitude. Knowing I had ancestors who made the journey I have fictionalized deepened my connection to my characters.

I thank all the members of my family and the many readers who have followed this journey for their interest and their support. It fills me.

To my publisher, Brooke Warner—I am grateful to bring yet another book to life in the house of sisters you have created. So thankful also to project managers Lauren Wise and Shannon Green, editor Krissa Lagos, cover designer Lindsey Cleworth, and the rest of the creative team at She Writes Press. To my publicist Caitlin Hamilton Summie, thank you for helping me spread the word about Isabela.

About the Author

Photo credit: Chris Loomis Photography

BARBARA STARK-NEMON is the award-winning author of short stories, essays, the historical novel *Even in Darkness*, and the contemporary novel *Hard Cider*. Barbara lives, writes, swims, cycles, and does fiber art in Ann Arbor and Northport, MI. For more information about Barbara's work, and book club discussion questions, visit www.barbarastarknemon.com

Looking for your next great read?

We can help!

Visit www.shewritespress.com/next-read
or scan the QR code below for a list
of our recommended titles.

She Writes Press is an award-winning
independent publishing company founded to
serve women writers everywhere.